SILENT DAWN

SILENT DAWN

Chasing Sunrise

Charles Avent

Library of Congress Control Number:		2014906556
ISBN:	Hardcover	978-1-4931-7824-7
	Softcover	978-1-4931-7825-4
	eBook	978-1-4931-7822-3

Cover Model: Katherine Marie Elliott

This book was printed in the United States of America.

Rev. date: 09/30/2014

To order additional copies of this book, contact:
Xlibris LLC
1-888-795-4274
www.Xlibris.com
Orders@Xlibris.com
541562

CONTENTS

I like to give credit, where credit is due. With that in mind, I give credit, by way of dedicating this book, to the following;

To my wife, Patricia, for believing in me and giving me encouragement: cheering me on.

To my mother, Helen Tate Mullendore Avent, who believed in me from the moment of my birth.

To my grandmother, Irma Onita Johnson Tate Mullendore, who was the first person who ever told me that I could do whatever I wanted in life.

To my mother-in-law, Rose Summers Miller, for encouraging my writing and smiling, even though she did not like vampires.

To my sister-in-law, Teresa Miller Elliott, who showed me I needed to develop the characters more, so the readers correctly interpret the story I intend to tell.

And to Mrs. Eugenia Dickinson, my high school science fiction teacher, who let me know I had a story to tell, thereby beginning my journey.

CHAPTER ONE

Poor Little Lamb

The few city blocks that made up the entertainment district became an entirely different world at night—one that most would never see. The pale light of dying neon signs bathed the streets, while the sound of merchants selling their illegal wares pierced the moist night air. The drug dealers and the pimps worked openly after sundown; not even the police would come into the area at night, much less anyone who wanted their protection.

This was Cami's world; it was all she knew.

She was aware that her protégé, Samuel, was somewhere nearby, watching her. Her own attention, however, was presently being given to the man who was walking slowly down the sidewalk. He was young—in his late twenties at the most, more than twice the age that Cami appeared to be—and dressed well in dark slacks and a matching blazer that would have done little against the evening chill. The girls whom he passed called out offers and solicitations, but he ignored all, except the youngest. Each time, he would get a close look at the girl then move on, still searching, hunting. Cami recognized his technique.

"Hey, mister," Cami said as the man approached. She was dressed in a very short skirt with knee-high socks. Her shirt was folded over on itself, revealing her stomach in such a way that it could be pulled down quickly to a more modest length, just in case the police did show up.

"Hey," the man replied in a well-practiced comforting tone. "Aren't you cold?"

"Yes, sir, I left my sweater at home."

His smile disgusted her, but she kept the feeling from registering on her young face. The man offered his jacket and threw it across her shoulders.

He asked, "How old are you?"

"Twelve years, sir." Cami could pass for twelve. After all, she had been twelve years old for a very long time.

The man glanced in either direction then peered into the shadows behind him. Seeing nothing, he continued. "How much?"

"How much for what, sir?" Cami asked.

Now believing that she was not a prostitute but just a lost little girl, he became a little more aggressive. "What if you went with me and played a game . . . would you like that?"

"Well, I should really be getting home, sir."

"I'm very lonesome," the man began. "I miss my little girl and just want to play a game to pass away my loneliness."

Both of those were lies, and Cami knew it. She could see the sores on his lips and knew exactly which of the girls with whom he had laid. People, however, tend to lie in such a situation—it was part of the process.

"I really should be getting home," Cami stated again.

Having thrown out the bait, she was now teasing him, just getting ready to set the hook and reel him in.

"It will only be a little while," the man taunted. "I'll even pay you $20! That's a lot of money for a little girl like you."

"Okay," Cami agreed. "I cannot stay long."

The man pressed a bill into her hand, and she slipped it into a hidden pocket. "Please call me Daddy."

Cami forced the sense of disgust deep within herself and pulled her lips into a joyless smile. "Okay . . . Daddy." She saw the pale skin where a wedding ring had only recently been removed, and she understood what he was looking for. "Come on," she said, leading the way.

The man followed like an obedient puppy, which had been promised a treat, as she wound through the twists and turns of the streets and alleys.

"How much farther?" he asked.

"Not far, just up ahead . . . nice and quiet . . . Daddy." She forced the last word—again. He did not answer, but she knew that her youthful tone and forced enthusiasm had convinced him. Of course, that, and the fact that he was certain he could easily overpower this young child.

Finally, she reached a dead end. It was a small courtyard, which had served the surrounding abandoned buildings.

"Right here," she said and turned to face the man.

He was already close, closer than she had expected, which made her gasp. She looked down to see his pants puddled around his feet, leaving him standing in his boxer shorts, with his socks peeking out. He had a look of determination on his face. Cami wanted to laugh, but she dared not, at least not yet. He pressed in against her and closed his hand around her thin neck, squeezing hard enough to crack his joints against her flesh. He pushed her against the cool bricks and ran his free hand over her body. She could not make out exactly what he was saying, but he muttered a steady stream of angry obscenities and vulgar threats.

Cami smiled, staring knowingly into his eyes.

This took him aback—for a moment. He had done this many times before, and the girls never smiled. They choked, screamed, and begged; some would even wet themselves, but they never smiled. Though *he* was confused, Cami knew *exactly* what she was doing. She had decided that this was not a human being but an animal and that he deserved to relish every moment of what was to come. She would, therefore, forgo allowing him the peace of being put under her hypnotic gaze and would simply have to endure the foul taste that the adrenaline gave when his fear came into full force. She threw her arm around his back and grabbed a handful of his hair. He started to scream when she pulled and instinctively clawed at her hand with his own, but she was able to quickly and easily muffle his screams. She pulled his face in close to her own. When she spoke, her voice had changed from that of a sweet little girl to that which sounded as though it should be coming from some type of a large animal. It was very deep and guttural as she looked into his eyes and said, "I may appear to be a child, but your feeble mind cannot grasp my real age nor what I truly am. Suffice it to say that I promise that not one more child will suffer at your hand, and I am about to send you to the fate that you so richly deserve!"

Then she flicked her tongue out to lick the tip of his nose and said, still in the deep, hollow, voice, "Tasty!"

She then quickly twisted her wrist to whip his face to the side, exposing the soft skin of his neck to her. She was so hungry; it had been too long. She could smell the blood that flowed through his pulsating jugular, and she could hear each heartbeat that made the vein dance for her.

"What the fu—" he started but finished with an anguished, muffled scream as Cami held his jaw shut with her tiny hand and buried her fangs into his meat, tearing the delicate membrane of the vein and spilling his blood directly into her eager mouth, pulsing with each beat of his slowing heart. The sensation was intense and immediate; her heart began to beat again rapidly. Her pupils dilated, turning her entire eyeball black, much like that of a shark during a feeding frenzy. His adrenaline had an effect on her as well as she fed hungrily from the man who clawed meekly at the young girl and choked on the blood that ran down his windpipe. She barely noticed when her protégé, Samuel, joined her in their feast, biting into an artery in the man's thigh. It was not quite as quick to give as the jugular, but it tasted the same. He winced slightly at the taste of adrenaline and made a face as if he had just sucked a lemon, but continued to feed all the same.

By that time, he was quiet and still, with the last of his life leaking from his body. As Cami felt his heartbeat slow then almost stop through her teeth, faded memories shot through her brain.

Romania (Wallachia), 1436

Cami burst through her bedroom door, gingerly carrying a concealed treasure in her small hands. She was too young to understand the misfortune of being born a Wallachian in Wallachia, which left her family mere peasants among the wealthier Hungarians and Germans. Her village of Olt, however, was quiet and peaceful, nestled in the shadows of the Carpathian Mountains. All Cami cared about now was the gift in her hands and the reaction that she hoped her mother would give.

Mother hummed quietly while she cooked breakfast on the terracotta wood-burning stove, which filled the small home with the sweet fragrance of baking *kiflik* and cooking eggs. The home was still lit by candles, the very early morning required by their vocation and the stormy weather combined to leave everything outside bathed in blackness. Her father busied himself with repairing a leak in the ceiling that allowed the rain that pounded at the rooftop to find its way inside the relatively dry home. He smiled at his beloved daughter as she passed to wait patiently behind her mother.

"Good morning, sweetie," she spoke softly. Her mother always spoke softly and always lovingly. She pulled the prepared food from the woodstove and pulled her daughter into a close embrace.

"I made you something, Mama," Cami said. She extended her hand to reveal a carefully crafted necklace made from flowers that she had never seen before in her most recent carefree exploration of the surrounding forests.

Her mother smiled. "It is beautiful!" She gingerly picked up the organic jewelry and wore it around her own neck. "Do you not think so?" she said laughing, placing her hands at her new necklace to accentuate her thoughtful gift. Cami loved the sound of her mother's laughter. It was soft and seemed to dance in front of her.

Cami started to agree before she realized that her mother had spoken past her. "Yes, quite beautiful." Her father's voice made Cami jump; she had not heard him approach. "Cami . . .," he started.

"Yes, Tata?" There was something in his voice. She was not sure what it was, but it scared her.

"Where did you get those flowers?"

"I got them in the woods, Tata, not too far away," she lied.

"Did you go to the hills?" His voice carried a mixture of fear and anger. He was referring to the foothills at the base of the Carpathian mountain range. Every child knew the legends and stories, but it was only the very young who still feared them. Cami, however, was the only one who had ever actually gone there.

She summoned all her courage. Her palms were slick with sweat, and a lump formed in her throat. "Yes," she answered simply, casting her eyes to the ground.

Due to her downcast eyes, she was not watching and was caught by surprise when her father's open hand slapped her cheek—not hard but enough to get her attention. Her mother gasped and pulled her close, while her father yelled, "You never go there!" He hissed, "I have told you *never* to go there!"

Cami's cheek stung; she fought against the tears that welled in her eyes. "They are only stories, Tata. There was nothing there!" she cried out. Her feelings were hurt—more than her cheek.

Her father kneeled down and looked her in the eye. "Little raindrop," he started. He used that affectionate name for her alone. He opened his mouth to speak, but a heavy knock at the front door interrupted him. The cadence was slow enough to be ominous, and each concussion shook the door in its frame. "Stay here," he told his wife and daughter. Cami had always seen her father as a tower of strength, but the fear in his eyes terrified her now.

"Who could be out in this weather?" her mother asked, pulling Cami closer to her.

She watched her father slowly approach the door, take a steadying breath, and pull it open. Her father shook; her mother screamed. The man in the doorframe was still. She could only see his silhouette, he seemed to wear the shadows like a thick cloak, but she could see that he was very tall, dwarfing her father with his size. He was thin, but something about him exuded power.

"You are not welcome here!" her father shouted. "Leave us alone!"

The man did not answer but extended a long muscular arm toward, but not passing, the doorway. Cami's father was not a violent man, and he was respected in the village for his patience and sage advice. Nevertheless, he was violent tonight. He reached for the long dagger that hung near the doorway and angrily pointed the serrated tip toward the stranger. Without a threat or a warning, he lunged at the larger man, disappearing into the pouring rain.

"Tata!" Cami called, tearing herself from her mother's grasp and running to the doorway. "Tata!" she called again into the night. She could see nothing in the darkness but heard the splashes and footfalls of a mortal struggle then nothing. The rain beat down from clouds that were uncaring as to what had happened below. "Tata?" she whispered to the darkness.

She heard the footsteps before she saw anything. They approached unhurriedly until she saw the figure emerge from the rain; it was the taller man.

"No!" Cami shouted. "Go away!" she yelled at the man.

He continued to approach, close enough that Cami was able to see that he carried her father's still form. She wondered if he was dead and if she would be next. However, the man did not return to the doorway; instead, he stopped far enough from the home to remain deep in the shadows. With unexpected care, he laid her father's body down on the ground and then kneeled next to him. After a moment, he stood and took one last look at Cami before disappearing into the night. She was not able to see him clearly, except for the glow of his eyes. It chilled her.

Cami's mother found the courage to join her at the doorway, but neither could overcome their fears of whatever lurked in the oppressive darkness. Before they found their courage, her father stirred. He moaned and made himself stand on his feet then slowly staggered toward the house. That was the moment when Cami found her courage and ran out into the rain to her father's side. He steadied himself by her aid, and Cami's mother slammed the door close as soon as they were inside.

Her father's fresh blood, which ran from a deep wound in his forehead, painted a stark contrast to his suddenly pale face. He sat, heavy and uncoordinated, in a nearby chair, while her mother worked gently to clean the blood from his face. Cami, however, noticed something else. "Tata, why do you have flowers?" He looked down and struggled to focus on the small bouquet that he clutched in his hand. He stared at them in mute horror as the significance of the forced gift sunk in. He threw them to the ground and sobbed—another event that Cami had never seen before.

Moreover, her mother just stared. "Six flowers," she whispered. Cami had never encountered the superstition, and she had no idea what it meant—in this case, a child's death.

Cami's father recovered quickly, but he did not return to the fields. He said that it was to rest, but Cami felt that he was watching over her for some significant but unknown reason. Whatever it was, it may have been the same reason that the neighbors kept their distance and that travelers altered routes to avoid their home. News, especially when based on fear and superstition, travels very quickly in the village of Olt.

Cami spent the first night back in her own bed since that fateful event. She had nearly fallen asleep when she heard the screaming. The sudden sound startled her, and she bolted upright in bed, while her tired mind struggled to understand what she was hearing. It was something that she had heard before—the terrified cry of a young lamb. When they were old enough to be unreasonably bold and adventurous, but not old enough to know how to care for themselves, they would often find themselves stuck in the fences.

"Tata?" she called. "The lamb is stuck in the fence, Tata." There was no answer. "Mama?" Again, there was no answer. Cami swung her bare feet over the edge of her bed and lit the candle that sat by her bedside. The flickering light cast dancing shadows against the wall as she padded toward her parents' bedroom. Before she reached them, however, she could hear the deep breathing of exhausted sleep; she had not known how many sleepless nights they had spent watching over her. She knew they had argued while they thought she slept, with half-heard discussions about the man and their fears, but she could never understand what they had debated. "Tata? Mama?" They did not stir.

The lamb screamed again, louder and more frightened.

That left only her before the lamb—a part of their livelihood—died terrified and alone. She pulled her lighthouse shoes onto her feet and made her way into the chilly night air. "I am coming," she called to the lamb and made her way around the home toward the pen. It was quiet and still; the fence was unbroken, and the lambs still slept peacefully with the ewes. She wondered if she had been dreaming or perhaps imagining the sound. Cami leaned against the fence and scolded the uncaring animals for whatever mischief they were playing. As she was turning around to leave, she stopped short because of a man standing silently behind her. She tried to scream, but he moved faster than she could create the sound. He covered her mouth with a firm, smooth hand. Her terrified gaze met his cold one, and she recognized him—the man that had come to their door only days before. She could see him clearly now. He was nearly angelically handsome, but the horrors in his eyes detracted from his physical appearance.

The strange man pushed her to the ground and covered her body with his own. She could not move and could only gasp when she felt the quick searing pain at her neck. She began to feel calm, bordering on euphoric, then began to give in to the sleep that pulled at her eyelids. The man, having considered the usefulness of having a child under his wing to avert villagers' attentions, raised his head and spoke in a low harsh screeching tone. "Young woman, I have drained your blood to a point where you have only enough blood to stay alive. If I take any more, you will die. However, if I replenish your blood with my own, you will live—live forever. Tell me, would you rather live or die?"

Please do not kill me! Cami screamed in her thoughts. *Mama, please help me!* However, she lacked the strength to form the words, and all she could manage was a very weak "Live . . ."

The man, her attacker, smiled; it was an evil grin, which showed his sharp and extended canine teeth. He brought his wrist to his own mouth and tore at the skin. His blood ran freely down his arm and spilled on to the soil. He allowed his salty blood to drip into Cami's mouth. It ran across her tongue and down her throat, running into her stomach. Pain shot through her body, almost immediately, making her writhe on the ground in silent agony. The minutes seemed like hours until the pain subsided, leaving her panting and gasping on the ground. Then she heard something that she had not heard before— she could hear every creature in the woods with a new clarity. The crickets chirped, and an owl screeched; the wind ran through the trees, and a predator stalked its prey. To her, it was now a well-thought-out orchestra, with flawless pitch and timing. When she strained her vision, she could almost see them as well as she could hear them.

"What did you do to me?" she asked.

The man did not answer. He only said, "You will need to feed soon."

Cami nodded, uncomprehending, as he disappeared into the night. Her memories were gone. She did not know who she was or how she had gotten there. She wandered alone through the woods and the foothills surrounding the Carpathians. She instinctively slept in the darkest areas during the day and roamed in the night. Nevertheless, each day, the hunger grew until it was tearing at her stomach and dulling her senses. She could feel herself weakening until she laid herself down to die. As she lay on the cool forest floor, vestigial memories started to emerge from the shadows of her mind. She followed them, rising to her feet and stumbling through the woods, until she found a small path cut through the brush. The path led to a road, which itself led to a small town. She made her way through quiet streets that she knew should have been familiar, passing row after row of quiet dark houses.

All were dark, except for one.

One home was lit up despite the late hour. She headed toward it, unaware of the image that she must have presented. To any observer, had there been any, she would have been a young girl in a dirty and torn nightshirt with missing shoe. Inside, she was something much more primal and wild. She reached the stoop and hit the door with her tiny fist only once before it was jerked open.

A woman stood in the doorway. Cami felt as though she should have recognized her but could not make a connection. The woman, however, clearly had a recognition of her own. "Camilia!" she cried. A man appeared next to her. He was as frightened as the woman was overjoyed. He pulled her back before she could embrace Cami. "What are you doing?" she demanded. "Cami has come home!"

"That is not Cami," he insisted. "Look at her eyes."

Cami could barely focus on their conversation despite the sense that she should. Instead, her entire concentration had expended on the flesh that stood in the home. She could smell their blood and hear their heartbeat. With each audible beat, she could see the skin of their necks and wrists quiver and knew that it was their rich blood coursing through their veins. The woman fought her way free and ran to Cami, dropping to her knees with her arms spread wide. Cami fell into them, and she was enveloped in the loving embrace.

The bite took the woman by surprise. She screamed and pulled at the child's hair, but her teeth had buried in the woman's neck. For the first time, Cami tasted a mortal's blood and immediately felt the physiological sensations of feeding. She ate greedily, holding on to the woman as she struggled to break free. Cami was so enthusiastically drinking that she had not noticed the dagger pierce her back and slide between her ribs until she saw the tip push through her chest. She dropped the woman, who fell silently to the ground in a crumpled heap, and turned to face the man, with the dagger still buried in her body.

He mumbled a heartfelt and half-remembered prayer. The sound of it stung in Cami's ears. When he turned to run, she leaped onto his back and sunk her teeth into the soft skin of his neck. She was even stronger now, and he was unable to pull her from his back. Soon, he too succumbed and fell to his knees then to the ground. Cami drank from his veins, feeling the strength returning to her body. Only then did she realize exactly what had happened and stared at the bodies in disbelief. She knew they were not dead—she could still hear their very faint heartbeats—but they would be soon. She kneeled next to her mother and ran her fingers through her hair. Her skin was already beginning to cool as the remaining blood had allocated to the base requirements for survival.

"I am sorry, Mama." Hysterics began to set in as the full realization of what she had done became clear to her. "Please, Mama! Please forgive me! I love you! Please, Tata! Please do not die! Please!" Then she fell to the floor in tears, bawling uncontrollably. "Please! I did not mean to!"

Behind her, she heard the words "But you did."

Cami was on her feet in a flash and whirled toward the sound. There stood the man who had turned her into what she now was. Her anger—her raw hatred for the man—exploded inside her. She felt the strength from her parents' blood in her as she leaped at him, her hands frantically tearing at his skin as though she intended to pull him apart. Her hands, however, did not find their mark. The man was fast—much faster than she was. He caught her by the throat and held her in his deceptively strong grip until she gave up struggling against him and allowed her body to hang limply.

"Who are you?" she asked.

The man smiled and released his grip, surprising Cami as she fell to the ground. He kneeled next to her. "My name is Boian Lupei. Relevant to you, I am your rebirther."

"What is that?" She wanted to understand what was happening to her.

He spoke patiently as a father would to a young child. "You are *vurdalak*. I am the one who gave you that gift. You were born once, but now you are born again—born anew—into something better than you ever could have been otherwise. Perhaps you would have lived a long and happy life, but one lifetime is far too short to live truly. I have seen things that you would not believe and which you never would have learned without me. I have seen the rise and fall of kings and empires. I fought in the holy wars and supported the great artists of the Renaissance. I stood by the side of your prince Vlad when he rose to power, and I will stand over his grave when he dies. Little Cami, you will live forever, and you will praise me for the life I gave you."

"My parents . . . you killed them."

"No, my dear, you killed them, and quite viciously I may add . . . my compliments. To blame me for their deaths is quite a stretch of your imagination. I only provided them with a quick easement, for which you should be thanking me. You were foolish to go to them!" Boian snapped. "You can blame no one but yourself."

Cami opened her mouth to argue, but no sound came out. He was right, and the guilt crashed around her like a heavy wave. She could only watch in mute horror as Boian crouched at each of the bodies and drained the last drops of the life from them, stilling their struggling hearts and giving them the closest thing possible to a merciful death and the peace that their eyes had been begging for. She sobbed uncontrollably, but it was the last time she ever would.

CHAPTER TWO

Cami's Saving Grace

Cami and Samuel walked in silence along the lonely highway, each lost in their own thoughts. Despite having done it for over five hundred years, Cami had never learned to take the same pleasure in killing that Boian had. Nevertheless, the guilt was assuaged by her choice of meal. She fed off the undesirables—the child molesters, drug dealers, and other criminals. She took the life of those who she felt no longer deserved it. She wondered sometimes how many she had killed. The number was easily in the hundreds of thousands, but she refused to keep count. Counting, as Boian had suggested that she do so long ago, made the necessary task seem too much like sport.

Lost in thought, she did not notice the police car pull up alongside them until it flashed its lights. She froze, ice running through her veins despite the warm blood that filled her stomach.

"What do we do?" Samuel asked. He glanced at the horizon, knowing that the deadly sunrise was steadily crawling toward them.

"I will do the talking." She walked to the car with Samuel close behind. The cop was an older man with a thick gray mustache and kind eyes hidden by thick wrinkled lids. She flashed her sweetest smile and batted her eyelashes. "Hello, sir. We are just out for a walk. It is a pretty night."

"Yes, it is," the officer agreed. "The nearest town's about fifty miles off." His voice was thick with suspicion. Cami quickly did the math in her head—there was no way they would make it before daylight. "You two homeless?" he asked.

"Yes, sir," Cami answered. She forced a look of shame to her face.

"What's the matter with him? He doesn't talk?" he asked, gesturing toward Samuel.

"No, sir, he does not. He was born that way."

"Is he your dad?"

"Yes, sir," Cami lied, taking Samuel by the hand. For all she knew, he could have been—time has a way of erasing old memories.

"I'll tell you what, how about I take you two as far as Madison, there's a shelter there that can take you in for the night and feed you in the morning. Hop in."

The rear doors unlocked with his button-press. Cami weighed the reality of the lightening horizon against the wisdom of locking themselves in the back of a police car. The older man's sincerity and good nature provided some measure of comfort, and the pair seated themselves in the hard vinyl seat. The doors locked behind them once closed. The tires chewed on the gravel as the officer pulled into the road, and the frame complained softly as he pulled a sharp U-turn to go back the way they had come.

"Sir, Madison is that way," Cami said, pointing the way they had been heading.

"A man was killed a few hours ago. Seems someone tore his throat out, and he bled to death before being dumped in an alley. You wouldn't know anything about that, would you?"

"I have no idea," Cami said. She desperately looked for an easy escape, but the vehicle was designed to prevent exactly that. "We can walk from here . . . Honestly, we do not need a ride."

The officer continued as though he had not heard Cami. "Whoever did it, they were pretty unlucky. It was the chief's son, so every cop in the city's on this one. It seems that a man and a girl were seen leaving the area, and you two fit the description. Here's the thing, if you did kill the chief's son, it's not going to go well for you. Things happen. People are put in the wrong cell—maybe the guards step away for a bit—and it won't be pretty. You confess now, and maybe I can make it easier on you."

Cami doubted that he had their best interests at heart but was rather trying to get them to confess. He probably had not called it in, so no one knew he had company. She was not afraid of him. He likely had no idea what she was, much less how to kill her. The approaching sun and official attention, however, could both be just as deadly.

Samuel leaned in close and whispered into her ear, "We're running out of time. If he takes us in, we will suffer the final death."

"I thought he didn't talk?" the officer said. His eyes narrowed in the mirror. "So why don't you just—"

Cami did not wait for him to finish. She leaned back and kicked at the clear partition that separated the back seat from the front, smashing it into the back of the man's head. He swore as he struggled to maintain control of the vehicle. He may have recovered too if Cami had not crawled through the opening. Her weight forced his head against the steering wheel, and he swerved with one hand while trying to push the partition, made heavier by Cami's weight, away from him. When the tires hit the soft shoulder, the vehicle spun violently to the side; the forward momentum continued to act on it and caused the car to flip violently. It rolled several times, turning every loose item in the car into a deadly projectile before coming to a stop on its roof.

Cami knew that the accident should have killed her—she was lying on the interior roof, surrounded by broken glass and blood. She looked at the officer; he hung limply in the seat with blood running freely from his face and pooling underneath. She raised herself to a low crouch and saw Samuel doing the same. She leaned in close to the dying man, barely able to hear his weak heartbeat. With a heaviness in her heart, she opened his jugular vein with her extended fang and gently sucked the small amount of life from him—not to feed but as an act of compassion. She had done it before, killing an innocent person, but the experience did not make it any easier.

When he was gone, she pulled his wallet from his pocket and opened it. He had pictures—a wife, some children, their children. He had a life, and she regretted taking it. "Greg Shumway," she read aloud. The man had family—people who would not know that he was dead until sometime later in the day.

"It was him or us," Samuel offered, cutting into her thoughts. "It still might be us if we don't hurry." He pointed to the distant horizon, which was already starting to glow with the uncaring flames of the sun. "We don't have much time, and I have no clue where we are." There was fear in his eyes. "I don't want to die . . . again!"

"We will not as long as we get out of here now."

She took one last look at the man then at the sunrise. She could already feel her skin starting to burn with the introduction of the impending dawn. They left him behind. The pair ran now, desperate to find shelter but finding none. Cami stole a look behind them—the crash scene had faded from view miles back, but the sun continued to advance. She felt it was ironic that, after all this time, this was the way her life ended. She cursed her own poor planning and resented the man who brought them so much further from their goal.

"Look!" Samuel shouted.

Cami whipped her head around to look but did not find anything that warranted his relief. "What?"

"Overpass," he said simply.

She could see it up ahead; there was an aged cement overpass that had fallen into disrepair over time. They ran faster, spurred by a goal, reaching the structure just as the pain became overwhelming. The shade offered immediate relief, both physical and emotional. A compacted earthen mound on both end supported the cement. Despite its age, the pair was able to dig into it enough to sink into the soft soil. Then they died, just as they did every day. Cami felt the sensations of death creep into her toes, which stiffened with rigor mortis. The sensation crawled into her legs and her stomach and then her chest. Just like the living, her body kept her brain alive, while the rest of her slipped into the cool embrace of death. Centuries ago, she would have thought of this as sleep. However, centuries ago, she would have dreamed.

Hours later, a very primal part of Cami's brain activated, releasing the hormone that would reverse the process. She repeated the same horror every night. Her brain awakes; the realization of being trapped an otherwise dead body. She could only wait and, meanwhile, feel the excruciating process of her own death in reverse. Her heavy eyelids began to loosen, allowing her to open her eyes. It took a moment for her to remember where she was, but she soon remembered the events of the previous dawn. She allowed her body to return to life, painfully reanimating her flesh and softening her joints. She heard Samuel groan and was strangely comforted by the knowledge that she was not going through the experience alone. Soon, they were both awake and alone under the overpass, rejuvenated by the rest and the previous meal.

"We probably shouldn't go back there," Samuel said. It seemed obvious to Cami, who did not bother with a reply. He continued, talking a great deal without saying anything of value. He did that when he was unsure or nervous.

Cami stopped him in midsentence. "Alaska," she said simply.

"The state?"

"No, the salmon." Cami's voice dripped with the unnoticed sarcasm. "Yes, the state."

"Oh. What about it?"

"We are going there."

"Why Alaska? What's there?"

"Nothing. That is the point. More importantly, however, there is darkness. In the winter, it is dark for most of the time. Imagine it, Samuel—no more hiding from the sunlight. We could blend in, almost like regular people."

Samuel thought for a moment, taking in the dream of normalcy. "I don't remember what it's like to be like everybody else. Cami . . . I'm trying but just can't."

"What?" she asked. She peered around their concrete shelter, her eyes piercing the darkness to ensure they were alone. They were very much alone.

"Why did you do this to me?"

She turned and then sat next to the man. "I gave you life—eternally. Do you not remember what you were before?"

"Not really. It seems like a long time ago."

"It was," she agreed. "Your family was dead, and you were dying. You survived the attack from the Powhatan tribe, and you only did that by hiding, while your family was being slaughtered. When I found you, you were crying for your loss and were about to die. I asked you if you wanted to live, and you said yes. I gave you what you asked for."

"Oh," he said.

"Besides . . . I do not like being alone." They sat in silence for a moment. She knew that he was remembering now and that he would have to mourn the loss all over again. "It is time to go," she said softly.

They avoided Madison, pressing on instead to the next town. It was a place called Carver, large enough that two more strangers would not arouse suspicion but small enough not to care about the crimes of the big city. It was a perfect hunting ground, and the two of them were hungry.

The selection of the victim defined the strategy they would employ. The man that they chose was studying the passing crowd the way a lion watches a herd. Like the other predators, he was looking for the weak and vulnerable. He even looked like a predator. His hair was dark and short, and he had greased it to make it harder to grab during a struggle. His clothes were loose enough, but not flowing, to allow for freedom of movement, and his expression was that of professional impartiality. Cami allowed herself to be his perfect prey—young, alone, and vulnerable. She stopped a stranger within earshot of the man, who casually listened to the brief conversation.

"Excuse me," she said to the older woman that had paused. "Where is the bank? I need to deposit some cash before it closes." Cami smiled inwardly at her performance, but the woman only shrugged and continued along her way. The trap had been set.

"Excuse me," the man said as he approached. His smile was wide, but his eyes were cruel.

"Yes?" Cami replied. She looked up at the man; the difference between him and her was that only one of them recognized the other for what they were.

"Are you lost?"

"Yes, sir, I am trying to find the bank. My dad asked me to deposit some money, but I got a little bit lost."

The man maneuvered his face into something resembling concern. "You shouldn't be alone out here. It's not safe for a little girl like you. I'll take you there. It's right this way." He turned and started walking, knowing that Cami would follow. She did but not for the reasons that he assumed.

Cami willingly stepped into his trap—a supposed shortcut through a quiet alley. He turned, ready to strike, but Cami was much faster. In a flash, she crawled up his body and was on the man's shoulders, with her teeth buried in his neck. He screamed and pulled at her small body, but she was too strong for him. She tore his skin open, spilling his blood into her mouth. He beat his massive fists against her, but she hardly noticed. He drew a knife and plunged it into her body, but it did not slow her. He succumbed to the blood loss and fell to the ground, struggling for breath and unable to move. Cami licked the blood from her lips as she stood, looking for Samuel to join her in the feast. He was not there. "Stay here." She smirked at the man. His eyelids fluttered open, and he looked at her with unfocused eyes. He tried to move but could not manage more than a quiver.

She made her way to where Samuel had been waiting. He was not there. She returned to the alley—the man was closer still to death—but Samuel was not there either. She finally found him after a brief search, sitting against the far side of a low wall. "What are you doing here? Did you lose count or just not hungry?" He did not answer, so she kicked him in the ribs. Instead of rousing him, he fell to his side. That was when she saw it—the wooden stake buried in his chest, directly over his heart. She refused to react, feeling eyes peering on her from the darkness. She peered into the shadows and saw the tall, thin man leering back at her.

Boian.

He turned and disappeared into the night. He wanted her to know that he was there. He wanted her to know that he could always find her.

Moldova, 1487

Cami and Boian never stayed in one area for very long because their ostensible father-and-daughter relationship would not withstand any degree of scrutiny when the young girl refused to age. There was also the associated increase in local deaths; they tried not to hunt where they lived, but it was sometimes unavoidable. So they moved—a lot. They walked together along an overgrown forest path in silence until Cami broke it.

"Why did you do this to me?" she asked.

"Do what?"

"You know what I mean. This! *All of this!*"

"Would you rather have died that night?"

That night—she barely remembered it. "Yes." Without answering or breaking stride, Boian left the path and walked to a young oak tree. "What are you doing?" Still, he did not answer. Instead, he carefully studied the branches before selecting the one that fulfilled his secretive purpose. She cowered inwardly—Boian had hit her before. It did not hurt her, but his raw savagery terrified her beyond words when he did so. "What are you doing?" she repeated, this time with all the force she could muster.

"I am giving you your wish," he answered as he pulled a branch from its socket. It was sharp; she knew what that meant.

"Please, sir . . ."

He approached; she ran. In a flash, Boian was upon her and had forced her to the ground. She screamed and struggled, but he was much stronger than she was. With her arms pinned beneath his legs, she could only watch as he raised the stake high above his head and gasp as he brought it down toward her. She felt the rough wood sink into her chest; she wondered what it felt like to die and waited for it to come.

It did not come.

Boian stood, freeing her but leaving the stake in her chest.

"Why am I alive?" she asked.

"It did not hit your heart. You thought it had." He reached down and pulled the stake from her chest; it pulled free with a suction sound. Cami screamed in agony. "Remember this lesson, little Cami, survive, no matter whom you have to kill for your own survival, no matter what you have to do. The one final death is something to be feared. You were afraid when I stabbed you, were you not?"

Cami nodded.

"You said you wanted to die, but when death stared you in the face, you blinked. You will always be afraid to die, and you are right to be afraid." He threw the stake to the ground and continued walking, leaving a shaken Cami to follow. As they walked, he continued. "It is okay to kill, little Cami. You are stronger and better than they are. They are your prey, just like deer or rabbits in the forest. If you are going to kill, you should enjoy it. It can be fun if you allow it. You will learn."

Neither of them spoke after that until they reached the city of Siret to secure a room for the day. The inn was small, but it was quiet and available, and they had no trouble securing a room.

Before the pair mounted the stairs to find their rooms, a voice stopped them in their tracks. "I know you." They were the three words that frightened even the unshakable Boian. They represented danger and death. To lose their obscurity was to lose whatever semblance of safety for which they had hoped.

"You are mistaken, friend. We have never come this way before." Boian offered a disarming smile; despite it, the man approached.

"Not here," the man replied. "It was in Bender. You and this girl arrived just before my beloved died."

"I am sorry for your loss," Boian said dismissively before turning to the stairs. Cami knew him well enough to see his fear, and she followed close behind.

"You are not human," the man said. It was a statement rather than a question.

Boian turned. Cami saw his fangs had started to protrude. She stood behind him, desperately wanting to run but afraid to do even that. Others had joined the man at the base of the stairs. Some were armed, but each had an expression that ranged from fear to rage. They had all heard the legends, and the man had told all who would listen about the tragedy of Bender. "We just want a room," he offered. "My daughter and I have traveled a long way, and—"

The man interrupted with an enraged scream as he rushed toward Boian, driving a short dagger into his gut. Men gasped and women screamed, but no one reached to restrain him or help Boian. They quickly realized, however, that Boian did not need help—he stood uninjured with the blade protruding from his flesh. The crowd murmured and pressed closer. Boian doubled over in an imitation of pain, but it was too late for theatrics; the growing mob knew what he was. Boian grabbed Cami from behind him and pushed her toward the crowd before disappearing up the stairs. Cami broke free from the men's grasp and followed Boian toward whatever safety he sought, but she soon realized that running toward the upper floors was going to buy time rather than shelter.

Cami had a redeeming feature that Boian lacked; she was, to all appearances, a young girl. When the other guests of the inn emerged from their rooms to investigate the commotion, she was able to hide among the other children. Boian, however, was unable to hide. She could hear the shouts and screams when they found him—and the heavy sounds of a fight. Then his scream pierced both the air and her heart. Then silence.

CHAPTER THREE

Tata

Cami hated being alone. More than that, she hated knowing that she was never truly alone. No matter how far or fast she traveled, nor how many times she hid or doubled back along her path, she knew that Boian was watching. She could feel his eyes, and she always felt to be just on the edge of a terrible disaster. So she ran as far and as fast as she was able. Not until she found that she was on Highway 61, outside of Memphis, Tennessee, did she realize where she was going—Graceland.

Elvis started singing rockabilly in the early fifties, and Samuel became an immediate fan. Something about the up-tempo tones captivated him, and he was devastated when the King died in 1977. He begged Cami to go there and bring back the King. She refused the request. Nearly every day since, he had begged Cami to take them on the pilgrimage to the estate. They had never made it—there was always going to be enough time to go later and never a reason to rush. Cami regretted that she had never taken him. She walked through the streets of Downtown Memphis, ignoring the cheap vendors and expensive hustlers, lost in thought and regret.

"Hey." It was a man's voice. Cami ignored it and kept walking. "Hey!" the man yelled again, louder this time. She heard footsteps behind her and spun to face him. He wore a low cap that concealed his face, but she could see that he was short and slightly overweight, with an ill-fitting, mismatched suit and shoes that were a size too small for his feet.

"What?"

"You dropped this." He pressed a $5 bill toward her. She did not take it. Her money was tucked deep in her pocket. Perhaps some had fallen out, but she was not going to give anything away by taking the rest out to count it.

"That is not mine," she answered. The man looked confused and pressed his hand closer to her. His fingers hovered just above her chest. She had fed recently, but something about the man left her willing to indulge. She felt her fangs begin involuntarily to extend from the anticipation. "I will check, but I do not want to count my money out here in front of all these strangers. Can we go over there and talk?" She motioned toward the unlit walkway that emptied into the street.

"Sure," the man replied with a smile, which she could barely see under his brim. She felt his eyes dart along her body before Cami turned and headed into the deep shadows with the man close behind. She waited until the darkness concealed them both. He stood very close to her. In any other scenario, his presence would have been oppressive and intimidating. For Cami, his closeness just made it easier to kill him. Before he could speak, she drove her small unnaturally strong fist into his gut. He moaned and doubled over, and she could feel his stomach rupture under the pressure. This brought his neck to her level, and she grabbed his head and pulled him closer to her. He whimpered when she bit into him and fell to the ground when she began emptying his veins.

Something about his taste was familiar; she recognized it. She released the man and heard the dull concussion when his head hit the concrete. He moaned and tried to call for help, but the plea only came out as a hoarse whisper. His eyes opened with fear and confusion, and they met her own. She saw his face and immediately recognized it as the face of *her father.*

"Tata?" she whispered. The man struggled to speak but was not able to. He was dying. "*Oh, Tata!* What have I done?"

She cradled his head in her lap and cursed the bittersweet fortune of finding her father under such tragic conditions. Thoughts of how this could come to pass bombarded her mind. After all, she had seen Boian drain her mother and father more nearly six hundred years ago. This could not be her father, or by some strange gift, could it be him returning? He moaned, and his eyes rolled back into his head. His body started shaking as his heart struggled to use the small amount of blood remaining. Cami tore the vein in her wrist with her teeth and allowed the blood to flow freely. She held his mouth open and directed the steady drip into it, filling his mouth before the wound closed. He swallowed, closed his eyes, and lay still.

Cami waited, hoping that any god of fortune would smile on her father. He did not move. She ran a tender hand along his face—with no response. She felt something that she had not felt in a long time—remorse. Tears started to sting at her eyes as they threatened to escape the ducts.

She screamed at the same time that he did.

His revival was sudden and violent. People walking along the main road pretended not to hear and hurried along their way as he bore the excruciating pains of rebirth. She held him close to her as his appendages froze in rigor mortis and slowly released until he was strong enough to push her away. He vomited a small amount of blood as his stomach repaired itself, backed against the wall, and looked at her with wild, terrified eyes.

"What are you? What did you do to me?" he stammered.

"Tata, it is me. It is Camilia."

He was becoming more lucid now. "I don't know you . . . I'm not . . . What's a tata?" He was still frightened of her—and horrified at what was happening to him.

Cami struggled to understand. The man was clearly mortal, so it did not seem possible that he could be her father, and yet somehow, she was looking in his eyes. The best confirmation, however, was in the taste. Every vessel had a unique taste, and she remembered how her father's blood tasted. Now she had a more serious consideration. She became the man's rebirther and was responsible for his well-being. That was the very reason that she had never taken an unwilling *copil* (a Romanian word meaning a child or, in this case, young vampire), of her own before now. It is difficult, if not completely impossible, to nurture one through their adaptation when fear and anger are their driving force.

"You are changing, Tata," she explained, ignoring the man's insistence that he was not the man. "I am not going to let you die. I am going to keep you alive. Oh, what happened to you? You got older, your clothes do not fit, and you spent your nights hustling little girls. You are lucky I found you."

"I don't want to die," he said after a long moment.

"Do you remember how old I am?"

"Ten . . . eleven," he guessed.

"You are being kind," she joked. "I am over five hundred years. Although this was a horrid way, I have seen things over the years that I could not have possibly imagined! I have watched kings rise and fall. I have seen the world's wonders and wealth and drank deep from all that this world has to offer." She watched those whom she cared for grow old and die; she saw the world change but was not able to change with it. She did not mention those aspects and refused to watch her father die again. "I can give you all of that if you want it."

"I don't want it. I want my life. It wasn't much, but it was mine."

Cami looked at him with loving eyes. "I would give you your life back if I could, but sadly, I cannot. I can only give you something better, dear one. I can give you an existence like no other! I have given you a pain-free existence, where you will never have to worry or feel pain or sickness again!"

Meekly, barely able to speak, he mumbled, "Okay . . . please."

"You choose to live?"

His voice was thick with resignation but barely able to form the words. "Yes, I choose to live."

She got him to his feet and helped him steady himself. Cami started shooting questions one after another. He introduced himself as Richard. His age was somewhere between thirty-five and forty. The reason he could not really be sure on his age was caused by being shuffled from one extended family member home to the next. No one kept up with his age or cared if he was happy.

She locked her arm through his as they walked down alleyways to his apartment. When they got to the front of the apartment, it was a run-down hole with more rats inside than residents. He explained that today was his last day at the apartment because tomorrow he was being evicted.

Cami hopes these sad memories will fade with time. She was confused as to why he had no memory of her. She vowed that she would patiently raise Richard in his rebirth, just as Tata raised her.

"You're really five hundred years old?" he asked.

"Give or take."

"Crazy. Why am I so hungry?"

"You need to eat."

"Eat . . . what?" Richard knew the answer, but he was hoping that it was not true.

Cami smiled. It was difficult for some at first. "Blood, of course—life source, sustenance, whatever you want to call it. I found it easier at first to just think of it as a warm liquid diet."

"I don't think I can. I can't kill someone."

Cami understood—it was not something that she enjoyed either. "Some people deserve it. Death supports life. Every living creature kills to eat, and we are no exception. The best we can do is to kill those who deserve it, when it's possible, at least."

"Did I deserve to die?" he asked.

"No, Tata, of course not," she said.

"So then who are you to play God? The one who decides who lives and who dies?"

She was taken aback by the question and his sudden aggression. Despite her surprise, she answered patiently. "If you do not eat, you *will* die. It is as simple as that. You make the best of it, or you starve." A rat scurried across the floor, looking for food. It stared at the pair unafraid. Cami moved faster than the rat could react, and it squealed in fear before she twisted its pointed head from its twitching body and pressed it toward Richard. "Drink it, please."

He looked both disgusted and horrified by the prospect. "Why?"

"Drink it, please," she repeated. "Quickly, before the blood dies. You need to eat . . . or would you rather go out and kill a human being? Your call, but it will be light soon. You need to eat before—"

"What happens when it gets light?"

"If it hits you, it burns your skin. More than a few minutes and you will burn to death."

Richard gazed longingly at the fresh blood that poured over Cami's delicate hands, as she gently squeezed the animal to keep its heart beating, and spilled on to the cheap carpet. She knew that he was starving and that his need would overcome his revulsion. It did not take long. He grabbed the small corpse from her and drank greedily from the wound.

"Thank you," she said, relieved that he had taken in the blood.

His expression changed from desperate to relieved and finally to something resembling nausea. "It's horrible," he gagged.

"Yes, it is, but it will keep you alive through the daytime until you can feed properly. That is your only other option. So if you want to live on that, you can." She did not mention pigs. They tasted almost human. Ironically, it was much harder to get away with killing pigs for their blood than it was to kill humans for theirs.

"People . . . taste better?"

Cami smiled. "Yes, much *better*. You choose carefully, and there is no reason to feel guilty. The drug dealers, whores, kiddie fiddlers— they are all fair game . . . Oh! But not drug addicts! Not unless you want to go for a trip that could leave you in the open when the sun rises."

Richard was listening to her with a perplexed expression. "What?"

"It's just . . . you just look like a little girl."

"I am not—not anymore. Please start putting blankets on the windows. These curtains will not keep the light out."

"You tried to kill me earlier, now you've got manners—'please' and 'thank you.' Why?"

Cami thought for a moment. "First of all, make no mistake. If I wanted to kill you, you would be worm food right now. Second, why would I want to be rude? You raised m—I was raised better than that. In my short life, my parents taught me to be respectful and courteous to people . . . all living things really, especially when I have the upper hand." Then she looked sad. "Besides . . . I did not know . . . I mean . . . I thought you were a bad person . . . I just . . . I did not know . . .," she answered, deciding not to press against his confusion. Richard thought that he would never get used to such grown-up words coming from the mouth of a child.

Cami pulled the unwashed blankets from his stained bed. "Come on, help me." She began covering the nearby windows, while Richard did the same. He peered out, seeing the sky starting to lighten with vibrant splashes of colors and soft textures. He could already feel his skin starting to sting, but it was not as bad as the realization that he would never again see the sunrise or sunset. A single drop of rain fell from somewhere in the sky and thudded against the window, refracting the colors and creating a private show for an audience of one. Richard looked longingly at the drop and spoke to it. "Oh, my little raindrop," he said longingly.

"Yes, Tata?" Cami said. Her voice was full of hope, remembering the time her father used to call her that.

"What?" he asked perplexed.

"You called me little raindrop, you said . . . I heard you, Tata. Why can you not remember?"

"I didn't call *you* raindrop . . . It's raining, and I know it's silly, but I was talking to the raindrop," Richard answered. Cami ignored his confused stare and pulled the blanket to the side, plunging the room into total darkness. Despite the lack of visible light, the pair was able to see clearly. "Why can I see?"

"You will get used to it. Now please lie down. You *really* do *not* want to be standing or even sitting up when your body begins to die for the day."

They lay together on the bed, and Cami explained the quasi-death process to Richard as they went through it together. He was still naturally frightened, but she comforted him as the rigor mortis gripped his muscles and stiffened his limbs. His mind was the last to go, and he drifted off to death. Before she did the same, she moved herself close to him.

. . .

When Cami's mind started to return, slowly and painfully, the first thing that she heard was the pounding. It was insistent and driving, and it took a moment for her to remember where she was and what was happening. She heard Richard moan beside her and knew that he was experiencing the same. She talked him through the process, while the pounding grew more insistent. She could barely make out the enraged shouts that accompanied the percussion.

"Get outta here, you son of a bitch!" the man bellowed between drunken slurs. "You better got mah moneh! I swear to God I gonna kick yo' ass!"

Cami turned to Richard, who pulled himself to his stiff legs and hobbled to the window. "We've gotta get out of here," he said as he pulled the blanket free. "That assho—" He stopped himself, still not seeing Cami as his elder. "That jerk's serious. He's nuts."

"Let him in," Cami said as she turned on the lights.

"Are you crazy?"

"No. Trust me. Please . . . let him in. You need to start learning sooner or later." Cami turned toward the door and called through it in a cheery singsong voice, "Coming!"

Richard was practically shaking as he made his way to the door. The man outside was as wild as a dog brought to a frenzy by a scent. Richard released the chain and threw several deadlocks before turning the final lock in the knob itself. He threw open the door and poured himself into the room. His massive frame, seemingly equal amounts of fat and muscle, barely fit through the frame. He pushed Richard against the wall and started shaking him while yelling an unintelligible string of threats and obscenities. Richard merely whimpered in the man's massive grip.

"Hello, mister!" Cami paired the greeting with her sweetest and least sincere of smiles.

While maintaining a firm grip on Richard's neck, the man turned his attention to this new development. Through an intoxicated haze, he tried to understand. He turned back to Richard with a wide grin. "Little ol' for mah likin', but she'll do just fine. Gimme a night and y'all can stay another week. Whatcha says?"

"It's not like that," Richard pleaded. "She's just a friend."

"Yeah, I'll bet she is," he sneered. He released Richard and closed in on Cami. She could smell the alcohol in his breath and the long-since-dried urine in his clothes. "Yer 'bout my dawter's age, you know that?"

Cami stared at the man, looking into his eyes and then through them. He fell into her deep eyes, almost drowning in them, and stared at them, oblivious of his surroundings or of time passing. She searched the man's very soul until she found what she was looking for—his will. She brought his will into her own and then returned it to him as her own.

"What's going on?" Richard whispered.

Cami ignored him and instead spoke to the large man. "He does not owe you any money. He has paid his rent through to the end of the year. Do you understand?"

The man nodded, repeating what he had been told, "He doesn't owe me any money. He has paid his rent through the end of the year. I understand."

"You spent all the money on whiskey or vodka or whatever foul intoxicant you use to pollute your blood." She watched as his mind forced itself to create the new memory and assimilate it.

"What about his daughter?" Richard whispered.

Cami knew what he meant, and she sighed, happy for Richard's interjection. "You will never hurt your daughter again—not even a swat." She turned to Richard. "There, happy?"

"Yes," Richard said. "No," the man answered simultaneously. Richard nodded solemnly. Cami smiled to herself, satisfied that she had done the right thing.

Good, Cami thought under her breath. She released the man, who walked away in a confused daze. Richard watched him leave and make his way to the apartment that he shared with his daughter. He grabbed the doorknob but did not go in. After a moment, he shook his head and walked in the opposite direction.

"Cami?" Richard asked after a long moment.

"What?"

"Why didn't you kill him?"

"Why should I?"

"He is an ass. He hurts people. Isn't that what you said?"

"Would *that* not be playing God then?"

Richard had not seen the hypocrisy in his views. "Yes," he said meekly.

"We kill when we have to eat. I mean, it is most definitely a happy coincidence when the two intersect, but we do not just kill for vengeance. It is important that you remember that, so you do not lose what is good in you. We do not kill for fun—we are not monsters."

"We kill people in the night. What do you call that?"

Cami quickly replied, without skipping a beat, "Survival. Think about it like this, Richard, humans will kill two baby chickens and slaughter a pig for one breakfast. We only kill one animal for a whole twenty-four-hour period." Richard nodded, finally understanding. Cami had spent centuries rejecting her rebirther's teachings and refused to allow his same vices to permeate others. "Besides, how long do you want to live?

"What do you mean?" he asked.

"Please think it through. What happens if he shows up missing? There is a child involved, and he has some money. The cops are going to start looking around. When they start looking around, they are going to talk to us, and if anything seems the least bit out of place, they will start digging deeper. The last thing you want now is attention. Attention means that you either have to kill a lot of people or you die." She thought of Boian again. She wondered how many people he killed in order to survive that night so long ago.

"Okay, I get it, but we have to eat, right?"

"Right." Cami grinned. "Let us go shopping."

Although the pair walked for miles, Richard was surprised to find that he was not tired. Normally, he knew he would have been wheezing and trying to catch his breath, even if they were not walking as quickly as they were. Aside from his nagging hunger, he felt stronger and healthier than he ever had before. Lost in his thoughts, he almost missed Cami's departure when she took a sharp turn from the sidewalk and entered a local hardware store.

The place was empty aside from the disinterested cashier that was reading a worn magazine. Richard was surprised to find that he could smell him and was acutely aware of the subtle pulse that made his skin quiver in the most delicate of areas. The shop itself was as run-down as its keeper is a victim of the larger retailer that had moved in just a few months ago. The inventory was sparse at best. It had what Cami needed, however; she selected a premeasured length of thick chain and several metal clamps. Each of the items was neatly stored in an off-brand duffel bag, which she slung over her shoulder after paying. The cashier never looked up from his skin-mag; he would not remember them.

They continued walking, Richard asking countless questions and Cami deflecting them with a sharp admonition that he just "wait and see." Finally, they made their way to a quiet stretch of the Mississippi River. Cami seemed to know exactly where she was going, and Richard followed along with a morbid sense of fascination. Finally, she stopped and pointed. Several women stood in a small group near the road. Richard was amazed at how clearly he could see against both the distance and the dark, but he still whispered as though they were nearby, "Hookers?"

"Yes—easy prey. That is what you are going to start with."

"You want me to . . . kill them?" he asked.

"Not all of them, silly. Just kill one. Do not get greedy," she joked. "Do not worry, I will be doing the deed." She scanned the road, looking for something. "You do not go after the pack if you can help it. You look for the one who has separated herself. Sometimes she is just new and does not know any better. Sometimes no one else wants anything to do with her. You take the one that is alone, and there is no one left to describe you."

"You've done this before," Richard observed.

"Yes," she answered flatly. "That one!" she said finally and excitedly. She pointed to a girl that had just come from the riverfront, ignoring the man that had left in the opposite direction. She had not joined the rest of the group but instead stood far off and closer to traffic.

"What do I need to do?" Richard asked.

She pulled a folded bill from her pocket and handed it to him. "Take this twenty. Here, you only need about a minute. She will take you somewhere private. I am guessing back where she had gone before. I will be waiting there."

Richard eyed the woman and her seemingly preferred spot at the water's edge. He turned to answer, but Cami was already gone. He sighed and made his way to where the woman stood. She smiled as he approached.

"Hey, cutie," she cooed.

Richard forced a smile. He had never even talked to a prostitute before, at least not that he knew of, much less killed one.

"Hey," he stammered. "I have money," he said.

The woman laughed; it was a light lilted sound. "Slow down a minute, hotshot." She looked around then leaned in close. "Fifty bucks and I got a place nearby."

He handed her the bill. She took it, studied it for a moment, and then slipped it into her bra.

"You seem nervous. No need to be nervous. You wanna go somewhere private and talk?" Her voice came out like fine wine. She was clever; she had not said anything incriminating yet. Richard nodded, and she led him down to the riverside—precisely to where Cami waited. Richard knew that she was talking, he could hear the sweet cadence of her voice, but he was not able to catch the words. He wanted to warn her, to tell her to run away and not look back. Every step brought her closer to her death as their destination drew nearer. Richard knew that Cami was hiding in the darkness, hungrily watching. He did not want to kill, but he wanted to eat even more. He could practically smell the blood that washed through her veins, and all he could think about was the steady heartbeat that he imagined he could hear from deep inside her chest. He wondered how she would taste. He wondered how much Cami would allow him to have. Richard groaned inwardly when the woman stopped. "You okay?" she asked.

"Just a little nervous is all." Technically, it was not a lie. He was literally watching a stranger walk toward her doom; he was about to kill her, and she had no idea. He blurted out, "I've never done this before." That also was true.

As she always did, the woman weighed the risks against the money that she had taken and decided that it was worthwhile. "Don't worry, sweetie. I won't bite."

The woman smiled as she reached the sheltered area. Cami, however, had made no such promise. Cami appeared from the darkness, leaping from where she hid and pressing herself against the woman. She did not even have time to scream before Cami's teeth tore through her flesh. She started choking on her own blood as the delicate network of veins and arteries were pulled from the soft meat. A few moments after that, she would be dead. Her life had been brief; she was fortunate that her death would be also.

Richard felt his fangs starting to extend, pushing the root of his canine teeth through the gums. "What now?" Each of his senses was brought to hypersensitivity. He heard the occasional growl of a passing vehicle and saw the headlights reflect dimly off the ground. He saw reflections of moonlight dance in the laughing waves. He heard the mosquitoes darting through the air, looking for a meal as well. The sights and sounds combined to form a masterful opus that only he could hear.

Cami looked up, her eyes glazed over with bloodlust. "Now you just bite into the juicy part. Your body knows what to do."

Momentarily, Richard was ashamed of the enthusiasm with which he bit into the body. That feeling was immediately replaced by a euphoric rush. He had never before tasted anything quite so delectable. By the time, the sensation washed over him, and he was brought back to bitter reality; Cami was done feeding and was busying herself with the chain.

"What are you doing?" Richard slurred.

"She had drugs in her system, so you might feel a little bit funny," Cami said. "It will pass quickly. We are going to sink the body—the chain and clamps will help us keep it there. Fish and others will start eating the body, and the water will do the rest. By the time she is found, there is no chance anyone will suspect a vampire. She will just be another dead prostitute." She handed him the chain. "Put the chain on her." Richard took it and began wrapping it around the woman's ankle. "Not like that, Tata," Cami said.

They were hiding a body, and Richard was panicking. He wondered how Cami could be so calm. "What did I do?"

"When the skin and muscles decompose, the bones come apart over time. If you attach it to the ankle, you have three opportunities for the torso to come loose." She pointed to specific points on the woman's leg as she spoke. "The torso—that is the part that tends to float. So if you want to buy some time, you keep that from happening." Cami pulled the woman's shirt up, exposing an unexpectedly expensive bra for such a cheap hooker. "So we go for the ribcage," she said. Cami pressed the last link of the chain against the space between the woman's visible ribs. "See?" She pressed inward, indenting and then tearing the skin and bending the ribs to accommodate the insertion. The wound did not bleed as she pressed the metal into the cavity—all her blood was already gone.

Richard winced at the sound of metal grating against bone. *She looks so young*, Richard thought to himself. *How in the hell does she know how to hide a body?*

Cami continued her work with the same emotional detachment as one who was gutting a fish. She pushed through the skin of the woman's soft stomach, grasped the chain from the inside, looped it around the lower ribs, and screwed the clamp into place. She stood and tugged at the chain to make sure it was secure—the body twitched, but the ribs held. "Wait here," she said. "I will swim to the bottom and find something to attach it to. Then maybe we can catch a movie or something."

Richard was shortly stunned but shook the sensation from his mind. "It's gotta be fifty feet deep here easy. You'll drown."

Cami grinned. "You are sweet to worry. It is impossible to drown if you do not need to breathe." She giggled. She felt nearly like a child again but did not forget that she had the responsibilities of a mother now. Then she picked up the body and waded into the river, leaving Richard alone with his thoughts. By the time she returned, he was gone.

Chapter Four

A Resting Place Fit for a King

Cami retraced her steps to Richard's apartment, but she could tell that something terrible had happened before she reached the building. Several police cars blocked off access to the building, while an ambulance pulled into the lot. The mournful wails in the distance told her that more cars were on the way. She could think of any number of ways that Richard could have died, but she was sure that Boian's shadowy presence was the most likely cause—taking another companion from her and leaving her alone again. She had mixed feelings when she saw Richard running toward her covered in blood. He was alive, but he was also the cause.

"What did you do?" she hissed when he slid to a halt next to her.

"I killed him. I wanted to try to do that thing that you did—with the eyes—but he flipped out. So I had to kill him."

"Oh no, you really should not have."

"It wasn't my fault. He attacked me," Richard stammered as he rose to his feet.

Cami gave him a stern look.

Richard looked to the ground. "I'm sorry. I just . . . I hated him."

"We kill to eat—no other reason . . . And even then, if we can simply feed, erase the memory and move on—that is best. Otherwise, we are just monsters."

Richard nodded. "I'm sorry."

Cami sighed. "What is done is done. We just need to find a place before it gets light."

"I guess I didn't think it through," Richard said softly.

Cami did not answer but instead reached for his hand and gave it a reassuring squeeze. They stood together in silence, watching the officers crawl over the scene like ants on a small amount of dropped candy. Cami knew that they would be looking for Richard once they started looking into the financials and noticed that Richard was missing. So they would need to leave the area, maybe construct an identity.

Richard interrupted her thought process. He asked, "What about a crypt?"

"What about one?"

"Shouldn't we be sleeping in a crypt?"

Cami giggled. "You have been reading too many stories. Of course, there are times when they are convenient, but for the most part, they are simply dirty, dusty places, where you may have to heal when you awaken because a mouse or rat has gnawed at your fingers, your nose, or other extremities."

Richard smiled, amused at her description. Cami realized that she had not seen him do that before, and she returned the gesture.

"No, I'm serious. When Elvis died, they put him in a tomb over at Forest Hill cemetery. Just after that, a story leaked out that someone was going to kidnap his body and hold it for ransom. They posted twenty-four-hour security until they could get permission to bury him at Graceland. A few months later, they took his body to his home at Graceland, which left the tomb empty. People still visit the tomb and leave gifts and flowers at the door, but it's empty inside. We can stay there."

There was little reason for Cami to say yes, but the idea appealed to her. She was not sure if it was because of her affection for Richard or her guilt over Samuel or perhaps the latent thrill of the King's celebrity status, but she readily agreed to his macabre plan. Fortunately, Richard had not parked close to the still-active crime scene, so they were able to leave the area unnoticed. He took a circuitous route along back roads and residential communities, avoiding the freeways and city center. The ancient sedan belched exhaust into the otherwise still night, and the radio alternated between two different songs interrupted by periods of static. Cami watched the world slip past through the dirty window. For the first time in a very long time, she felt nearly at home.

"We're here," Richard said, pulling Cami from her thoughts. They had reached the closed gates of Forest Hill Cemetery. "I guess we'll need to climb . . ."

"We need to hide the car first. The car is in your name, right?" Richard nodded gravely. "Then it is in our best interest to keep it out of sight, for a few days at least. Do you not think?"

"Where?"

Cami thought for a moment. She replayed the route they had taken in her mind with crystal clarity, mentally marking potential hiding spots. Finally, she decided on a nearby location. "There was a warehouse or something, not far from here. Let us try there."

"They won't just let us park. How are we going to get in there?"

Cami grinned. "It is time you learned something new. Drive," she said, pointing down the road.

They were driving in the opposite direction, away from the factory, but Richard did not question her directions. He drove along the avenue until Cami stopped him, directing him to pull alongside a police car that contained a single occupant. Richard was very nervous but did as Cami told him. The officer rolled down his window, and Cami did the same.

"Evening, miss," the officer said.

Cami did not return the greeting but leaned closer to the smiling man. She stared silently until his broad smile faded, his face fell flat, and his eyes opened wide. Only then did she speak, "Sing a song for me."

Without hesitation, the officer began to sing. It was a tune that Cami had never heard, but she recognized the words as being flawless Italian.

She turned to Richard with a wide grin. "He is a falsetto." She laughed. Richard stared in stunned disbelief as the officer completed the song. Once finished, he merely stared once again. "You see, you can change people's behavior. You can make them do things."

"Will he remember what he did?"

"I do not know. They do remember sometimes. It depends on the person, some are stronger than others."

"When you told Logan about his daughter—"

"Logan?" Cami interrupted.

"My landlord back at the apartment. Would he have done what you said?"

"Yes. When you plant a seed, it will grow. You have seen that you can control the mind. The mind is just another organ in the body. Once you realize that you can control the body itself, you can affect the health or function of it. You have to understand the ramifications—the responsibility. You can stop someone's heart or keep their lungs from drawing breath." She turned to the officer. "Vomit," she said simply. The officer's body convulsed as his stomach violently contracted, forcing its contents on to the ground and against the car's door. Despite the physical reaction, his face remained impassive, and he stared blankly ahead. "Leave now, you never saw us."

The officer turned his head, rolled up his window, and disappeared into the night.

"How did you do that?" Richard asked awed.

Cami patiently explained the technique. She taught Richard how to collect his own will and project it on another. She explained how to captivate his target by adding depth to his own eyes. Most importantly, she explained the difficulty and importance in wielding such a powerful ability while resisting its corrupting influence. Finally, when he had absorbed all that she had to teach, he was ready. They drove in silence toward the distribution center. Richard was mumbling reminders to himself, and Cami allowed him the time to do so. They turned on to the narrow road that would lead to the gate. The night guard looked up from his smut rag, surprised to see anything smaller than a big rig.

Richard rolled down the window as the man approached. He was a small man, not much taller than the car itself, and his facial expressions and features were reminiscent of a panicked rodent. "No entry," he said. Cami wondered if he was old enough to even legally be employed, much less carry the pistol that clung to his hip.

Richard stared at the youth, and Cami watched as his face began to relax and his hand drifted away from the pistol. Richard maintained a deep eye contact and started to mutter specific commands and vague concepts. "You'll let us in now," Richard commanded.

The man repeated, "I will let you in now," as though speaking through a dream. Despite his seeming agreement, he did not move.

"Open the gate," Richard said again, more forcefully this time.

The man shook his head. His eyes refocused, and he brought his hand to the pistol. Cami was suddenly at his side, which surprised Richard, as he had not seen nor heard her leave the vehicle. She jumped in front of the man before he could react and locked his eyes into her own. His body froze as she gazed intensely and whispered with a lover's passion. Then it was over. She relaxed; the guard stared blankly ahead.

"Let us in now. You will show us where to hide the car so that no one will find it."

The man returned to the tower and pressed a button, raising the gate to allow them to pass—Richard driving the car, Cami as its passenger, and the young guard leading them on foot.

"What did I do wrong?" Richard asked. He whispered as though the man would be able to hear him even if he was not entranced.

"You lost your focus. It only takes a moment, and then the influence falls away. It happens, Richard. You did fine, sweet man. You just need more practice." Cami smiled up at him and brushed the hair on his temple.

They followed him to the far side of the facility, which housed the rusting carcasses of abandoned and unserviceable trailers. The man judged carefully, looking over each one as if through a magnifying glass, before selecting the one that seemed to meet his expectations. The axels had broken, leaving the container resting directly on the ground. Even with Cami's immense strength, coupled with Richard's developing ability, the trailer was difficult to open. Once they did so, they were able to store Richard's car before resealing the door behind it. There was no way to tell that the doors had ever been opened, much less recently, and Cami gave the effort an approving nod.

"You will forget that you ever saw us. There is nothing interesting in these trailers," Cami projected. The man turned and walked back to the gate. She knew that he would come back to reality shortly and led Richard past the man. As they walked, she explained. "Sometimes they retain a little bit of memory of what it is that you made them do or what they had seen. If the last thing that you say to them is an order to forget, that goes away, so you do not have to worry."

Richard nodded, absorbing her lesson. They moved quickly, knowing that the dawn was fast approaching, and made it to the crypt in a few minutes. It was not as Cami had expected. The building was massive and stately and carried an aura of sorrow despite the cheerful mementos left by recent visitors. Richard pulled uselessly at the crypt's gate, and Cami watched with amusement as he tried to force his way inside. She knew he would not be able to. Being so young, she allowed him to experience the minor failure for the learning opportunity that it presented.

"I can't," he huffed resignedly.

"I know." Cami smiled. "Did you really expect to? Those are iron bars, silly."

She produced a set of lock picks and studied the thick tumbler lock. Richard, upon seeing this new set of tools, said to Cami, "I'm not even going to ask where you've been hiding that." She shrugged and used one to push the pins into the shear line while using another to provide the tension as she twisted the tumbler. One by one, the pins locked into place until the tumbler was able to turn freely and the clasp snapped open. Cami grinned to herself as they stepped into the cold chamber. "Amazing," Richard muttered as he ran his hand along the cool stone walls. "I always wondered . . ."

Cami frowned, her expression contrasting the one of wonderment that Richard kept. "There are a lot of windows," she noted.

"Well, sure, out here but not in the vault itself. That's where the bodies are kept or would be if they were still here."

They made their way to the vault, which had once housed the American royal family—the King and those closest to him. It was sealed, secured from the public by a massive steel door which was itself secured by thick steel bars. The building was maintained meticulously as a testament to the legend's memory, and the flowers that remained on and around the doors were fresh and fragrant. She was lost in the sea of colors and the waves of scents that washed over her before she shook herself free from the immersive sensations, remembering both the steadily approaching sun and the goal it necessitated. She carefully studied the door and busied herself, freeing the latching mechanism without visibly damaging it—no easy feat and not a quick one.

"Cami . . .," Richard called.

"I am a little busy," she answered.

"It's getting light . . ."

Cami did not answer, forcing the thought from her mind as she focused on the door instead of the approaching dawn. It was a race that she was tired of running in but one that she could not safely end. She could hear Richard nervously pacing behind her, and the sound of his footsteps and breathing was distracting.

"Would you be still?" she snapped. It was harsher than she meant, but she was already feeling the uncomfortable effects of the approaching daylight. She had come to understand very well what Boian had told her, *"Every blessing has a hidden curse. Every curse has a hidden blessing. Which one you find is as much a matter of fortune as it is inclination."*

"Sorry," Richard mumbled.

Cami reminded herself to apologize later, provided they could get inside in time. She knew that they had to because there was nowhere else to go. Finally, with great effort, she was able to open both doors without damaging the flowers that surrounded them and revealing the intrusion. They stepped into the silent resting place. The stale still air reminded Cami of the last time she had entered a king's final resting chamber. It had been a long time ago, and it was a very different king. They carefully set the bars and the door in place, which sealed the room in an oppressive darkness—so dark that even Cami had difficulty seeing in it which was much more than the muted colors that Richard was able to discern. Cami sniffed at the air, sensing something that she could not quite place.

"What do—" Richard began, but he was silenced when Cami pressed an urgent finger against his lips. He knew to trust her senses and instincts, and he stopped speaking without understanding why. All that he knew was that something was wrong. He backed against the cool wall of the vault. He held his breath and strained to listen but could hear nothing, except for his own heartbeat. He reached for Cami, instinctively trying to pull the girl close to him, but his hands caught only empty air. He pushed himself into the room's corner and allowed himself to fall to the ground in a crouch. He heard the brief angry percussion of a footfall on the stone floor. Then silence. He heard the sharp intake of breath and the sound of bone on flesh. Then nothing. He knew that there was an unseen battle raging around him—one that he knew would prove deadly for him if he were to participate.

His unpracticed eyes slowly began to adjust, allowing him to make out a figure in the darkness. That indiscernible figure was pursued by another; he could only assume that one of them was Cami. He could not make out which one was she or who the other was. The fight raged in near silence within the small room, with neither gaining the upper hand. Blows were exchanged, and clothing was torn; the two shadowy combatants tore at each other in a frenzy until one made a fatal error. Richard could not see how but knew only that one gained the advantage and forced the other violently to the ground. The struggle on the ground was brief and punctuated by snarls and hisses from the inevitable loser. The topmost figure raised both arms overhead and brought down whatever they held into the other. There was a brief screech, a raspy moan, and then silence.

The victor rose unsteadily on his—or her—feet, approaching Richard, coming closer one step at a time. He pressed himself tighter against the wall, trying uselessly to push through it to safety, trying to will himself further from the terror that could kill so reflexively. He flinched when the light exploded in his eyes, blinding him for a brief moment, then died down. The match cast aggressive shadows on the walls and, to Richard's relief, on Cami's face. She was bloodied and torn. The skin of her face had been ripped deep enough to show bone underneath, and her arm hung limply at her side. She was the victor, even if only barely. Richard watched in amazement as her flesh began to repair itself; the wounds started to close, and the skin stitched itself together, while the bones of her arm fused and formed to make her whole.

"What happened?" Richard asked, eyeing the body. He followed Cami, who kneeled next to it and directed the light on to its face. After a moment, she lit a second match and discarded the first. The body was that of a young boy, maybe six or seven years at the oldest, although Richard suspected that he too was much older than he appeared.

The dead child's blank face had twisted in a mask of pain, most certainly caused by the wooden stake, which Cami had obviously forced into his chest. His skin had already grown pale, and his limbs were stiffening in death. Cami prepared herself for what would come next. She had only seen it happen a few times, and each time was slightly less jarring and disturbing than the previous one. When a vampire died, the life force that kept them in an ageless stasis was severed. It always seemed to Cami that Mother Nature finally noticed that her most sacred rule—that all things should age—has been violated and thus corrected centuries of oversight in a few intense moments. The body would rapidly pass through the ill-gotten years, compressing growth, rigor mortis, putrefaction, and decomposition before turning into an explosion of dust and larger particles that was at the mercy of even the slightest breeze. It was difficult not to be soiled by the explosion if one was too close when it happened. The sensation of being covered in recently ancient remains was difficult to forget.

Cami, however, had never seen it happen to a vampire that had turned in childhood and was not prepared for the fresh horror she was to face. The child grew into adolescence and passed into adulthood in a terrifying moment. He was a corpse at each stage in what would have otherwise been normal development, and his body grew and changed as though it were being unnaturally stretched and shaped by Mother Nature, but somehow, it appeared normal at each stage. The boy became an adolescent then a man and then aged into senescence.

A part of Cami wanted to hold the unfortunate child and comfort him in death, or somehow find a way to stop the process, before she remembered that he was already gone. She dreaded the next moment, but it came anyway. What was once a child grew into a twisted, gnarled corpse—a perverse parody of what he had once been—and then turned into dust. She saw every particle of what had once been a child and quietly wished him peace in death. She could not help but see herself in the same way. She saw her body quickly aging, turning from a girl to a woman, from a woman to a crone then a corpse, and from corpse to dust. For one to be forcefully faced with their own mortality, it is terrifying for any sentient creatures. For one who had grown used to denying it, it was overwhelming. She could see that Richard was speaking, but she could not make out his words. She was lost in a sea of regret and fear. As she focused on the sensations, she allowed them to wash over her. She became an island in the middle of a tumultuous sea, and she forced herself to stand firm against the relentless waves of her own thoughts. Eventually, the sea settled. The waves grew smaller and ceased their violent crashing, and she was able to restore an internal sense of normalcy.

"It seems that someone else had the same idea," Cami said. She answered the last question that she had heard and did not ask Richard to repeat what he had said. Richard took a moment to understand what question it was that she was answering.

"He was . . . one of us?" His face showed the same fear and trepidation that Cami felt internally.

Cami remembered the first time that she had seen a vampire die. It was at Boian's hands, and he was merely a threat to Boian's status in the small group that had become something close to a family. The death was brutal and violent, and it left a permanent scar on Cami's previously unsoiled mind. She pulled Richard close to her, comforting him. "He was like us. He was not one of us. There are those who are feral, wild—those who forgot that they still have a heart, even if it does not beat any longer. Stay away from them. More importantly, do not *become* one of them. Promise me this. *Promise*, Richard."

Richard nodded. "I won't." His eyes never left the loose pile of dust. A small mass remained behind, partially buried in the dust. It looked like a lump of petrified flesh, which Cami believed was left due to the traumatic death and the age of the creature.

Cami forced Richard's eyes to meet her own. "Swear it."

"I swear." He ran his hands over the stake that had killed the boy. "Did you have this the whole time, this stake?"

Cami lifted the small mass in her arms as she stood. "No, it is his. He had it with him. He planned to use it on me . . . then probably you after that. I just got him first." There was no remorse or pity in her voice; she spoke as though it were the only practical solution. Reluctantly, Richard agreed that it likely was. He knew that it was either the feral creature or them.

Cami opened the door once again and carried the mass into the main hall of the crypt then out into the cemetery grounds. She could not understand the reason that she would take such a risk, except that she had no desire to share the resting place with the remains. She moved quickly against the dawning horizon and, with an underserved reverence, laid the small item in a concealed location where the morning sun would find it, reducing it to unidentifiable ashes. She allowed herself one last look at what was left of her misguided elder before returning to the vault.

"There are no windows," he said as she sealed the door once again from the inside.

"That seems to be a plus." Cami forced a smile.

"How do we know when it's getting light? You know, when it's time to sleep?"

"Just like many things, your body knows. It will start shutting down when it is time. Once it starts . . . you need to make sure you are somewhere the sun will not reach."

"What if you're outside?"

"Do not be."

They rested in comfortable silence, each reflecting on the strange events and experiences of their recent past. As their bodies began to accept their daily death, Richard lay flat on the floor and Cami joined him. She leaned in close to the man, placing her head against his chest and an arm reaching across him. Then like a child, she slept.

CHAPTER FIVE

Cami's First Drive-in Movie

They naturally awoke with the nightfall, and their bodies and minds were restored in the now familiar process. The first thoughts of each were related to their relative mortality. Cami knew how close she had come to being killed the previous night, and she was chilled by the realization that her death would have resulted in Richard's as well. Richard, however, was less concerned with what could have been than he was of what could be.

"We can be killed?" They were the first words he spoke. They echoed off the walls and hung heavy in the air.

"Yes, we can," Cami answered.

Richard sat quietly, considering the implications. "Why didn't you tell me?"

"I told you that we can die."

"By the sun, I know. You said we're immortal! By definition, immortal means 'can't be killed'! You did *not* tell me *that we could be killed*! I would have remembered that!"

Cami thought for a moment. "You are right. I am sorry. Yes, Richard, we can be killed. It is not easy, but it can happen."

"How?"

"There are a few of ways—fewer ways than humans' at least. A stake through the heart obviously, you saw that last night. Burning also works, but the body has to be completely destroyed by the fire. There is something even greater, something that we all fear. When the power of God moves through the faithful, it is deadly."

"What do you mean?"

"Silver blessed by a priest, holy water, a crucifix—these are all things that can be wielded against you. It is not the action of blessing that matters, as much as what the blessings represent. If the faithful accepts that God exists and calls upon him against what he knows to be . . . one of us . . . then almost anything can be a weapon. However, they have to do it intentionally wishing us harm. My own rebirther told me a story once, about a man that he said he knew. In this man's human life, he was a priest—a true man of God. He wore a massive crucifix around his neck and filled his mouth with holy water. Any vampire that crossed him, anyone that came against him, he had simply to call on God and spit the water on them, and they would burst into flames!" Cami accented the story with an excitable hand gesture.

Richard frowned, trying to understand. "If he's a priest, he knows that God exists . . . So how can he touch a cross without being hurt? How can he take in holy water without dying?"

"Intent—that is the key. He does not want to hurt himself, so God is not going to force it on him. It is that whole 'free will' thing. It was his cross. He did not want to hurt himself, so he was safe. I always saw that as more of a legend you tell around a campfire, so to speak."

"So what does that mean? Does God . . . hate us?"

"No. What we are is up to us, just like anyone else. We can be good or evil. We can *do* good or evil, but what is inside us, we cannot change. God intended for man to live and die—sunrise and sunset and all that. However, we do not die. We control others' minds, so we negate free will. He does not *hate* us, Richard. It is just that he cannot allow us to live."

They both fell silent, Richard reflecting on what he had learned and Cami on what she already knew. She seemed older in that moment, and for the first time, Richard was able to believe that she had lived for centuries before. He wondered how heavy that knowledge must weigh on a person and how long he could bear it. Watching her internal struggle—and fearing the loss of the little girl that he had come to know—was nearly too much for him. He wanted to bring her back.

"You want to go get some ice cream or something? We can eat regular food, can't we?"

Cami giggled. Her eyes were still sad, but her laugh was warm and welcoming. "Of course, we can. You will just get sick for a few hours while your body rejects and absorbs it, that is all, but . . ." She paused.

"What?"

"Can we go see a movie?"

Cami looked at Richard with hopeful eyes, which fell when Richard laughed. "I'm sorry," he said between peals of laughter. "I'm not laughing at you. It's just . . . you're very complex, just when I think I have you figured out . . ."

He lifted her into the air, just like he had done with his little niece a lifetime ago. She giggled again, but this time her eyes found the laughter as well. Richard used to have a passion for movies but had not been to one in a very long time and was excited for the distraction.

They borrowed a car—it was Richard's idea to attempt at manipulating the mind of another person. Although it was not needed, Cami stood nearby to assist him and swelled with a strangely maternal pride when it was successful. Soon, they were driving down the street in the nondescript white sedan. The stranger would pick it up again at the same spot in a few hours, once he was done at the party that he felt the overwhelming desire to crash. Richard remembered the Summer Twin drive-in from his childhood—from happier times that he cherished endlessly. It was the sort of place where management checked the trunks of the cars but did not care whether you were old enough to watch the movie. When finances permitted, his parents would take him there on weekends. His mother would spoil him with popcorn, sodas, and candy that she would hide in her purse. In a strange way, he felt as though he were passing along the experience.

"When was the last time you went to see a movie?" Richard asked Cami as they pulled into the lot and found their spot. Richard scanned the lot. Aside from the few cars that packed in the back shadows of the lot, they were alone. He looked at Cami, who had her face pressed against the window, transfixed by the massive screen and the images that danced across it. Richard repeated the question.

"I have never been to the movies," she said finally. She looked nearly embarrassed by the admission.

"Never?" Richard asked surprised.

She shook her head with her eyes downcast. "I mean, I have heard of them. I have seen movies on television, just never on a big screen like that. I have always wanted to, but—" She stopped and stared out the windshield, transfixed by what she saw. Richard joined her in the experience. The previews played and the sound filled the car from the speakers. They were watching the same generic romantic comedy that Richard had seen countless times before under different names, but Cami watched mesmerized by the action on the screen. He had just started to get into the unfolding plot when Cami leaned in and whispered in a conspiratorial tone, "She is going to end up with the best friend, not the rich guy."

He smiled in response. There was something refreshing about seeing the girl act the age that she appeared to be rather than the centuries old that he knew her to be. At intermission, they played a cartoon of candies, soft drinks, and popcorn dancing across the screen. The large soda started drinking from the straw of the little soda, and Cami took note, laughing aloud, "Look! It is a vampire soft drink!" When she laughed, he did as well. Hers was an infectious laughter. When the movie started back, she laughed some more and for a movie that did not deserve it, but he joined her gladly, laughing until his sides began to ache and his lungs started to burn. This surprised Richard, who had not felt pain since his rebirth. Despite his confusion, he elected not to mention his concerns to Cami, who was still genuinely lost in the magic that she saw on the screen. Eventually, the movie ended, and Cami seemed genuinely surprised to find that her predictions were correct. She excitedly recapped the plot, while Richard listened patiently. The lights came up, the screen went blank, and Cami fell silent.

"What's wrong?" Richard asked. "It had a happy ending."

"I know, but . . . it is over. I hate it when good things end," she answered.

They sat together in silence for a heavy moment until Richard reached across the armrest and dug his fingers into Cami's ribs. She jumped and squealed when he did it again; he tickled her ribs, while she giggled just the way a little girl should. Soon, he was leaning across the car's seat, tickling her sides with both hands. He knew that any curious onlooker would get the wrong impression from the shaking car and the movement veiled by steamed windows, but the childlike laughter was all he cared about at that moment.

"Stop!" Cami giggled. "Please, I cannot breathe!"

Richard stopped and stared at her in disbelief. She stared back, equally shocked. "I thought we didn't have to breathe at all," he said.

"We do not . . . We should not," she answered, trying to make sense of the sensation that she had felt. "I cannot believe it . . . I do not understand it . . . but I felt like I could not breathe."

"When we were laughing—you know, earlier—my sides started hurting . . . *actually hurting* just like . . . like before." They both knew what he meant.

"What do you think it means?"

"I do not know," Cami answered. They sat in silence, deep within their own thoughts. Richard started the engine and drove toward where they would be leaving the car for its owner. They slipped through the night, passing by the streetlights and landmarks unseen, until Cami finally spoke. "I had forgotten what it is like . . . I did not remember . . ." She offered the fragmented words as an explanation. Richard did not fully understand, but he knew she did not understand either. She collected herself then explained, "It has been so long since my rebirth that I guess I forgot what joy felt like. It felt as if I was a little girl again. It felt . . . good. *It felt right.*"

Richard smiled and patted her hand as they stopped at their destination—the corner where they would be abandoning the car.

"Thank you," Cami added.

"For what?" Richard said, looking puzzled.

"I do not know how, but you have already given me so much. I have felt alone for so long that I have started to forget what it felt like to belong. Thank you."

Richard was at a loss, shocked at his own surprise. This was the little girl that had brought him such horror and pain, the creature that had protected him from the danger that she brought, the friend that he would die for if it would save her from danger. In that moment, she seemed nearly human. "We saw a movie. I guess all this night is missing is dinner." He smiled.

Cami agreed, and they left the car for the familiar shadows of the darkest night. They were in very high spirits from the movie, and she excitedly recapped the plot while they selected their prey. They both knew him when they saw him. They had little to go on, but sometimes hunger necessitated quick judgment. They made short work of him while he weakly pleaded for his life, growing stronger as the life ebbed from his eyes. Richard still had not grown accustomed to having to kill in order to survive, but he was able to ignore his prey's pleas now. Cami strategically mutilated the body to hide the evidence of vampirism, and they removed his wallet to suggest a mugging gone wrong. Richard tried to resist looking inside, but his curiosity got the better of him. He closed it quickly, trying to forget the happier times that were captured inside. He slipped the wallet into his pocket, where it would wait until it could be discarded.

"It is best not to look," Cami said. He had not realized that she was watching his reaction. "If you think too much about it, and you will not be able to function."

Richard nodded, and they went their separate ways—Cami to hide the body in a conspicuous location where it was likely to be found and Richard to discard the wallet in a location where it was not. He took a series of twists and turns, his footsteps echoing off the aging concrete, focusing only on the way back and the unknown destination. Because of this lack of attention, he was surprised when he heard a voice.

"You are Cami's new toy, are you not?"

Richard spun around like a wild beast when cornered, but there was no one there. He knew he had heard something, but without a source, he briefly doubted his own sanity. "Is someone there?" he whispered. He tried to sound brave but was quietly terrified.

"Yes." The voice was behind him now, and it spoke directly into his right ear. Richard spun around to come face to chest with a tall thin man dressed in loose dark-colored clothing. Richard cowered as he looked up to the man's pale face. The man smiled.

"Who are you?" Richard demanded. He took a step backward, but the man pressed forward. He did not touch him, but he towered over him and stayed close.

"My name is Boian Lupei, and I survived Cami."

"What do you mean by that?"

"Did she not tell you what happened to her last companion?"

Richard looked for a place to run but found that the man had position himself between him and the alley's outlet. "He was killed."

"Did she tell you who did it?"

"No, she did not mention it."

Boian laughed. It was a shrill-cutting laugh that chilled Richard. "That is because *she* did it. She has killed each one before, except for me. If you are with her, then that means that you are next." He seemed to relish each word, forming the syllables as though he were making love to them. Boian continued speaking. His voice washed over Richard, invading his mind and intruding on his thoughts. Richard had no reason to trust the man, but his words reminded him that he had little reason to believe Cami. He started to see that he had not known her for very long at all, that what the stranger was saying was possible, probable, the truth.

"Boian!" It was Cami's voice. Richard fell to the ground, released from the spell. His mind was still clouded by Boian's influence, and he could not concentrate on the argument between the two creatures. They circled each other as they spoke—two apex predators fighting over a prize. "How did you survive?" Cami demanded.

Boian laughed. "Humans! They are weak and foolish. Do you think those puny villagers could kill me? Each one of them died painfully, slowly. First, I swept through them, cutting off and breaking their limbs, then feasted until I was full. I then drained the rest for the pleasure it gave me and spat their blood on the ground so I could watch the horror on the faces of those knowing they were next . . . just like when I killed Samuel."

Richard could see the pained expression in Cami's eyes. He also saw the subtle movement in Boian. With Cami distracted, he reached back and grasped the wooden shaft of a carefully crafted stake hidden behind his back.

"Cami, duck!" Richard managed to say. However, Cami was not where she had been. She moved with supernatural speed as Boian drove the stake through where her chest would have been. Richard could not follow her movement but caught a glimpse as she circled behind him and brought her small fists down on his head. He snarled and turned, lunging again with the stake. This time he made contact. The tip pressed against her chest, just to the side of her heart. He pressed, and she pushed at his hands with every bit of her strength. Richard could see that she was in pain, with the wood having some unknown effect on her, and rose unsteadily to his feet. He knew that the man was transfixed on Cami and paid no attention to his perceived victim. He also knew that he had only have one shot, one opportunity, to end the terror that had dominated Cami's life for far too long. He pulled a sharp broken plank from a pile of discarded wood and stood behind the massive figure. While the pair struggled, he raised the makeshift stake. While they hissed and cursed at each other, and while Boian's greater strength began to overwhelm Cami, he brought it down into the man's back.

Boian pushed Cami away. The stake, partially buried in her chest, went with her. His eyes blazing with hellfire and his fangs extended and dripping with anticipation, he turned to Richard and scowled. The back of his hand took Richard by surprise and sent him sprawling to the ground. Before he reacted, Boian was on top of him and clawed at his skin. Although he tried to protect himself, it did little against the enraged creature, who tore at his skin and pulled muscle from bone like an enraged beast. The wounds screamed, and the pain threatened to steal Richard's very consciousness as he weakly fought back. He did not know if he could die in such a way, but he was beginning to hope that he would.

Suddenly, Boian stopped. Cami had leaped on his back and was viciously biting at his neck with her fangs. He screamed and stood, taking her with him as he threw his body against the wall with her own cushioning the blow. She groaned and locked eyes with Richard. "Run," she whispered.

Richard did. He ran, leaving the girl locked in violent conflict with a terrifying creature. He ran because the person that he had come to trust told him to. He ran because he was afraid. He ran because he did not know what else to do. He kept running until he reached the crypt. In his panicked speed, it only took a few moments, but it felt like an eternity, as the intrusive thoughts railed against him.

It was open.

The metal moorings had been pulled free and bent, making the intrusion obvious. Richard realized that Boian had done it intentionally as part of a calculated plan to deny them their refuge, if not their very lives. Richard stared at the door and looked deep within himself. He knew that Cami could have gotten away or ran before Boian even saw her, but she stayed for him. She put herself at risk for him. Despite her instruction, Richard was going to do the same for her. He could not explain the feeling. He had never been the type to put himself at risk for another person's benefit, and he certainly would not consider himself the heroic sort, but something about knowing that Cami was in danger awakened the feelings within him. He was enraged; he was emboldened; and somewhere deep down, he was terrified.

He found the pair where he had left them, and it was clear that the battle had been fierce. They circled each other warily, each deeply wounded and exhausted. To an outsider, it would look very odd to see a grown man locked in a life-or-death struggle with a little girl, but Cami had held her own so far. Richard, however, could see it in her eyes—she was close to defeat against the older more experienced fighter. Boian feinted to the right, swinging wide with a solid fist toward Cami's bloodied face. She took the bait and blocked high, not noticing that Boian had brought his left hand directly toward her thin neck. Her eyes bulged when he made contact, squeezing her neck with his abundant strength. She clawed at his hand, desperately trying to free herself but to no avail. She knew that she was defeated, and she hung limply when he lifted her into the air. Although she remained prideful and silent, her eyes hoped for mercy.

Boian read what has in her eyes and laughed. "Mercy? This world has no place for mercy, and neither do I. The weak need to die to make room for the strong, especially for our kind. Yet you take them in. You coddle them like infants at their mother's teat." Richard approached, carefully and quietly. He knew he would have one opportunity. Cami struggled to speak, but Boian silenced her with a tight squeeze around her vocal chords. "After I kill you," Boian continued, "I will find your friend and kill him too. I know who you think he is." He savored the taunt.

Richard gathered every bit of courage and strength and jumped on to the larger man's back. He wrapped his arm around Boian's neck and locked it into the crook of his elbow. With his other hand, he grabbed his own wrist and pulled tight against the flesh. Boian howled with surprise and anger and dropped Cami heavily to the ground in his effort to deal with this new threat. Cami struggled to stand, while Richard struggled to maintain his tenuous hold. Soon, that hold broke, and Boian pulled Richard off his back and sent him flying to the wall. The world exploded in pain and colors for him, but Richard rose to his feet and stood over Cami.

"You can't have her," Richard said weakly.

Boian smiled. Even under the fresh wounds and old scars, he was intimidating. "I do not need your permission," he growled, taking a step forward. He stopped when Cami started to stand. She pulled herself to her feet, her face fixed and resolute. She stood in front of Richard.

"It is over, Boian," she said. She stood on unsteady legs, like a newly born animal. "You have never understood. You have only ever really lived for yourself, so you have never lived at all. When someone is willing to die for another . . . even you cannot break that." Boian scowled and opened his mouth to speak, but Cami interrupted him. "Besides, I have more fight than you have night." She pointed to the sky, which was already beginning to lighten. His face betrayed the internal struggle between reason and emotion and then his resignation to the decision.

"I will see you again," he swore. Then between the blinks of worn and heavy eyelids, he was gone.

Cami collapsed into Richard's arms. She had bravery in abundance; it was only strength that she lacked. He carried her close to his chest, just as a loving father would carry a young child, and ran into the sunrise. His skin burned and his body ached, but still, he ran.

CHAPTER SIX

More Fight than Night

"How long was I out?" Cami shook herself awake. It took her a moment to orient herself to her surroundings. She was in the back seat of Richard's car, and he was leaning against the driver's side door.

"You were unconscious for two sunrises."

She sat up carefully. Her skin had healed, but the grievous nature of the internal wounds had taken more time. She could see the concrete pillars that supported the massive structure. Air smelled of pollutants and urine. "Where are we?"

"We're just outside of Des Moines, Iowa. More specifically, we're on the lowest level of an underground parking garage, just outside of Des Moines, Iowa. I thought it was best to get away from Memphis, and I didn't know where else to go, so I just started driving. You had talked about Alaska a few times, so I guess I was headed that way."

Cami sat up and smiled. "You did well." Her face turned with the fresh memory. "I told you to run," she scolded. "You could have been killed, coming back like that."

"You *would have* been killed if I hadn't," Richard reminded her. "Besides . . . I couldn't just leave you there."

Cami knew that it was true. If not for Richard's intervention, she would have suffered the final death that night. She also knew that she would have done the same for him, even though the sense of mere obligation had long since passed. She changed the subject after accepting what he said was true. "Richard, I need to heal. To heal, I need to eat."

"I already thought of that." Richard grinned. He left the vehicle and helped Cami to do the same before leading her to the trunk. Each of their sounds and movements echoed off the concrete walls and pillars. She leaned against him and watched as he opened it, revealing what was inside. It was a man—bound, gagged, and terrified. He screamed against the gag and struggled against the ropes, but he was unable to free himself.

"Let me guess . . .," Cami said. "Wife abuser?"

"Nope," Richard said. "Beat and robbed a little old man who was towing a tank of oxygen behind him." Richard shook his head in mock disgust. The man in the trunk backed himself against the interior seat, only prolonging his life by mere moments. His will to survive even in the face of certain death was a powerful force.

Cami's fangs gleamed when she smiled. She reached into the trunk and pulled the man toward her. He muttered muted prayers until she pressed her fangs into his soft neck. His eyes opened wide, and he tried to pull away, but Cami held him close and feasted on his blood. Richard could see the difference in her as she was rejuvenated; her color returned, along with her stature, and she stopped when she was full. The man was not dead yet but was very close to it. Richard accepted the remains and drank deeply until the man gave in to the embrace of death. They left the body submerged in one of the pristine fingers of Saylorville Lake before continuing on their journey, trusting the water and the scavengers to cover their tracks.

They hugged briefly then got into the car and drove on into the night, pressing toward their shared goal and the promise of freedom and safety.

. . .

Boian watched the pair dump the body into the lake at its edge. Every part of him wanted to attack them at that very moment to take them by surprise and ravage them for their perceived crimes. He, however, was cautious. He had underestimated the pair and the bond they shared. Once, it had nearly killed him, and he refused to make the same mistake again. Instead, he remained silent and still while they made their way on foot through the woods. He then followed at a distance until they entered their car and drove away. He watched the car disappear, staring until the dim taillights disappeared from his view.

"Excuse me, sir, park's closed. You're going to have to leave." Boian turned. He towered over the park ranger. The ranger should have been afraid. If he had known what he faced, he likely would have been terrified. Despite his short stature, he was solid and muscular, and he subtly flexed his biceps in an effort to intimidate the trespasser. "What are you, deaf?"

Boian smiled. He loved this part. He took the ranger by surprise when he closed in and grabbed the man's wrist. The ranger tried to pull away, but Boian twisted his arm behind him, snapping the wrist and pulling his shoulder out of the socket. The man screamed, but Boian was not finished. He pressed his knee into the man's back and forced him to the ground, landing on top of his body. Unlike Cami, Boian did not believe in a quick, merciful death for his victims. He enjoyed their suffering, feeling that their pain, and the adrenaline made their blood taste even sweeter. The ranger's death was prolonged and painful due to Boian's culinary tastes—his latent rage and his innate hatred for humanity. He tore at the man's neck and allowed the blood to flow, holding him to the ground while he struggled. He fixed his mouth over the wound and drank deeply until the struggling stopped. The man's eyes were dim, with barely a small spark of life inside them. Boian stared into them for a moment, savoring the final moments before he snapped the man's neck and drained the rest of his blood, keeping the heart beating until he had finished the last drop.

He left the body next to the other, accepting both the necessity and Cami's resourcefulness, before starting down the road. He walked in the direction that Cami and Richard had driven. He was in no hurry—he had all eternity to exact his revenge.

. . .

Cami and Richard could not remember the name of the small town in South Dakota, but the hotel was quiet and clean, and the clerk did not ask too many questions when they checked in and paid with cash. The room was simple, with muted colors and a neutral floral wallpaper pattern. The television was the only modern addition to the room, and it was playing a very old black-and-white movie. They had pulled the heavy curtains shut, hung the "Do Not Disturb" sign, and waited for daylight to peak its feared rays into the darkness.

Cami was slowly spinning in the cheap office chair when Richard emerged from the bathroom, freshened and cleaned from the shower. He wore the new clothes that Cami had chosen for him, and she had to admit that he looked much better than he had before. The clothes fit properly, for one thing, and the style was from the current decade.

"I want to show you something, Richard," she said.

"Okay, what?" Richard answered. He shook the last of the water from his ears.

In a flash, Cami was on her feet, running toward Richard. He did not have time to react before she reached him and could only close his eyes tightly when she leaped at his upper body with outstretched arms and a fierce expression.

The anticipated impact did not come. Richard opened his eyes, but Cami was not there. He glanced nervously around him, but he was alone—alone, that is, except for the small lone bat that circled overhead. Cami had changed her form into that of a bat. While she could have chosen from many different forms, she felt that the bat was an ideal introduction to the concept. Richard jumped when Cami landed on the ground at Richard's feet, upon which her clothes were carefully laid, and burrowed into the fabric. His jaw dropped when she seamlessly changed back into her human form. He marveled as her clothes seemed to fill with her body. Then her head, still having some of the features of a bat but without hair, popped out, and out sprouted her beautiful locks and became the angelic face of his Cami again. She quickly got to her feet, stood before him, and smiled up at her friend.

Richard opened and closed his mouth as he tried to form the words. Finally, he managed to say, "How did you do that?"

Cami giggled. "It is simple. I am going to teach you. Lie down." Richard lay on the rough comforter, and Cami sat next to him. "Now your body is going to change a bit. It is going to hurt but not much. Are you ready?"

Richard gulped. "Hurt? How much?"

"Not a lot. It is more like a bad leg cramp. Then it is over."

He nodded. He trusted Cami completely, but the idea of pain was not very appealing to him.

"Close your eyes. We are going to start with a bat. The bat is a small and fast animal, so it is not a bad way to travel. Remember when we talked about the daytime, how your body knows what to do?"

Richard nodded. He still did not fully understand, but he knew that it was true.

"Transformation is pretty much the same way. You have thousands of years of history in your veins, and your body knows how to change. You just need to get your mind out of the way of it."

Cami's voice became deep and driving. Richard recognized this as the same tone that she would use to control a mortal. He allowed her dulcet tones to lull him in by the sound of her voice.

"Imagine that there is a bat inside you, built from the same flesh that makes up your current form . . . Get rid of anything that is not 'bat.'"

Richard allowed his mind to let go of his notion of self and trust in Cami. She kept speaking, but her voice became an undercurrent in the river of thoughts and images that filled his mind. He could see his body changing and could feel the physical effects that lagged the mental acceptance. He wanted to scream but was unable to as his bones softened and painfully reformed themselves. His arms shortened and his fingers elongated as his body rapidly shrunk. The skin between his fingers broke then grew and fused together to form wings, and his bones hollowed to allow them to function. His head sunk into his shoulders, and his legs pulled toward his body. Finally, his skin erupted with a fine coat of hair that pushed through every inch of his now exposed flesh. When the pain stopped, he opened his eyes. His first thought was one of wonder. The room was massive, with walls that towered over him and furniture that seemed too large to be real. He was surprised at how well he was able to see and even more surprised when he found that his vision was significantly supplemented by echolocation. He was acutely aware of every area in the room and was able to track the erratic flight of an insect that he had not even seen before.

Cami smiled down at her eager student. "Amazing, is it not?" she whispered, understanding his sensitive hearing and inability to filter loud noises. Suddenly, Richard realized he was naked and tried to cover himself with his wings. Cami giggled and said, "You are completely covered in fur, nobody could see anything. Go ahead, try to fly."

Richard, taking Cami at her word, stretched his newborn wings and allowed them to catch the air. He rose slightly and then settled back on to the bed. The feeling was amazing. Even that small movement was a freedom greater than any that Richard had imagined. He tried it again, forcing his wings downward and allowing them to catch the surrounding air. He rose but faltered at the apex of his rise before repeating the movement and filling his wings once again. He found that by varying the strength of his wing's flap on one side, or by changing the shape and position of the wing, he was able to control his speed and direction. Although far from graceful, he was soon able to fly around the room in a lazy circle without hitting the walls. He tentatively dove, just a small dip, enough to feel the exhilarating rush of wind hitting his face and blowing through his fur. He did it again, deeper this time, diving lower to the ground and pulling upward before hitting the floor. The dive was successful, but his recovery was not. His wing clipped the cheap office chair and caused him to lose control. He recovered but was unable to change his trajectory before sailing through the open window and into the cool night.

Cami acted quickly, cursing her own lack of foresight and leaving the window open. She quickly changed her own form and darted out the window. She looked down first, hoping not to find him on the ground, but did not see him. Instead, he hung in the air above her, desperately trying to remain aloft despite the light breeze and heavy nerves. She flew behind him and carefully guided him back into the window. Her presence was calming to him, and he was able to navigate his way into the room and on to the bed. Like he had seen Cami do before, he burrowed into his clothing and waited, knowing that Cami would guide him through the process of returning to his human form.

"Not bad for your first try," Cami said. She had already changed her own form and kneeled next to the bed. She spoke to him softly, describing how his body will change again, how his bones would soften and grow, and how the skin will tear and reform itself around his fingers. He could visualize the process then felt the agonizing sensations of growth and change as his body rebuilt itself into what it once was. Cami turned her back before the process completed and reached out to catch his pants in midair as they sailed past. She threw them back over her shoulder, and he hurriedly put them back on.

"Thanks . . .," he muttered. "How did you know?"

Cami laughed. "No one ever gets that part right on the first try. The pants take a little bit of practice." Richard laughed with her, the levity a welcome break from the fear that had tugged at his most private thoughts. They fell asleep, enjoying the rare peace.

They awoke at dusk, with the joy from the previous night spilling into the new one. They walked through the quiet streets of a poor section of the city. Most cities had such a place—a world entirely its own, where families struggled to survive in the shadows of the city skyline. They were ready to feed, and the harshest reality was that such places received very little attention from law enforcement. However, they tended to police themselves, so there were always risks. They enjoyed the clear night; the stars were twinkling through the atmosphere, and the moon was casting pale shadows in their path. The soft breeze carried the smell of firewood and spices, and even the light echo of their footsteps seemed to have a musical quality. As they walked, they talked about everything and nothing, simply enjoying each other's company. Life was easy in that moment, and Cami was thankful that she could finally enjoy it.

"So Butch and Sundance are hanging on to the cliff face surrounded by the posse," Richard continued. He had pulled every movie he could remember from memory and entertained Cami by telling her stories that she had never heard. He took joy from the way her face lit up when he talked. "They have to choose between jumping in and trying to fight their way out. So Butch, he—"

Richard stopped, noticing that Cami was no longer with him. He turned and found her standing in the middle of the street, straining to hear something that he could not. "What is it?" he whispered. Icy fingers of fear gripped the back of his neck, and his eyes darted around him nervously. He thought of Boian and wondered if he had found them again.

Cami ignored the question, which only heightened Richard's tension. She turned her head one way and then the other, honing in on the sound. Her direction chosen, she started to walk slowly and carefully toward the source. Eventually, with Richard in tow, she reached a small run-down home in the middle of the block. The fence was adorned with a "Beware of Dog" sign, but she ignored it as she opened the gate and went inside.

"Cami," Richard hissed. He was frightened for her, as well as for himself, but he knew he would not leave her alone in the yard. He only wished that she would not force him to make the choice.

The dog that came bounding around the side of the house was easily seventy-five pounds of justification for the sign. It was a mix of breeds, but its bared teeth and angry eyes were the only characteristics that worried Richard. He put a hand on Cami to pull her to safety but soon saw that there was no need to do so. The dog had stopped, frozen in place. Its eyes were locked with Cami's, who gently shook free from Richard's grasp and slowly walked toward the creature until her face was mere inches from its own. Despite Richard's fears and expectations, it did not bark nor bite but instead lowered its head and lay down at her feet. She gave the dog a quick scratch on the belly before rising to her feet and continuing into the yard. As they approached the window, Richard finally heard what had attracted Cami—it was the quivering voice of a little girl, lost in her earnest prayers.

"God . . .," the girl began. She was wearing pale blue pajamas and kneeling at her bedside. The room was bare, with very few toys and a nearly empty closet. The girl clearly had not bathed in some time. "I know you're busy and all, but I need your help. Ever since Mommy died, Daddy has been sad. Can you make him happy again? If it's not too much trouble, can you give me a new mommy so Daddy will stop touching me that way?"

Richard stared at the little girl through the window. She climbed into bed over to her nightstand to turn the light off. Only then did it occur to Richard how late at night it was. He looked at Cami and saw something in her that he had never seen before. He saw white-hot rage.

"I guess we found our meal then," Richard suggested.

"No. As much as I would enjoy it, this little girl needs a father—her *real* father. We take that from her, who knows where she will end up. I have another idea."

She looked in each window, moving silently from one to another, until she found what she was looking for. She pulled the window open and climbed inside. The air inside the home was stale and oppressive, and every surface seemed as if coated with a thin layer of dust. Richard followed behind, uncertain and nervous. Together, they picked their way through the stranger's home until they reached the living room. The overweight man was asleep in front a soft-core pornographic movie, with a beer in his hand and a pile of discarded cans surrounding his recliner. He snored softly, and drool ran freely from his opened mouth. His face was unshaven, and a lonely cigarette burned itself out in the ashtray.

"What now?" Richard whispered.

Cami did not answer. She drew back and slapped the man across the face. He snorted and was startled awake then blinked uncomprehending until he realized that he was in his own living room and surrounded by strangers. With that recognition, his eyes blazed with drunken anger. He stood swaying and towered over Cami and Richard. His mouth opened to shout but was immediately silenced and was surprised by Cami's small hand. She grabbed his jaw and pulled him to the floor with a surprising force. As he fell, she twisted his body, so she fell on top of him, with her face a mere inch from his own. She forced his mouth to remain closed despite his struggles and opened her own mouth wide. When he saw her gleaming fangs growing toward him, he stopped. Only then did she remove her hand.

"What . . . what are you?" he asked. He seemed suddenly very sober and very afraid.

Her skin drew tightly, her nose shriveled quickly, and her beautiful locks gave way and fell out, partially covering the man's face, giving her face and head the appearance of a skull with a light coating of dead skin. "Death," Cami answered with a low-pitched guttural tone to her voice which Richard had never heard. The hollow, animalistic tone, not unlike a large dog growling into a barrel, chilled Richard to the bone. Nevertheless, he stood silently and watched as her eyes became solid black and her face became that of a large hairless vampire bat. Then it quickly turned back to the skull. He understood what she was doing, as well as why she was doing it, but it still frightened him. "I am the angel of death," Cami continued. "You deserve my full wrath. I know what you have been doing to your little girl—issue of your own body, flesh of your flesh."

The man's face ran through the entire range of emotions, finally settling on a forced anger. "Did she tell you that? She's a liar!"

Cami drew her fingers over his neck. Her razor-sharp nails cut the skin cleanly but not deeply which allowed the blood to flow freely but not threateningly. He winced but fell silent. "No . . . you godless waste of human life, she is *not* a liar. The Lord, our God, has heard her prayers and sent me to fulfill them. Only because your daughter loves you, despite your horrific crimes against her and against heaven, I will spare your life tonight. This is what is going to happen." She leaned in close and whispered into the man's ear. She maintained her grip on his neck, and his eyes bulged when she tightened around his windpipe. "You will be the father that your little girl deserves. Clean yourself, get yourself together, and clean her while you are at it. Moreover, if you ever touch her again, in a way other than a truly loving parent, I swear to you, by all that is holy and with the Almighty Father as my witness, that I will dispatch you to the fate that you richly deserve. I will not only dispatch you with a great joy and oh-so slowly that when I finally do allow you to die, you will be grateful for that sweet release, but I will also peel the flesh from your bones over a period of days while keeping the wounds fresh with salt and lemon rinds. I will allow the true hounds of hell to feed on your extremities"—reaching back and between his legs for effect—"while you watch helplessly, unable to do anything but scream in your freakish agony. Let us not forget that when your torture is done on earth, that your torment will just be beginning. Although Lucifer is a fallen angel, he does perform a service, and that service will be your damnation and torment for all eternity. That is a very long time, so think carefully about your decision. Do you understand?"

The man nodded. His eyes were wide and terrified, which confirmed his sincerity. Cami stared deeply into his eyes before rising to stand above him. She was gone in a flash, moving so quickly that the man's eyes could not follow. To him, it appeared that she had simply vanished—a specter, certainly as real as death itself. Richard followed shortly after, stealing one last glance at the man they had left behind. He wept quietly. He was completely sober now, perhaps for the first time in months. Then looking around, he said aloud, "Was that a dream? No! No, it wasn't. God sent an angel to save my baby from me. Oh, God, please forgive me." He continued to weep. They watched unseen, peering through the windows as he stood and wiped the tears from his eyes before walking toward his daughter's room. Cami's face looked as if it was made of stone as he entered the bedroom and gently shook his daughter awake. Her reaction was that of fear then resignation as she sat up and began to pull her pajama shirt over her head. Then she showed confusion when her father stopped her. He pulled her shirt back into place, pulled her close in the embrace that a father reserves for his beloved daughter, and repeated heartfelt and tear-filled apologies and regrets, begging her and God to forgive him. Finally, the little girl embraced him in return. The tears in her eyes, for the first time either of them could remember, were tears of joy and not of fear, anguish, or regret.

As Cami and Richard walked down the quiet street, curiosity finally got the better of him. "Why didn't you just hypnotize him?"

Cami thought for a moment. "Sometimes you do not need to pour truth into a person. Sometimes you need to reach down their throats, into their hearts, and snatch it out."

CHAPTER SEVEN

Mama's Song

Cami was running, but she was not sure what she was running from nor where she was going. The dense forest trees whipped by in an organic blur and her legs burned. She caught her breath and stole a glance behind her—the man was still chasing her, and he was catching up. He was not angry. He was smiling and laughing. Cami realized that she was laughing as well. She was running from her tata, who was playfully chasing her through the woods. He caught her, and she giggled as he lifted her high above his head and then pulled her close in a loving embrace. She could smell the unique smell that her father has and feel the safe warmth that his rough hands provided. She looked again and stared into Richard's face. She held him until the moment that she slipped away.

Cami blinked. Her vision had left her disoriented, but reality slowly settled into her thoughts. She was in a car; the snow-covered trees and rolling hills slid silently past, all bathed in the soft moonlight of the clear night. The speakers sang a quiet tune until static took the noise away. The static gave way to some hardcore rap song, which grated on Cami's ears.

Without taking his eyes off the road, Richard turned off the radio. "Hey, you're awake." He smiled.

Cami blinked. "What? I was not sleeping."

Richard laughed. "Sure looked like you were asleep to me. Unless you normally mumble to yourself while you're awake." Cami did not answer, and Richard stole a glance in her direction. Her eyes seemed concerned at best, frightened at worst. "What's wrong?"

"You do not seem to understand . . . We do not sleep at night. I could not have been asleep. It is just . . . It is not possible." Cami remembered dreams. What she had seen felt very much like that. She sighed; questions without answers always frustrated her. She took a moment of silence to convince herself that what she had seen was somewhere between a wish and her imagination. "How far are we from Fairbanks?"

"We should be there in a couple of days at most." He looked out at the vast expanse that had surrounded them. They were very much alone. In addition, Richard felt a joyful peace, which he had not felt in a long time fill his heart. "Is it really dark all the time there?"

"For part of the year, it tries to get light, but it only brightens up a bit. That is only for a couple of hours at most. It might burn just a bit, but we could go out in it and be fine."

"So we'll be . . . like real people?"

Cami stared dreamily out the window. "Yes, Richard . . . like real people."

Fairbanks itself, when they finally reached it, was nothing like what Cami had imagined it to be. From Boian's myths and lies, she expected a strange world lost in time—a collection of hardy survivors fighting against even harder elements. What she found instead was a modern city, with all the hidden stories and public faces as in any other. They made their way along Parks Highway, and Cami was able to forget all the pains and worries of the past. The city looked friendly; it looked like home. Over the next few days, the pair carefully constructed a life in Fairbanks. They found a small apartment with two bedrooms, which was perfect for their public image as father and daughter. Although the bedrooms would not be used, they were kept cleaned and ready. They made small purchases in the local stores, donated the food that they were not able to eat, and gave every impression of being a happy young family, which, in Cami's heart, they were.

Cami watched television, something that she had not done in a very long time. Richard watched as she laughed at the cartoons and cried at the movies—just like a little girl. They went for walks. They would walk for hours, exploring the city and the surrounding countryside. They dressed warmly when they did so, only to blend in rather than for any actual protection from the elements. A few times, they even had to go back for their shoes because walking barefoot in the snow would cause a sensation. Feeding, however, presented a particular challenge. They were in a relatively small city, which they planned to make their home. They had no choice but to feed but very carefully.

"What about the morgue? We could just drain the rest out of the corpses," Richard suggested.

"No good. I told you that. We cannot feed from the dead. Let me explain so that maybe you will understand. If you drink from a living being, human or otherwise, the living blood brings life into our bodies, which animates us. If you drink from a corpse, you are introducing dead blood into a dead body, and it only makes our bodies die faster." She looked up at him in that condescending stare.

They walked silently. They could both feel the hunger gnawing at them, weakening them. "Well, we have to do something. I mean, if we're careful, we could feed without anyone catching on. There are plenty of bad people, even in a small town like this." Even in the face of starvation, the thought of killing anyone innocent was repulsive to them both.

"Thirty-two thousand people in this town and we are probably just about the newest. If people start turning up dead, where do you think they are going to look?"

Richard once again fell silent. He was beginning to wonder if the seasonally perpetual darkness was worth the hunger that he now felt. They walked aimlessly then, hoping that an idea would come to them. Instead, they came to the idea. Fairbanks Memorial Hospital was relatively small but large enough for the community it served. Most of the windows were dark, given the late hour, but the lobby glowed like a beacon. A hospital, as a necessity, would have to have stores of blood. Of course, Cami reasoned out, they would be far less likely to notice blood disappearing than they would the morgue filling up. Even if they did notice, the level of concern would be far less. It would probably be thought of as a clerical error rather than theft. The two looked at each other. A plan was already forming in the air between them.

They entered through the main entrance and made their way to the gift shop, where they purchased a small bouquet of flowers. In a hospital, a bouquet of flowers is a key that will open most doors, or at least explain one's presence in the patient areas, even after visiting hours if someone looks like they do not belong. The more difficult part was making their way into the restricted areas where the blood was stored. For that, they enlisted the unwitting help of the janitorial staff. The night janitor was an older man. His wrinkled scalp could be seen easily through his thinning wisps of white hair. Cataracts dulled his elder eyes, but he led them steadily toward their goal. Every time that someone would come close, Cami and Richard would hide while the old man carefully mopped the floor. Each time, it worked to assuage any suspicions, which would have been otherwise raised. No one ever thinks to question the janitor.

Finally, they reached the refrigerated storage where the hospital kept their blood supply. The janitor followed his implanted compulsion to clean the surrounding hallways, which left him available to escort the pair out the same way he had brought them into the storage area. Collectively, they took only enough to survive, but they hoped not enough that it would be missed or, worse, required by patients. They found a discarded transport container, which they also appropriated for their use, before carefully slipping from the room and following the janitor toward the nearest exit. They resisted the nearly overpowering temptation to take the blood immediately, feeling that time remained a greater factor than their hunger. Finally, they made it into the cool night and ate greedily. They feasted that night and several nights that followed.

"How much is left?" Cami asked. She poured the bottle of tomato juice into the sink and rinsed the glass clean. Then she carefully emptied the package of blood into the container. The end product vaguely resembled a bottle of tomato juice. In a low-lit area, no one would question it. Cami had taken to drinking it in public, saying that it made her feel as though she fit in.

"This is the last of it," Richard answered. He would not have said anything if Cami had not asked. She cleaned a second bottle and poured half into it. All good things must end, and they each savored the last of the fluid. Despite their most sincere intentions, they had not yet found a better solution for their most basic biological need and soon found themselves back at the hospital. At the hospital, they followed the same elderly janitor through the same pathways to the same storage room. The pair collected the precious bags of blood from the replenished supply and again quietly left the room and followed the janitor toward the exit. The difference this time was the voice that stopped them before they reached it.

"What are you two doing here?" The voice was deep and authoritative, and it echoed off the clean white walls. Cami spun around to find the security guard closing in on them, focused only on the trio to the exclusion of anything else. He was as massive as he sounded to be. His uniform struggled to contain his form, and he wore a dark beard that was closely trimmed. The overall effect was that of a clothed bear charging at his prey. He reached them and poked a meaty finger at the frail janitor. "Mitch, what the hell are you doing?"

The old man blinked. "I . . . I don't know," he said. He looked around as though he had no memory of where he was or how he had gotten there. He looked at Richard and Cami. "Who are you?" he demanded. Somehow, he seemed even older and more fragile when he was upset.

Cami sighed sadly and spoke deeply to the guard. Richard noticed her strategy and spoke similarly to the very confused janitor. Before very long, the guard had reluctantly caught the janitor that had been stealing from the blood storage. It was an elegant solution but one that Cami and Richard regretted having to put in place. Cami, however, was nothing, if not pragmatic. She knew it was the only way to explain the missing blood supply without raising more questions. Unfortunately, it also closed that source to them, so this time they were more careful with their supplies. An infinite hunger paired with a finite supply did not work to their favor. After denying it for so long, they began prowling once again, instinctively looking for the dregs of society upon which to feast. There were those that were promising, those that lived in the grey between right and wrong, but the opportunities consistently failed to manifest.

"What about trappers?" Richard suggested. They were alone and walked in the middle of the empty street.

Cami thought for a moment. "That is not a bad idea. They are out there alone. Accidents happen, so it would not be too suspicious as long as they never find a body. As long as we do not overdo it, it might work."

Richard beamed inwardly feeling proud of himself for the suggestion. Cami smiled as well; her little bird had learned to fly. "So how do we find them?" Richard asked. He waited for an answer but soon realized that he was walking alone. He turned to find Cami standing alone in the middle of the street. Snow had begun to fall, dancing in the air between them, giving her a somewhat angelic appearance. Richard was reminded of the time when she overheard the tiny prayers of a scared little girl, but something in her face was different this time. He came closer, afraid to speak and break the spell. Her eyes darted to him, only for a moment, before they returned to the soft haze of her ethereal thoughts. She swayed slightly, much like a cobra mesmerized by a snake charmer. Richard reached out to touch her, but before he could, she started running. He followed, falling behind and losing her in the twists and turns that she navigated effortlessly. He rounded a corner to find her standing very still, much like she had been before.

"What the hell are you doing?" Richard demanded. He was confused and frightened by her strange behavior and blank expression.

Cami looked at him and brought her finger to her lips, shushing him like an errant child. Then suddenly, she was gone again, running in a full sprint in the direction she had chosen. When Richard caught up to her next, she was standing on the sidewalk outside of a church. Richard stood next to her and stared, as she was doing, without understanding why. The Immaculate Conception Church was as white as virgin snow. The church's walkways were cleared carefully and meticulously. The spire rose high into the air, rising higher than even the tall bare trees that grew from the snow-covered lawn, and the windows glowed with an inviting warmth. Angelic singing cut through the snow and floated on the breeze; it was pleasing to Richard, but it was something much greater to Cami.

Richard followed her as she slowly walked to the door. Now that she had found her destination, she moved with a sincere reverence toward the entrance as though she were savoring each step. Richard was no longer frightened; whatever had affected her in such a profound way had drawn him in deeply as well. A few heads turned when Cami walked inside, with Richard following close behind. Each person was lost in his or her prayers or thoughts. The mass itself was lightly attended, but Cami could see only the choir that sang sweetly from the choir loft. She walked closer, trailing her hand along the pews and breathing in the sweet incense as she approached. While Richard trusted Cami completely, he began to wonder if she was hunting now—or if she had gone mad. He was nearly certain of it when she broke into a dead run into the choir, which scattered from confusion and surprise at the little girl who tore into their midst. A woman screamed, the priest jumped, and the parishioners murmured. She held on to a woman who was resplendent in her ornate white robes and entirely unsure of the girl that held her so tightly. Confused, the woman hugged her back. She did not let go, and no one stopped her, while the choir resumed its hymn. Cami did not know the words, but she sang along as best she could while looking up adoringly at the woman. By the end of the final hymn, Richard thought he could see tears welling in Cami's eyes. Reason convinced him that it must have been his imagination.

After the service, the three sat together in an overpriced coffee shop. Cami aggressively captured every part of the memory—the air was thick with the smell of brewing coffee beans, the grinder whirred and competed with the sound of the blender, and people laughed. A barista called out the name of the morbidly obese young man who collected his drink and dropped a few coins into the tip jar. A sudden gust of wind shook the door, allowing a few delicate snowflakes to slip inside the door as it swung, caught by the shot of wind. The woman introduced herself as Mary, and she and Richard quickly warmed to each other and talked like old friends. Cami watched them happily. She understood now. She knew that death was only the end of the physical form, but the spiritual self would live on in another body as the reincarnated self. Her family was together after all, but only one of them knew it. Cami allowed herself to know it as a fact. She could not bear to think of life being any other way. When she slipped her hand into Mary's, she was relieved that her hand was being held as well.

"So is it just the two of you?" Mary asked. The question would have been personal in another context, but the question was comfortable, and the answer would be a comfortable half-truth.

"Yes, just us," Richard answered. "Cam's mother died a long time ago. We kind of take care of each other now."

"I'm sorry," said Mary. "If you don't mind me asking, how did she die?" Cami closed her eyes against the memory. Mary recognized the pain, although she did not know the real reason for it, and squeezed the child's hand. "I didn't mean to ask that. I shouldn't have."

Richard answered, truthfully and quickly, "She had a blood disorder." He did not mention that the disorder was the absence of it or that Cami had been the cause. "What about you? Is it just you, or is there someone . . .," he trailed off. Cami smiled; Richard had no idea how to flirt.

Mary smiled as well as she and Cami shared a brief unspoken moment that Richard missed entirely. "It's just me. I was born on Fort Wainwright, but my mom died of complications from having me. Dad raised me as best he could. We were very close." Her voice trailed off with the unwelcome memory.

"Were?" Richard asked.

"He died a few years ago—heart attack. He was a tough old man. It took his third one to bring him down. So I stayed around, a whole lifetime to move just a couple of miles from where I was born." She chuckled to herself. "I never thought about it like that before."

"What do you do?" Cami asked, trying to steer Mary toward a more pleasant thought.

Mary was lost for a moment before she came back from her mental journey and smiled. "I'm a nurse. I work at Alaska Memorial, which isn't too far from here. I actually saw you two there before. Looked like you were visiting someone. Do you know someone who's laid up?"

Richard and Cami glanced at each other. Although they had developed a suitable alibi while inside the hospital, they had not considered that the question would be raised outside of it. Richard stammered, but Cami interrupted, with her voice confident and sure. "We do not know anyone there. Daddy and I travel a lot, so we know what it is like to need friends. We visit a new city, we like to go to the hospital and see the people who do not get many visitors so we can cheer them up. We just do not think that people should be alone." Cami smiled inwardly. Not only did it explain their presence in a way that Mary would appreciate, but it also provided a suitable excuse to visit again.

Richard stared at Cami with awe, while Mary stared at Richard with affectionate respect. "That's sweet." She smiled.

Mary opened up about her life, and the three talked until the manager forced them to leave so she could close the store. She was soft-spoken and loving but became animated and passionate on certain topics. She had tried to enlist in the air force when she was eighteen but was disqualified by a slight heart murmur. It did not affect her life, she said, but it was enough to keep her out of the service. She always felt that her father was disappointed by that—his only child was unable to follow his example. However, he always told her that he was proud of her, no matter what. She had twin freckles on her neck, which she jokingly called her bite marks, and her short dark hair was pulled into a tight ponytail. She was everything Cami wanted in a mother and everything Richard wanted in a partner. It did not matter, not right now at least, that they did not know it yet.

The three were soon inseparable. Richard and Cami each saw the change in the other without seeing the extent of it in themselves. When the weekend came, and Mary was free of her demanding work schedule, they saw a double feature movie at the Regal. Cami had never been to a walk-in theater and had only the drive-in experience to draw from. She was amazed by the more immersive experience of both the theater with stadium seating as well as the sound system. She followed them to the apartment where they played the proper social games; she complimented the décor while Richard offered her drinks. They talked until the late hours, enjoying both the company and the conversation, until Cami realized that she was up well past any reasonable time for a girl her apparent age. Reluctantly, she wished the two good night and took a moment to remind herself which bedroom was supposed to be hers. She listened through the door, enjoying the sounds that accompanied the experience.

The next time they saw each other was on the next Sunday, when Richard and Cami joined Mary at her church. Cami had been looking forward to hearing Mary sing again, and she was excited for the experience. The pair sat in the first few rows, joining the steadfast and the faithful of the community. Richard was familiar with the ceremonial expectations of the church. Cami looked to him for the behaviors that the community would expect from her as the priest, the Eucharistic minister, and altar servers paraded up the aisle, with the priest in procession. The priest called, and the crowd replied; he spoke, and the crowd did the sign of the cross in unison. Richard did so with no discomfort, but Cami felt her finger trace the burning path of a cross into her chest. She winced but ignored the sensation. She looked to Richard, who stared ahead with a peaceful expression, which she tried to match, despite her own fears and concerns. She saw Richard reach do the sign of the cross again, and she was afraid—afraid that it would hurt again, afraid that she would not be able to do it, afraid that someone would notice her reluctance. She did it again. The pain was worse this time, and a small puff of steam rose from her chest and burned her nostrils. She winced at the pain. However, she could not help but feel that she deserved it.

Mary joined them before they lined to take communion. It had only been a week since they first met, so she was surprised at how close they had become. Cami watched her and Richard carefully as they accepted the sacrament then nervously stood before the priest to accept it herself. When she accepted the body of Christ, she was, for the first time that she could remember, able to swallow solid food. Then she prepared for the priest to wave the sign of the cross at her and knew it would burn. It did not, and in fact, it was comforting. She felt blessed, as if a burden had been lifted from her. Next, she received the wine. Said to be the blood of Christ, its effect was immediate and surprising. The wine touched her tongue, and its flavor was as though it were the purest blood that she had ever tasted. It was something unique, with no trace of the familiarity to which she had grown accustomed. There was no salty or sour flavor, which she expected from the wine. She swallowed and felt the fresh blood slide down her throat and fill her stomach with a comforting warmth. This warmth spread from her stomach to her arms and legs then to her fingers and toes. Any hunger that she had felt was gone, and she felt completely satisfied, energized, and refreshed. She shuddered and sighed with a rush of pleasure then sheepishly returned to the pew when she saw that she had held up the process. She sat between Richard and Mary, holding each of their hands in her own.

. . .

Father McCullough was a stern and serious man, with respectably peppered graying hair and deep blue eyes. He wore thin-rimmed, silver-framed glasses and kept his thin mustache carefully trimmed. Although he was slightly below average height, he carried himself taller than his physical size. He watched the little girl carefully from the pulpit. He had thought that there was something odd about her since the first time he saw her, when she burst into the service and attached herself to Mary's waist, and her behaviors only confirmed his own suspicions. She winced when she crossed herself, and she recoiled from some unseen assailant when she crossed herself again. However, it was her reaction to the blood of Christ that had allowed him to make up his mind; he did not have such a perspective, but he was about to ruin the comfortable life that Cami had started to build.

Father McCullough saw this occasionally in Fairbanks, due to the unique winters and cyclically endless nights, and took no personal joy in the task. He knew what Cami and Richard were—they were the undead, the enemy of all that is pure and holy. The last that had come through had been ostensibly an elderly woman. She was very sweet, and he deeply regretted having to report her through the ecclesiastical chain, but he knew that their very nature was to corrupt. If they were allowed to exist, they would spread. As their influence—their very presence—spread, people died. Although he took no pleasure in the task, he fully accepted the reason for it. *Souls are at stake*, he reminded himself. *This community relies on you to do the hard thing right*. Although he knew it to be true, making the phone call was still very difficult to do.

It was the pope's direct edict that a direct contact with a *striga*, the Holy See's name for a vampire, would be reported directly to his trusted, designated cardinal in order to preserve the secret of their existence. Father McCullough's voice quaked during the brief conversation. The cardinal listened carefully, saying nothing until Father McCullough had finished. The cardinal thanked him and ended the call without a word; he listened to the dead line for a moment before seating the receiver in the cradle. He shivered, knowing that that call would bring *the dark man* back. Father McCullough feared very few things, relying on the power of God to protect him from any mortal or supernatural evil. Ever since his conversion, God has upheld his end of the bargain. He feared that man, however, and dreaded his arrival.

Friedrich Nietzsche wrote, "Beware that, when fighting monsters, you yourself do not become a monster . . . For when you gaze long into the abyss, the abyss gazes also into you." This man has gazed unflinching into the abyss. He has become terrifying himself. The church, nonetheless, entrusted him with dispatching the darkness of the world and permitted him the internal darkness that allowed him to do so.

. . .

The young nun stood outside the door for only a few minutes, but each of those minutes seemed like hours. She had not spoken to the man who inhabited the simple room and was not aware of anyone who had. All that she knew of him was what little she had seen of him and the rumors that reached her humble position. His very presence carried a terrifying aura, and many of the sisters were too afraid to be near him. He was tall and dark, not in complexion but in the sensation that enveloped him. Deep scars webbed his pale complexion, and his eyes were two deep dark pools. He was unnaturally tall, and his muscular frame gave him the appearance of an alpha gorilla. She took a deep breath and knocked. "¿Señor?" she called.

"¿Qué es este?" What is it? The man's voice was deep and seemed to penetrate her will.

She answered, "Acaba de llegar un mensaje para usted. Lo ha traído un mensajero." A message just arrived for you. A courier brought it. She held the parchment envelope in her shaking hands. She turned the envelope in her hands and looked at the pressed seal.

"No quiero ser molestado." I do not want to be disturbed.

She replied, "Señor . . . es del Santo Padre." It is from the Holy Father. Even holding the envelope—it did not seem real. They were a small monastery, and having a visitor was unusual enough. Having a communication from the Holy See was unprecedented.

The man replied, "Puede esperar." It can wait. The nun was shocked; the idea of refusing such a message was inconceivable to her. She turned to walk away but returned to the door. She raised her hand to knock but lowered it in fear. She opened her mouth to protest but closed it without speaking. "¿Todavía estás ahí?" You are still there, are you not?

"Sí, señor."

She jumped when the man opened the door. He filled the frame and towered over her. She felt very small in his presence and very frightened by his gaze. He said, "Dámelo." Give it to me. He held out his large hand, and she carefully laid the message in it. Her task complete, she backed away from the man and did not turn around until she rounded the bend in the hallway. Only then did she hear the door softly close.

On the other side of that door, the man carefully broke the seal on the envelope and removed its contents. He studied them carefully before lighting one end with a match then dropping the burning paper into the metal trashcan that sat next to the plain desk. He packed his few belongings into his simple black bag, replaced the bandage that he had taped carefully to his chest, and left that very night. In the morning, another frightened nun would come to the room to bring him breakfast. She would find it clean and empty as though no one had been inside it at all. They would whisper about him for many years to come until he was eventually forgotten. For now, he had a target. Hunting was the only real purpose he ever had.

. . .

"Is that the last of it?" Mary asked. She took one last look around the now empty apartment.

"I think so," Richard grunted as he lifted the final box. They would load it into her truck and then unload it at her house, which was nestled in the forest outside of town. He could not fully understand how Cami had engineered it, but Mary had happily agreed to her suggestion that they move into her home. It was true that her family home was too large and lonely for one person, and it was true that they had bonded together in a way that Mary could not explain or understand. She had always been fairly conservative and traditional in her choices and decisions, but the arrangement somehow felt natural.

Despite the pain associated with the ceremonial actions of mass, Cami was excited about that Sunday's service. She enjoyed watching Mary sing but also eagerly accepted the delectable blood of Christ and the sensations that came with it. She was so excited that it was not until after she accepted communion and allowed the phenomenon to wash over her that she noticed the man sitting next to Father McCullough. Their body language suggested that the stranger had no interest in Father McCullough, while the father's own revealed his discomfort—even fear. Cami studied the man, who merely stared directly ahead of himself and sat as still as a carefully carved statue. She wondered who he was and what he was doing in Fairbanks. She wondered about the scars that crossed his face and hands. She stared until his eyes shifted, leading his head as it turned. He was staring directly at her, his face deeply impassive. Although devoid of expression and discernable thought, something about the way the man looked at her made Cami very nervous. Richard and Mary did not seem to notice, so Cami elected not to say anything. They seemed far too distracted with each other to notice anything else.

Father McCullough, as was his tradition, stood at the exit and wished each parishioner well at the conclusion of the service. His farewells were traditionally warm and sincere but not today. He greeted each member mechanically, and each member returned the greeting reflexively without acknowledging or making eye contact with the man that stood behind him.

Cami stood in the greeting line, with Richard and Mary behind him. She noticed that they were holding hands, but the emotional impact of that otherwise joyous observation became diminished by their steady progression toward the dark stranger. Father McCullough shook one hand after another, nearly rushing the goodbyes as though he wanted to get through them as quickly as possible. Cami thought about running but weighed her fear against the difficulty in explaining her actions to Mary. She remembered then what Boian had told her so many times, *"Attachments breed weakness. If you care for anyone but yourself, it will eventually kill you."*

She hoped that he was wrong, that she did not have to choose between family and safety. She hoped that she was wrong about the man and that she could get outside and into the cool air and put her fears behind her. She started breathing heavily, and the room started closing in on her. Through the hazy tunnel of her vision, all she could see was the dark man, and he grew larger as she grew closer. When she reached Father McCullough, she locked eyes with the dark man for the first time. She knew that he recognized her for what she was; his expression revealed his complete recognition. In addition, she, similarly, knew what he was. She had heard legends but assumed that they were just that—stories told to frighten the younger vampires. She had no idea that they were true, but she did not doubt it now.

All mortals carry a stench of death because they are all slowly dying of age or some other frailty. This man, however, smelled of too many deaths and none yet his own. The scent clung to him like a vengeful spirit, and it pressed heavily upon her. Her entire body was tense, ready to strike or defend. Without taking her eyes off the man, she shook Father McCullough's hand and shot out into the night. She wanted to run, to shout, to cry. She had started to build a life, and now it was all threatened. Mary and Richard talked happily while they walked together; Cami allowed Richard the memory and hoped that he would treasure it and hold it fondly.

CHAPTER EIGHT

The Reluctant Christian

Richard moved into Mary's bed and bedroom and lay awake next to her. He pretended to sleep, until he was sure that she had drifted off, and stared up at the ceiling as he settled deep into himself. He would have been bored if he was not so content, and he allowed his thoughts to ebb and flow like tides. He was so lost in his own thoughts that he jumped when he felt the soft small finger tap his arm. He turned and saw Cami staring back at him. There was something in her eyes; she did not need to speak. He carefully left the bed and followed her down the dark hallway. She checked again all the windows and doors before sitting at the dining room table.

"What's going on?" he asked.

"We need to leave," Cami answered. "Tonight . . . tomorrow . . . soon, we need to leave."

Richard could not believe what he was hearing. "What do you mean leave? We're happy here. *I'm* happy here. Why should we leave?"

Cami explained. She told him about the dark man and what he was. She recounted the legends that had been solemnly passed from one to another and how those legends had turned out to be true. She told him why they were in so much danger and why they had to leave. The legend said that those men were themselves half vampires and were entrusted with tasks that no mortal could hope to achieve. Cami doubted that was strictly true, but the story alone revealed the terror that they demanded. Even Boian spoke of them in hushed, reverent tones, which always frightened Cami more than anything else did.

"He's just a mortal. Why should we be afraid of him?"

"For the same reason a burglar fears a police officer. *It is not the men that you fear*, but what stands *behind them*. Maybe we could kill this man before he kills us . . . maybe. Honestly, the chances are in our favor for that part. If we do, however, he will not be the last. Our best strategy is to run. We leave now, and we run as far and as fast as we can." Cami strained her senses, sure that every sound from the outside was the man coming for them. She peered through the curtains, her vision cutting the dark like a knife.

"Well, what about Mary? Are we just going to leave her during the night? No explanation?"

Cami stood upright and turned slowly. "Yes, that is exactly what we are going to do. We are going to leave, and we are never going to see her again. If she comes with us, she will be in danger every moment of every day. She will always be running. What sort of chance do you think she would have against those who are chasing us while our bodies are resting during the day? If you love her as you say you do . . . as I do . . . you have to let her go. We do not have the luxury of choosing."

Richard turned and stared down the hallway at the closed bedroom door. "I don't want to . . .," he whispered.

Cami rested her hand on his shoulder. She understood; she felt the same way. "I know," she consoled. "It is best for her. Maybe someday we can see her again." She turned Richard's head to face her. "Richard . . . never be afraid to love or to open up. It may hurt for a little while, but it is the only way you can ever truly live. When you rely on another person, you are twice as strong as you were before." She spoke carefully, each word erasing Boian's influence. She smiled, knowing that she had freed herself just a little bit more. It was a continuous effort.

Cami looked out the window again. Her paranoia was twisting each breeze into a voice and every snowflake into a footfall. She gasped when she saw him—the dark man. He was standing in the fresh snow, staring at the house. She knew that he saw her also and pulled the curtains shut as though the thin fabric would protect them from the terrible reality that was just outside. She closed her eyes and cracked the curtain—he was gone.

"What did you see?" Richard asked. He was standing close behind her. He willed himself to wake from the nightmare, to wake up and find that none of it was real, to get back to his old life, where the only people that wanted to kill him lacked the means to do so.

"He is out there," Cami answered. She felt her throat tighten that her voice choked with emotion. It was not fair; they had been careful not to raise suspicion, and they had not hurt anybody. They had built up a life, and it was about to be taken from them before her eyes. "Listen . . . he is going to come in. There is nothing we can do about it. We do not know anything about him, but if half of the legends are true, the chances are good that he could kill at least one of us before we can take him. When Mary comes out, he will likely kill her too."

"He's from the church. Would he do that? What about 'thou shalt not kill'?"

"Men like him—they might be even beyond redemption. Of course, since he is actually working for the church, the pope could simply give him absolution for doing 'the Lord's work.' They get the job done. It does not really matter how. He is not going to worry about Mary, not if it gets him a chance to get us. We have to draw him away from her. It is the only way to keep her safe. When he comes in, go out the window. I will try to get him to follow me. When I am sure that I have lost him, I will meet you in Juneau."

"Why travel all the way to Juneau and not just go back to the apartment?" Richard knew that he should have simply agreed, but he felt that he could almost delay the inevitable by discussing it. He wanted this to make sense, but none of it did.

"We have to assume that anywhere we have ever been, he knows about it. I have no clue how long he has been watching us or what he has already seen, so we are not taking any chances. Richard . . ."

"Yes?"

"I love you." She looked up at him as a young girl would look at her father. Richard took her into his arms and hugged her tight.

"I love you too." He wanted to cry but could not find the tears. Instead, he found his hatred and anger toward the man that was shattering his new existence and held it tightly for the strength it gave him. "You're sure that he'll leave her alone?"

"He will chase us. We are the ones that he wants, and he will not let us get too far away. Once we are gone, he will have no reason to kill her . . . She will be safe." Cami desperately hoped that it was true. Given the circumstances, it was the best plan that she had.

Richard nodded. Neither of them voiced their doubts and fears, but he felt them. He walked over to the mantle and removed the small frame. In the frame was a picture of the three of them from the day they moved in. They were smiling, and Cami was making a silly face. He carefully removed the backing, pulled the picture free, and slid it into his pocket.

"He is coming," Cami said. She said the words with an eerie calm, which contrasted against the fear that they both felt. Richard heard nothing, but the pair stood and readied themselves. Suddenly, the heavy door splintered noisily at the frame and flew inward, unsettled by the heavy boot that led the man inside. In one smooth motion, he used his forward momentum to hurl two wooden stakes through the air, which sailed toward their marks—the still hearts of Cami and

Richard—like angry hornets. Cami pushed against Richard, sending the pair sprawling in opposite directions. The stakes buried themselves in the wall.

Lacking the time to open the window, Richard jumped through it. The glass shattered around him and cut into his flesh, and he fell to the hard ground. He should have been terrified, but his only thoughts were for Cami's safety and wondering how Mary would stay warm until she could get the glass repaired. He shook his head and jumped to his feet. He could hear the struggle inside and ran to the front door despite his own fears. He saw that Cami had lowered herself to a crouch, and she ran toward the man at full speed aiming for the clear route on the man's left side. He was ready for her, however. In one motion, he pulled a heavy wooden crucifix from a concealed pocket and brought it upward in a high arc that connected violently with Cami's head. He caught her with the holy weapon, which burned her flesh and sent her flying against the wall as she howled in pain. She struggled to rise, but the man was upon her before she could. He pressed his boot against her neck as she groaned and pushed against him, and he raised the cross high over his head for the killing blow. It had all happened faster than Richard could react, but he rushed forward now. He knew that he was sacrificing his only chance for survival and that intervening would likely result in his own death, but his love for Cami knew no bounds, and he did it without hesitation.

The bullet caught the dark man before Richard could. He jerked to the side and fell against the wall, leaving a bloody pattern from his wounded arm. He did not scream and looked more annoyed than frightened. Mary stood in the hallway, clutching her father's pistol in a white-knuckled grip. She was crying with terror and could not form the words to warn or comfort, but she aimed her weapon for another shot. She was surprised at how quickly the man moved; she did not expect him to move at all after the first shot. He was too quick for her to take aim, and she fired off a useless shot behind him as he ran. In a moment, he was upon her. The pistol was gone, she did not know where, and he was pressing on her jugular vein. In a brief moment, the world went dark as Mary slipped into unconsciousness.

The man was not ready for Richard, who had chased after him in a vain effort to prevent him from reaching Mary. He jumped on the dark man's back with an angry shout, but the man's reflexive response was too quick even for Richard. The dark man stood to his full height, rage in his eyes, and closed in on the injured Cami and the incapacitated Richard. Richard and Cami locked eyes; the both knew that they had to run. They knew that they had to draw the man out away from their unconscious loved one. They both hated the thought of leaving her alone but knew that removing the threat from her home was the only chance that she had, and her heroism had removed the barrier that had previously prevented them from doing so. The dark man noticed that as well and charged after them. They ran outside together. They could hear his footsteps behind them, but they grew softer as the gap widened. He was running for his quarry; they ran for their lives.

They knew, no matter where they ran, he would follow, but at least he would follow them away from Mary.

. . .

The jarring sound of crashing wood, splintering against a boot, crashed through the house. She awakened with a jolt and instinctively reached for Richard, but he was not in the bed next to her. She feared the worst and pulled the covers over her head like a frightened child. She peeked outside of the protective cloth fortress when she heard two thuds against the wall and saw a bizarre sight: two sharpened tips that had penetrated through from the opposite side. She was breathing so heavily that she was afraid she would not be able to speak, but she picked up the phone to call the police anyway.

The line was dead.

Through the thin interior wall, she heard shouts, crashing glass, dull thuds. She had no idea of what was happening but knew that something was very wrong. Mary was grateful for her habit of sleeping with a nightlight because it provided just enough light for her to cross to her chest of drawers and retrieve the cigar box that she kept inside it. Inside that box was her father's gun—an old revolver that he had kept meticulously cleaned and oiled. Given Mary's dislike of guns, the weapon had not been well maintained since her father's passing, but she knew that it would fire. Her hands shook as she loaded six rounds into the chambers, and the sound of sliding it back into place seemed to echo off the walls.

She took a deep breath and peeked through the bedroom door. She was terrified and confused by what she saw but knew only that she wanted to protect Cami and Richard. She loved them as her own and knew that she would gladly die for either one of them. She only hoped that she would not have to. Mary crept down the hallway toward the furor, letting the pistol lead the way. She gasped when she saw the intruder—it was the man from the church, and he had his foot on Cami's neck. Despite the tears blurring her vision, she took aim and fired. What happened next was a blur. She fired another shot; she missed. Then the man was upon her and then darkness.

Mary awoke, in a daze and disoriented. She winced at the pain that shot through her head. Her blurred vision began to clear, and the memories came flooding back. "Richard!" she shouted as she tried to sit up, which was when she realized that she had been restrained. Her hands were tied behind her back, and her ankles were secured together.

"Don't think I enjoy what I do." The man's voice was deep and rolling. He had a slight accent that Mary could not quite place, but she was more concerned with discovering where the voice originated rather than the speaker. He walked from her periphery into her view. She recognized the man from the church—the one that had attacked Cami and Richard. "I do it because I have to. I would have preferred for you to stay in the bedroom, but what's done is done."

"What do you want from me?" Mary sobbed. She shivered with cold and fear. She knew that she would do the same thing again but wished that the outcome could be different. Her mind raced, imagining the terrible things that were in store for her.

The man crouched next to her, directly in her line of sight. "I don't want your body," he said. Mary wondered if he had heard her very thoughts and tried to silence the others that stormed in her mind. "I want information. If you give it to me, I can be on my way and leave you alone, no worse for the wear." His face twisted into something resembling concern. Mary doubted it was sincere. "If you don't give me the information I want, I'll have to take it from you. You don't want to go through that, and I really don't want to spend that much time getting what I need. So let's make it easy, tell me where they're going, and I'll be on my way. Of course, I'll have to leave you tied up for a day or so, just to make sure you don't contact them. Aside from being hungry and possibly soiling yourself, you'll be relatively unharmed."

"What do you want with them?" Mary demanded. She tried to sound brave, but she knew that her voice betrayed her fear.

"You don't know, do you? They didn't tell you?"

"Tell me what?"

"Your friends, they're *vurdalak. Strigoï.*" Mary looked confused. "Your friends are vampires."

"There's no such thing," Mary replied.

"That's where I come in. That thing—that's not a little girl. That creature is a cold, hard-hearted killing machine. The only reason they kept you alive was that they were probably planning to feed off you, a little at a time. I checked you out everywhere while you were out. You don't have any bite marks, so I'm sure they hadn't tried it yet. Trust me, they would have drained you like a bathtub." He did not have any direct knowledge of that, but he dealt with their kind before, or so he thought.

"That's not true. You're lying."

"You saw it yourself, you know you did." The man smiled. "What's your name?"

"What's yours?"

She did not even see his hand coming but felt the sting when he slapped her. "I don't need you," he said. "I won't be able to catch up to them, but I can find them with or without you. It's what I do. If you're going to waste my time, I will discard you." He pulled a large knife from another hidden pocket and laid it at his own feet. He smiled as her eyes focused and widened in fear. "What's your name?" he repeated.

"Mary."

"Much better. So where are they going, Mary?"

"I don't know, I swear!" Strictly speaking, it was true. It seemed that there was a lot that she did not know, but she could not accept that Richard and Cami were anything other than what they had claimed. She knew about the apartment, she knew where they kept their car, now seemingly suspiciously out of sight, and she knew how Cami loved Juneau when they visited earlier in the week using her good friend's plane. Most importantly, she knew that she loved them.

The man frowned. "I'm disappointed in you. You unknowingly open your home to two vampires. They lied to you, you saw that yourself. Next time they got hungry, they would have killed you—"

"They wouldn't," Mary interrupted.

"As quickly as they would have looked at you," the man continued as though he had not heard her words. "They're nothing short of evil, and you're accepting of them. Tell me, Mary, what does that make you?" Tears stung at Mary's eyes. She felt frightened and betrayed. All she had to do was open her mouth and speak—tell everything that she knew about them—and the man would leave. She could not do it. Although a very real part of her wanted to save herself, even at their expense, she could not make her mouth cooperate. "If they truly cared about you, why did they leave you here with me?"

The simple question pierced the last of Mary's resolve, and she wept bitterly.

. . .

Cami stopped before they crossed the freshly salted road and tore a deep wound in her skin. She allowed the blood to flow freely and stain the fresh snow.

"What are you doing?" Richard asked.

"I am making sure that he has a trail to follow. He cannot see our footprints in the road." She looked back into the dark woods. She was sure that he was behind them somewhere, but she had no idea how fast or far he could run. She wanted to make sure that he had something to chase.

Richard was shocked. "Why would you help him?"

Cami turned to him and spoke as an impatient mother would speak to a dim-witted child. "We keep him coming after us, and that takes him further away from Mama—Mary! I mean, Mary. As long as we are running and he is chasing us, she is safe. At least we stand a chance if he catches us. If he went after her . . . I would be afraid that he would not leave her alive."

Richard stared into the tree line and tore at his wrist in the same way. His blood joined Cami's in the pure white snow. It was unnecessary from a practical perspective, but as an act of defiance, it was clear. They continued running, their bare feet scattering the road salt and sinking into the piled snow on the other side. They ran north, grateful for the time afforded to them by the long Alaskan nights.

. . .

"So, my fine little Mary, I'm going to ask you again, and I want you to think very carefully about your answer. Are you going to tell me what you know?" He picked up the knife and rested it against her stomach. The metal was cold, and she instinctively backed away from it. The man grabbed her arm and held her in place.

"I don't know anything. Please let me go."

The man sighed and pressed the blade into the soft flesh of Mary's stomach. It was only a quick, shallow surface wound, but it was extremely painful. Mary screamed in shock, hurt, and again tried to pull away. Again, the man's strong grip held her firmly in place against the bed. He pulled the blade free and allowed the blood from the blade to drip on the floor. She could feel the cold air entering the wound and began again to sob quietly. She expected another question, but none came. Instead, he drew the sharp edge of the blade against her stomach a second time.

"Barrow," she gasped. "Try Barrow—I think they went there."

"Can I trust you?" the man asked.

"Yes . . . please . . ."

He sighed. "No, I can't. You gave it up too easily. That makes me think that you're probably lying," the man said. "When someone resists as much as you did, they don't give up the truth right away. The first thing they're going to do is try to lie about it. You were afraid, as you should be, but you held fast. So now you're going to try to save yourself without giving up the monsters. Now since I can't trust what you say, which tells me that I need to get you past the point of lies, I need to break you. Only then can I believe anything that comes out of your mouth. I'm sorry that you made me do this."

Mary tried to disassociate herself from what would come next. She closed her eyes and tried to ignore the pain, to get deep enough into her own head that she could forget about her body. She was pulled back into her body when the man brought a heavy fist down on her thigh. She screamed. He brought down his same fist on her opposite thigh, tearing muscle and shattering blood vessels. She screamed again. She spouted lies and half-truths, desperate to get the pain to stop as he continued torturing her fragile body. He beat her, cut her, stressed her joints, and broke her bones—enough to cause unimaginable pain, but he never let her lose consciousness. As the injuries and wounds mounted, and as the pain grew, Mary's very sense of self began to change. Her thoughts flashed to Cami and Richard, who had come into her life so suddenly and left just as quickly. She thought of how they had lied to her and how they left her alone with a different monster. She had a life. It was not the happiest, but it was hers, and it was safe. She wanted to keep it.

"Juneau . . .," she said simply. Under her breath, she whispered, "God, forgive me . . . God, forgive me . . ." She closed her eyes, preparing for another blow that did not come.

The man stopped. "How do you know?"

"I know," she whispered. She could not look the man in the eyes. She could not put her knowledge into words, but she knew that is where they would head. She was not sure how, but she thought that it may have been the way Cami's eyes lit up when saw the tramway, or the memory of walking hand in hand with Richard through the Rainforest Garden, but she knew it to be true. She hoped that she would someday forget those memories but doubted she ever would.

"Thank you," the man said.

"I need help," she begged. She could feel her wounds burning in the cold air, and she knew she would not survive if left alone. The man that had done such harm had become her only hope. He did not answer, and she turned to look him in the eyes. For the briefest of moments, she thought she saw sincere regret.

"Mary, there're certain things that can never be known. This is one of them. I'm sorry."

"No . . . *Please* . . .," she begged. However, it was too late. He pressed the long knife against her throat and flicked his wrist. She felt a sting as the blade opened her vein then warmth as the blood spilled down her skin.

"I'm really very sorry," he said. Then the world went dark.

. . .

The howling wind and the dark skies provided a fitting backdrop for Cami and Richard's joyless drive toward Juneau. They did not speak to each other but lost themselves in their own thoughts. They struggled to come to terms with what had happened and what they had lost. Cami had finally gotten her family back and had only started to heal from the guilt and trauma of losing her parents for the first time. Richard had finally found a home and a love that he never knew could exist, and it was all taken from him in a few tragic moments. He hoped that the dark man had come after them. He hoped that the man had not lost their scent.

Numb and afraid, they drove on. By the time they stopped for fuel, they had only begun to share their wealth of feelings and thoughts. A small part of Richard blamed Cami for leading him to such a semblance of life, and a small part of Cami blamed herself for the same thing. They were both grateful that they had the opportunity to love as deeply as they had, but they also mourned the loss of it. Their feelings and thoughts became less coherent and less lucid as the time since they last fed grew longer. Cami, especially, needed to eat to recover from her injuries and self-induced blood loss. They began to discuss their plan for settling into the community. Then they would have to figure out how they would feed without drawing suspicion.

Cami looked at Richard quizzically when he pulled off the road and parked in the near empty lot of a rest area. He answered by gesturing with his head, and she followed his gaze. There was one other vehicle in the lot. It was a run-down orange station wagon, with deeply tinted windows and surprisingly expensive rims. A bent metal prop held the hood open, indicating some sort of mechanical distress. Having seen their approach, the man exited his vehicle and waved eagerly. He was very obese, which was only accentuated by the heavy winter coat that barely contained his mass. His face was hidden beneath a thick beard, and his forehead was beaded with sweat despite the cold. He smiled as Cami and Richard approached.

"Big guy like that . . . he will have a lot of blood," Cami whispered. Richard nodded.

Richard whispered back, "He looks like a nice guy. I don't think I'd have the heart."

Cami, keeping low tones, said, "We will see."

The man, as it turned out, was not what he had seemed. When they came in close, he raised a pistol and demanded they give him all their money. Richard just laughed. The man lowered the pistol briefly then shot Cami in the leg and yelled, "Does this look like I'm joking?"

Cami looked up and, instead of grasping her leg in pain, spoke quietly in that low growling tone. "Not one bit, but you do look delicious!" He was not only a source of sustenance, but he was also a target for Cami's and Richard's misplaced rage. His death was so brutal and violent that it would later be attributed to a wild animal. They continued on their journey, leaving the man's body on the frozen ground. Their bodily pains were gone from having fed, but the fat man's death did nothing to sooth their aching hearts. It was very much the opposite, as another death was on their heads. Neither of them voiced their feelings, but they feared that they had taken a step toward becoming what they feared.

Chapter Nine

Vampire Hunter

As the pair made their way into Alaska's capital city, they could not help but notice that there was a small homeless population in Juneau. It was large enough, however, that an ostensible father and daughter could live in their car for a few days without drawing too much attention. Centuries of experience had given Cami the broad perspective that allowed her to accept the loss just a little bit better than Richard, who had hardly spoken since they left Fairbanks. She allowed him to grieve; she knew how it was to lose someone you cared for. There was nothing for him, except for the twin deceptions of hope and despair, along with the ageless little girl who was trying desperately to break him out of his protective emotional shell.

"Richard . . .," Cami said out of nowhere. They were still sitting in the car, isolated and alone.

Richard stared straight ahead through the windshield. He did not turn his head. "What?"

"Do you want to see a movie?"

"No."

Undeterred, Cami tried again. "Maybe we should go for a walk. Get some air."

"Why do we need air? We don't need to breathe, you saw to that. No . . . Thanks," Richard replied. Merely speaking took willpower that he was not sure he had any longer. He wanted to shut down, to let the pain crash over him and drag him under. He could not explain why leaving Mary had devastated him. He only knew that it had.

The silence filled the car. The discomfort was palpable. "Listen, I know how you feel. I—"

"How would you know?" Richard interrupted. He was suddenly very passionate and animated, giving full vent to his emotions. "You don't know what it's like—not any of it. You made me into this. You did this to me! You have no goddamn idea. You're just a little girl. You've never been in love before."

Cami stared at him. Her voice was even and measured—the opposite of his. "I have loved more deeply and more intensely that you have ever known in your meager life. As for pain and loss, dear Richard," spitting his name like a foul taste in her mouth, "I killed my parents more than five hundred years ago. I killed them and drank their blood. I was new at being a *vurdalak* and had no control over either my hunger or my emotions. My body died one day before that, but I die inside every single day because of it. Do not tell me that I do not know about loss. I think about it . . . about them . . . every single day."

Something resonated in Richard. He could not explain it, but her revelation spoke to him. He knew that he should have been afraid of her then, or possibly disgusted or angry, but he felt none of those things. He dropped his head, ashamed that he had completely ignored her thoughts and pains. "I'm sorry. I didn't know." He was drawn in by Cami's very raw emotion. "What happened?"

She told him the story. It was a story that she had never told before. He hung on every word. Cami did not know when Richard had reached for her hand, but she held it gratefully while she poured her heart into him. He listened and then shared the silence with her when she finished. Giving voice to the pains that she had kept inside had been cathartic for her, and she felt that a weight had been lifted from her shoulders.

Richard smiled. It was a close, comforting smile. "How about that movie? I saw a theater on the way into town . . ."

Cami returned his smile. It felt good to smile after what they had so recently experienced. "Let us go."

The engine roared to life when Richard turned the key, and the tires crushed the dirt and rocks as they began to pull away. Suddenly, the wheel jerked to the side and the tire went soft. Richard slowed to a stop, and the car rested at a slight angle. "Damn it!" Richard swore. After everything they had been through in the last few days, the inconvenience of a flat tire seemed almost comical. They looked at each other, and Cami shrugged before they both erupted into laughter. "When it rains, right?"

They exited from their respective sides. Richard opened the trunk for the spare, while Cami looked at the damage to the tire. Although it was very flat, it took her a moment to find the cause. Buried deep in the vulcanized rubber was a hollow steel tube that had opened an unrestricted air channel. She understood why the tire had gone flat so quickly but could not imagine where they had picked up the tube that had opened the tire in such a way.

"Hey, Richard, look at this," Cami called. There was no reply. Cami heard the wind rustle through the nearby leaves. She heard an animal skitter through the brush. She heard the wind gently run past her ears. "Richard?" she called again, and again, there was no answer. She stood and looked around. Nothing moved. She circumnavigated the vehicle. She was alert and frightened. Something was wrong.

"Hello, Cami." Her skin crawled. She knew that voice. When she reached the open trunk, she saw that she was correct. The dark man stood with Richard. The man held him in place with a firm hand clamped tightly over his mouth and a wooden stake pressed tight against his chest. Cami could see a small trickle of blood from that ran along Richard's shirt from where the stake had pierced his skin.

"Let him go!" Cami snarled. She had already lost her mother incarnate and refused to let this man take her father's spirit from her as well. She rushed at him—her only desire was to pull him apart with her bare hands. He smiled and pressed the stake deeper into Richard's chest, stopping her in her tracks. Richard's eyes opened wider with fear and pain. Cami looked into them, doing her best to offer some form of comfort. She looked at the dark man and willed all her hate to show in her eyes. No one moved; it was a standoff. "So what do we do now?" She could not understand why he had not simply killed Richard when he had the clear opportunity. It did not make sense to hold him hostage when he could have simply killed him and fought Cami alone. She considered her options and rejected each one in turn. The dark man seemed to wait until she realized that she had none left.

"That's up to you. I want your help, little Cami, so I'm going to make you an offer. Your rebirther, Boian . . ."

"How did you know about him?" Cami demanded.

"I know many things. I have an interest in catching him alive, but that's proven to be a somewhat difficult task. You know him far better than I could hope to, so I want you to help me. I get the feeling that there's no love lost between you two, so I don't think you'd have any objections to trading his life for yours."

"If I help you, you will let Richard and I live? How do I know you will keep your promise?"

The man laughed. It was a dry, humorless chuckle. "You're not hearing me. I'm offering you, and you alone, a chance to live. I don't need him. Frankly, having only one of you gives me less to worry about."

"If you do not let him go, it is no deal. Let him go, and I will bring you Boian myself. I give you my word."

Richard did not trust the man. He slowly crept his hand closer to the stake, hoping that the man was too distracted with Cami to notice.

"Then he still dies, and you follow him into hell."

Richard brought his hand closer to his own chest, moving excruciatingly slow in order to remain undetected.

"Understand this: if you kill him, you will not walk away. I will kill you slowly, draining you one pint at a time."

The exchange was the verbal equivalent of two deadly animals squaring off for a fight to the death. Richard brought his hand even further upward along his body. He was nearly to the stake but did not dare strike before he was ready—as ready as he could be at least.

He stopped when the man pushed the stake into his chest. He felt the point slide between his ribs and cut through his muscle. He screamed against the man's heavy hand as the tip came to a stop just short of his heart. He could feel the burning wood pressing against his heart but not quite piercing it. "Put your hand down, my dear fellow," the man scolded. Richard complied. The dark man backed the stake out of his chest. Not enough to eliminate the pain completely but enough that it was barely bearable.

Cami desperately made one last effort. She stared deep into his eyes and allowed herself to fill them. She collected her own wishes and wants and impressed them upon the man through her gaze. She searched his eyes but could not find his will.

"Did you really think it would be that easy?" the man asked. He sounded almost disappointed at Cami's attempt. "You can't hypnotize me, you can't fight me, and nor can you escape. You can either help me or you can die the eternal death."

Cami knew that she had run out of options. She knew that he had beaten her. Resignation was written all over her face when she replied. "Yes," she answered finally. "Yes, I will help you." She saw Richard's eyes flash with a mixture of fear, disappointment, and surprise. "I am his rebirther. I brought him into this plane of existence. If he is going to suffer the eternal death, it should be by my hand and mine alone."

"A touching sentiment," the man sneered. "You'll understand if I don't trust you." He pressed the stake further into Richard's chest until it was once again pressing against his heart. It burned in Richard's chest, but he could only watch as Cami walked closer to him—to kill him. "The slightest touch will pierce his heart. All you have to do is press. Moreover, if you change your mind, it will not be possible for you to pull it away before I can finish him and then you, in turn. Think very carefully about what you want to do. You won't get another chance."

Cami walked confidently toward the pair. Richard begged her with his eyes, but she avoided looking at him. She put her hand on the end of the stake and breathed in deeply. *Please, Richard . . . please understand that this is for your good. I cannot allow you to suffer.* Then she saw it—the subtle subdermal motion that indicated that his muscles had relaxed along with his guard. Cami had never before moved so fast or felt so powerful, but the motivation of protecting Richard had sparked something within her. The man was ready and pulled inward to thrust the stake into Richard's heart. Cami's strength surprised him, and she pulled the wooden weapon from both his grip and Richard's chest.

Richard fell to the ground in a half-dead heap and rolled in the snow as though he was trying to run away from the pain in his chest. Cami did not have time to check on his well-being and could only hope that he would recover, if they even survived at all. She did not want to take her eyes off the dark man, who lowered himself into an aggressive stance. She could see his eyes dart across the battlefield as he noted the various assets and liabilities that he needed to account for. Cami did the same, and the two regarded each other carefully. Cami attacked first, launching herself at the man like a wild cat eager for blood. The man swung his massive fist in a wide arc, which connected with Cami in midair and sent her falling to the ground. She sprang up and dodged his next blow then drove her fist into the man's stomach with every ounce of strength that she could muster. The man fell against the trunk of the car, and Cami took advantage of his momentary disorientation to climb on top of him and pound him with wild, aggressive punches and scratches. She leaned in to bite him, not to turn him or even expecting to kill him but just to do as much damage as she possibly could before he could recover. Her fangs pressed through her gums in eager anticipation, but before she could connect, he caught her by the throat and threw her to the ground. She landed hard on the frozen terrain, which caused her to become temporarily disoriented.

The man towered over her, smiling. "It's been a long time since someone was able to hit me, little Cami. You should be proud of that. It's regretful that I'll have to kill you. I can offer you a quick and noble death, however, if that is any consolation." He raised his boot high into the air and took aim for Cami's head. Her eyes widened when she saw the two silver crosses embedded in the sole charging toward her. His boot seemed to fall in slow motion, and Cami watched it grow larger as it approached her face. She weakly threw her arms in front of her face to protect it and felt her forearm crack and her skin burn with the impact. The man pushed downward, forcing Cami's arms against her face and causing her flesh to boil. In a desperate move, she hooked her feet under the bumper and pulled. Her skin tore as she broke free, and she gasped from the pain. She ignored it and climbed to her feet. The man was ready for her and swung his heavy wooden cross into her chest. She felt her ribs crack and her breath robbed from her as the holy relic seared her skin. She fell into the opened trunk as he raised his weapon for the final blow.

The man had ignored Richard, whom he considered to be very near death. Richard knew this and gathered the last of his waning strength for a single blow. He knew that he only had enough energy for one chance, and he prayed quietly that it would be enough. If nothing else, he hoped that it would be the distraction that could save Cami, if only for a few precious moments. The man brought his weapon down. Richard saw his opportunity draw near as the large cross swung toward Cami's head. She saw it too and stared in wide-eyed horror as it came closer. Richard struck. It was weak and barely effective, but it was enough. The cross glanced off the metal rim of the trunk, barely missing Cami's vulnerable head. The man twisted his wrist to control the ricochet, sending the heavy wood into Cami's face and sending her wailing to the ground. She gasped for breath and tenderly grasped at her wounds.

The man turned to Richard, who stood on very unsteady feet. He wanted to run, but he lacked the strength. He wanted to fight, but he lacked the ability. He wanted to live, but he doubted he would. The dark man's expression was flat and joyless as he freed a fresh wooden stake.

"Please," Richard said weakly. It was all he could manage.

The man did not answer. He struck like a cobra, with the stake leading his powerful arm into Richard's chest. Richard screamed and clawed weakly at the wooden intrusion. He looked at his wound and then at the man and then fell limp to the ground. Cami screamed both in raw hatred for the monstrous dark man and from the pain of seeing the man she envisioned as her father impaled and unmoving. She let the anger wash over her and fill her, giving her strength and purpose. She steadied herself on the car's bumper and pulled herself to her feet. Her face was fixed with determination, and her body was poised to attack.

The man this time was faster.

He caught her by the throat, stopping her before she could realize his intentions. His muscles pressed against her skin as he lifted her small frame into the air. She pulled at his fingers and kicked at the air, but it was useless to struggle. The man pulled his third and final stake free from its sheath and aligned it to Cami's heart. She closed her eyes—she did not want to see death coming. She, of course, did not want death to come at all, but the choice was not hers to make.

She felt her body jerk. She felt herself fall and hit the ground. She felt the man's grip relax. She waited for death; it did not come. She realized that the stake had not found her, and she carefully opened her eyes, wondering at the sadistic trick that the man was playing. She jumped when she saw that she was staring straight into his eyes. She tried to back away from him, but there was no need. His eyes were empty and dim, without any life left in them. He was dead, and above him stood Boian.

Boian kneeled next to Cami, who was completely at his mercy.

"Why?" Cami asked. It was all that she could manage.

"Why did I save you? Cami, when you die, it will be by my hand. I am not going to give someone else that privilege. That, my dear Cami, is reserved for me and me alone." He cut a small incision in his vein and allowed a single drop to pool on Cami's lips. She closed her mouth, unwilling to accept even life-saving sustenance from the demon, but the small amount that leaked through provided her with a very small amount of strength. "Besides, I have done something far better." He smiled at the thought of what he had done. His smile would have made Cami shiver—if she had the strength to do so. Boian stood and pointed to the nearby tree line. Cami followed his gesture. She wanted to smile, to cry, or to yell but could only manage a tortured amalgamation of all three responses, none of which could be heard in the sound that she made. Walking slowly toward the car was Mary, wearing a very sheer dress that would have done little against the harsh elements. Cami understood the message—the cold did not have an effect on Mary because she had been rebirthed. Yes, Boian had rebirthed her as a *vurdalak as well.*

"No . . . Please, no . . ." Cami sobbed quietly. "You bastard . . . you son of a dog," she managed between tears.

"Me? You are the one that left her to die, Cami."

"We were trying to save her . . . We were trying to bring him out."

"I am afraid she remembers it differently. He did things to her, and you did not save her. When he was torturing her, it affected her mind. You left her to die, and I saved her from death. There is a sort of symmetry to it, do you not think?"

Cami did not answer. She stared at Mary, who stared back with cold eyes, lifeless and uncaring.

"Some of the things that I told her . . . they might not have been completely accurate, she believed them wholeheartedly just the same. You believed that she was your mother, did you not? You had this entire family unit built up in your frail little mind. You just wanted it so badly that you fooled yourself into believing it. Nevertheless, they are not your parents, Cami. Your parents are dead—you killed them. Are the two people who you brought into your life to assuage your guilt? You killed them too." He stood and motioned for Mary to join him. Mary obediently came to his side and looked down at Cami.

"Mary, you need to get away from him," Cami pleaded in tears, choking. She pulled herself up to a sitting position using the bumper for support. "He is evil, Mary. You have to trust me!"

Mary's expression changed to anger and betrayal. It stung Cami's heart to see her angelic face distorted in such a way. "Trust you? I did trust you! I let you into my home . . . into my life, but you lied to me. You let me . . . you let things happen to me. I loved you, and I loved . . ." The thought finally occurred to her; she had not seen Richard. She scanned the ground and saw his still body covered by an uneven layer of snow. "Richard," she finished. Her face was betrayed by her heart's sorrow before reforming itself into a stoic gaze. Cami knew that Mary's perception was an impregnable combination of Boian's lies and mental manipulations—he was very good at both.

"Mary . . . you are my mother." Cami gave her greatest, most personal secret. She was desperate to break through the veil that Boian had placed upon Mary.

"Did I not tell you that she would spew lies, hurtful stories to try and persuade you?" Boian said, shaking his head in a very convincing semblance of humility. He had preemptively turned Cami's own revelation against her.

"How dare you!" Mary screamed. Her voice splitting the frosty night air and believing that the truth, now twisted to appear as a lie, served as confirmation for the other lies that Boian had told her. It was a very old psychological trick used by traveling salesmen and psychopaths alike for a very good reason—it worked well. "I know what you are. I know that you killed your friend Samuel, and I know how you made Boian into a vampire and left him to die, the same way you left me."

"Mary . . . *please remember!*"

Mary continued, ignoring Cami's simple plea. "He's not going to leave me alone like you left him and me. He saved me . . . He saved me from you." Mary stood upright and took a small step backward, emblematically deferring to Boian.

"We are going to take our leave now. You see, the wolves are coming." Cami listened carefully but heard nothing. Boian smiled and leaned back. He released a loud mournful howl that echoed through the surrounding forest and made Cami's skin crawl. Boian smiled and turned, and then walked into the tree line with Mary in tow. Mary turned and took a final look at Cami and then disappeared into the darkness as well.

Cami, for the first time in too many centuries, cried. She listened to the claws scrape on the stones as the unseen creatures approached. She had nowhere to run and no ability to do so. "I am sorry, Richard," she whispered. "I am sorry."

Richard groaned.

"Richard?" She was not sure if she had actually heard him or if she merely hoped she had. She was afraid to hope, but her impending death allowed her the luxury of doing so. Cami knew that Juneau was below the Arctic Circle, and daylight would be coming soon. They would not be able to get to the safety of artificial darkness by the time it did, and the approaching wolves would only make certain that their last night was as painful and terrible as the daylight would be. It was a terrible way to die.

Richard groaned again and struggled to form the words that caught in his throat. He could not move, and yet he could feel the tip of the stake pressed against the soft muscle near his heart. The tip had scraped against his heart but had not pierced it. His body burned, with fresh waves of pain spreading through him every time he tried to speak.

Cami was sure that she had heard him this time, and everything else was, for the moment, forgotten. Richard was alive, if only barely, which gave a small amount of satisfaction to the hope that she had dared not allow just moments before. "Richard . . ." Her whisper was hoarse, but the encouragement that she felt was sincere. She dragged her body closer to him. Her movement was punishing her body. It took every bit of willpower that she could muster, but still, she forced herself to continue. She reached Richard as the wolves entered the clearing. While she came to him eagerly, the wolves approached cautiously, stalking their prey and moving in as a single unit. Cami knew that she would not be able to fight them and instead focused on the man who lay helpless on the ground. She rested her hand on the protruding stake and looked into her heart. She wondered if she should push the stake further into his body to give him a quick and relatively painless death or remove it and leave him to the coldhearted beasts and the burning-hot sunrise.

She knew what she had to do—she had to spare him the pain of Boian's plan. She had to give him the escape into the comforting embrace of death that she was not able to take for herself. She knew that, but when the decisive moment arrived, she could not do it. She still held to the fragile thread of faith that something would intervene, that some sort of miracle would save them. Straining, she was able to pull it free, only after several exhausting attempts and aborted efforts.

Richard gasped as the movement relieved the pressure on his heart, and he groaned when she had finally pulled it free from his chest. The pain caused by the object's removal and the void it left behind was intense, far worse than even the immense pain that he had experienced only minutes before. "Cami . . .," he managed to say.

Cami offered a weak smile. She was trying to tell him that everything would be okay, even if she did not believe it herself, or possibly offer some small amount of comfort as he approached death. She turned her head and saw that the wolves had reached them, with the leader of the pack sniffing at Richard's foot. Richard was not aware of their presence and retuned her smile with an insincere one of his own. Cami, emboldened by their impending death, gladly gave the last of her reserves of strength to pull herself on top of Richard's body and to kick and punch unconvincingly at the animals. Her attack did little against them, except to get the attention of most of the pack members. They bit at her legs and her hands, tearing the skin and ripping muscle. Cami wanted to scream, both from pain and the desperate need for help, but she could not make the words form. The wolves tore at her and at Richard, where Cami could not protect him, and the pain was freshly renewed with every piercing from the sharp jagged teeth. Cami was certain that hell was very real, but she doubted that it could by any worse than the tortures that she was experiencing at that moment.

She closed her eyes, trying to ignore the pains and horrors as she was being eaten, and tried to welcome death before the rising sun guaranteed it.

Crack!

A gunshot echoed off the hills; the alpha wolf yelped and fell to the ground. *Crack!* Another gunshot rang out, and another wolf fell to the ground. The survivors were confused, being threatened by an enemy that they could not see or smell. They forgot the torn and ragged Cami and Richard for the moment and ran back and forth in the clearing in their vain effort to find their new target. Finding none, and taking two more losses, the rest of the pack retreated to the safety of the forest. The approaching dawn was cold and eerily silent, the former made worse by their near dead state and the latter broken when the sound of heavy boots crunching light snow approached. Cami forced her eyes open and watched as the thick fur-lined boots came closer, one steady step at a time, before stopping near the dark man's body. The boots' owner, unseen through Cami's blurred and fading vision, bent over and checked for life. Finding none, he approached Cami and Richard, stopping next to them.

"It is okay . . .," Cami whispered to Richard. *We are going to be okay, Tata*, she thought before giving in to unconsciousness.

CHAPTER TEN

Imani's Home

Cami awoke with a start. She was in a small windowless room. She was hungry. She could not move. She almost immediately fell back into unconsciousness.

She awoke again. She had no idea how much time had passed. Her entire body hurt. Her injuries and wounds itched and burned. Her mouth tasted like blood. Richard was beside her; he was not moving. She drifted back into her deep slumber.

Cami woke up for a third time. She opened her eyes and waited for the room to stop spinning and for her vision to clear. She felt sick, but she was alive. More importantly to her, Richard was alive as well. He was stirring next to her. "Richard!" she called. For a moment, she did not care that they seemed to be trapped in a windowless room with no recollection of how they got there. Whatever fresh danger they had found themselves in now, she had at least saved him from the last one and accepted that small victory. She thought of how close she had come to killing him in an attempted act of mercy, and her thoughts overcame with a mixture of emotions.

"Cami . . . where are we?" Richard asked. With much effort, he sat upright and tried to make sense of his surroundings. "How did we get here?" He ran his hands over his chest. Although still fresh and tender, the wound had started to heal.

"I do not know, but we are alive, so you know . . . we have got that going for us . . .," she quipped with a smile.

"Yes. You are alive, and you're lucky to be so." The woman spoke while opening the door as though she had been listening to their entire conversation through it. She was small and thin, not much larger than Cami in frame and stature, although she appeared to be in her early forties. Her dark skin, perfect and unblemished, was pulled tight across her high cheekbones as though she were carefully and lovingly sculpted by a master artisan. Her hair had been carefully arranged and pulled back into a tidy bun, and she was dressed in a very simple black dress. She was beautiful, and she walked with the confidence of one who held great internal or hidden strength.

Cami was instantly alert. "Who are you?" she demanded. "Why are you keeping us here?"

The woman smiled, a warm and sincere smile that echoed in her eyes. "I'm not *keeping* you *anywhere*, child. You've already been here for a week. We've kept you clean and fed, most importantly—safe. You're welcome to stay as long as you want, and you're welcome to leave when the mood takes you. Until then, you are guests in my home, and you will be treated as such. My name is Imani." She extended a hand to Cami, who took it gingerly.

"Cami," she answered. She was still surprised by the revelation that they had been there for so long. "This is Richard." Richard nodded in her direction but did not respond.

"He doesn't talk much, does he?" Imani asked.

"Sometimes there is not too much to say, especially when we do not know where we are or what you want."

The woman smiled again. She seemed to do that a lot. "Ah yes. As I said, this is my home, but it's much more than that. You see, you are not the first of the vampires to come to Alaska. It is somewhat of a popular destination because of the day/night patterns. Sometimes they are just looking for refuge—a place where they can exist in peace and harmony—without worrying about discovery or about the eaters . . ."

"The eaters?" Cami asked.

"There are some vampires who are nothing but eaters. They consume, but they never create. They never improve the world—they only take away from it. They are simply loathsome creatures. You are just lucky that you didn't go on to Barrow, up north. I wouldn't be able to help you there."

"What do you mean?"

"They *own* Barrow. They are, in every aspect, the life of the city. They are in the city hall, they run the businesses, and they are in the schools. It is theirs. It belongs to them. There is a sort of uneasy truce between *them and us.* They don't come south of the circle, and we don't go above it. Frankly, the eaters got the better end of the deal, but we are not really after territory and it is not worth a war. We probably wouldn't win it anyway."

"Why not?" Richard finally spoke.

"You *do* speak!" Imani smiled. "We're not warriors, Richard. We're artists and philosophers, thinkers and adventurers. They are greater in numbers and eager to kill. We avoid confrontation when we can—and fight when we must." As she spoke, an older teen girl, barefoot and wearing a tunic, with shoulders, arms, and legs exposed, entered the room. The girl, using a razor knife, carefully sliced the skin of her wrist to open the vein. She offered the blood to Cami, who drank eagerly. Imani then did the same to her own wrist and allowed the girl to drink from her. She told Cami and Richard that it was not fair to take and never give back. The girl then offered her wrist to Richard, who drank deeply but was not greedy. He could have drunk more but stopped when he felt her discomfort.

Offering one's own blood supply was the most sincere gesture that one vampire may offer to another. The pair accepted Imani's blood gratefully. They took little but felt its restorative effects spread through their bodies like a miraculous, healing warmth. Imani waited for the natural euphoria to pass before she continued. "Before we reached this truce, there was a war. Hundreds on either side, the lines stretched as far as you could see in either direction. We just . . . stared at one another from opposite sides of a shallow valley until we attacked simultaneously. I have replayed it in my mind a million times since then, and I have no idea what started the charge. It was savage and brutal . . . It was horrible. One after another we fell, taking one of theirs for every one of our losses. Blood stained the snow, and the ash filled the air." She paused, reliving the memory. "Those of us who survived that day agreed to the truce, and it has held . . . pretty much at least."

"Pretty much?" Richard questioned.

"Yes, pretty much. There are some conflicts now and again, but generally, we keep to our own and they do the same. Now you know our story. Someday I will hear yours. For now, I will introduce you to the others."

Cami and Richard followed her into the large ornate estate. The furniture and decorations were elaborate, obviously imported antiques, which gave the home the overall feeling of a cross between a mansion and an ancient castle. The occupants were cordial but stiffly formal and clearly uneasy with the additions to the home. Cami was surprised at how few they were, and she realized that the war must have been more terrifyingly devastating than she originally thought. She could immediately see that they are not only unwilling but also unprepared for another war. They were a close group, and they had elected to hide themselves away in isolation rather than expose themselves to destruction. Imani was the only one who seemed to be able to accept war—and then only reluctantly. Therefore, she had become the caretaker of this group, holding herself responsible for the maintenance of her own safe haven.

Imani showed the pair the rest of the home and the grounds. Richard, being the youngest among them, was in awe of the collection of various treasures and antiquities. The library was particularly impressive, with massive stacks of books that ranged from priceless to contemporary and centuries of artwork that lined the walls. Imani, however, seemed nonchalant about the entirety of the tour. Only when they reached the detached servant's quarters did she start to become animated. She explained that there were humans who lived inside— actual living humans, some on their second generation. The humans were not only being kept for food, which was obvious, but also for companionship. Those who had accepted vampires as their superiors actually enjoyed becoming live-in servants and companions. It was almost like having human pets.

They stopped at the door. "Why do you keep them here?" She knew the answer but had yet to understand her moral outlook on it.

"No one here is *kept* here, not against their will anyway. I'm no eater," Imani answered. "They're free to go at any time. They are here purely because of their greed . . . or their need to provide for a family. The two can look very similar. They earn a salary, above average for the area, and live like kings and queens. Every one of their needs is met, and they are given free run of the grounds. In most of the cases, it's a much better life than the one they left behind to stay here."

"For what? What are they here to do?"

"Nothing other than what they do naturally. While they sit and eat, play games or watch videos, their bodies replenish their precious blood supply. We feed them well, and they do the same for us. We never take enough to harm them—just enough for us to live."

Cami was impressed by the efficiency of the arrangement. Imani was growing her own willing victims that kept her community and herself fed without exposing them to the risk of discovery that comes with hunting. The reaction among the mortals was mixed when Imani introduced Richard and Cami. While all were open and friendly, some seemed to resent the addition of two more vampires. Presumably, this was because it was two more that they would need to feed. They were welcoming, and Cami could see that the arrangement truly benefited both groups in different ways. The collection area was as sterile and clinical as the living area was warm and welcoming. There were half a dozen reclining chairs, each seat next to a metal post to hold the collection bags. The process was no different from the collection on any blood bank or hospital. There was a large whiteboard mounted to the wall, on which a series of names and dates were written in immaculate handwriting. Only one of the chairs was actually occupied, in this case by an overweight blonde with rosy cheeks and smiling eyes. She ate happily on chocolate chip cookies while watching the new arrivals with a passing curiosity.

"Are you supply or demand?" the woman asked, spitting crumbs as she spoke. She had a thick Southern accent, which Cami had not expected.

"What do you mean?" she asked. Cami was having difficulty focusing on her own question but was instead distracted by the swelling plastic container that held her blood like a clear, artificial tick. The blood swirled around itself as it was withdrawn, and Cami watched with an eager fascination.

The woman noticed Cami's fascination. When she spoke, her voice lacked the warmth and enthusiasm that it had only moments before. "I guess that answers my question then."

Cami shook herself free from the distraction, tearing her eyes away from the package of blood, and looked at the woman. Her expression was somewhere between annoyed and insulted. "I am sorry, did I do something wrong?"

The woman sighed. "You're new here, so you're not used to our culture. Our culture considers it very rude for you to talk about blood while the blood is inside or coming out of a person. It's insulting.

You only see us for what we can do for you rather than real people with more to offer than just some blood cells. It's for everybody's protection—the less the vamps associate us with blood, the less the temptation."

"I see. Thanks."

The woman smiled and took another bite of her cookie before picking up her dated celebrity gossip magazine and flipping idly through it. Cami had not realized that Imani had left until she returned with a small brown bag. She patted it gently. "I thought you two might be hungry," she whispered. They bade the woman farewell, along with the other mortals in the smaller home. Cami was touched by the sense of family that filled the home and, to a lesser extent, the estate as a whole.

Once outside, Cami leaned in close to Imani as they walked. "They stay willingly? Are they really free to go? They seem . . . happy enough."

Imani smiled. "Yes, they're absolutely free."

"Then why do they live in a separate home?" Richard asked.

"It avoids . . . any problems," Imani answered.

"If they leave, aren't you worried that they'll tell someone?"

"No. I kill them if they leave. They don't know that I can track them. Of course, their reporting us is not a risk I am willing to take. They're free to leave, but there are necessary consequences. I don't threaten them, so they only know that they are free to leave whenever they like but not that they will die for exercising that freedom."

Freedom . . ., Cami thought to herself. *That is a funny word for it.*

. . .

Cami and Richard grew comfortable in the home. Their needs were being met, and they were fed regularly. Neither of them was artistic, so there was always a sense that they did not exactly belong, almost as if they did not exactly fit in. There was always a gentle aloofness from the others, who would engage in their own pursuits and passions and tolerate the two newest members of the home. There were conversations that were silenced when Cami or Richard would walk into the room. It was without malice, but it was clear that they were not a part of the family.

Cami and Richard were sitting in the library, comfortable in the oversized chairs that flanked the fireplace, when Imani entered. Cami had found a collection of children's books and was devouring the old fables and contemporary tales that she found in it. She was reading one of Aesop's collections and was reading the tale of the hare and the hound when she noticed the woman standing quietly nearby.

"We need to talk about that night," Imani said. There was no greeting, and her usual friendly nature had been replaced by utter seriousness.

"What do you mean?" Cami asked.

"The night that we found you, the night you nearly died. That woman meant something to you, didn't she?"

"How do you know about her?" Cami asked. She rose as the thought occurred to her. She closed on Imani, who did not retreat or react. "Were you there?"

"Yes."

"And you did nothing? You did not, at least, try to help?" Cami's voice was a low guttural whisper.

"I told you, we never fight unless we have to. It's not our way—it's not who we are."

"Watching us die and you did not have to do so." Cami tensed her body as though she would attack. She thought of how close Richard and she had come to death and how Mary was still under the control of Boian. She only relaxed a little bit when she felt Richard's hand rest on her shoulder.

"You saw what happened," Richard said. "What more do you need to know?"

Imani repeated the question. "Did that woman mean something to you?"

"Yes," Cami and Richard answered in unison.

"Do you want to find her?"

"Yes," Cami answered. She felt the slightest glimmer of hope but pushed it deep inside. "Why?"

Then Imani smiled. "We know where she is."

Richard was less able to conceal his hope, which came out in his voice. "Where is she? Is she safe?"

"Yes, she's fine, relatively speaking, of course. However, she's still with the eaters, and she's exposed to their corrupting influence. Unless you want to lose her forever, you are going to need to get her back soon. Get her, bring her here, and we can help her remember who she was."

"Where is she?" Cami demanded.

"All in good time." Imani walked to the fireplace. She stood before it and watched the fire crackle and spit as it consumed the wood. "Fire . . . it's an interesting thing, isn't it? It can be used to create— heat, life, food—or it can be used to destroy. The fire doesn't know good or evil or right or wrong . . . It just is."

"What does this have to do with Mary?" Richard asked. Cami could see something in his eyes, something she had never seen before. He was panicked and wild, but he forced himself to remain calm.

"I'm going to help you, but we need something from you first."

Cami was enraged, but Richard reached Imani first. He closed in on her and reached for her delicate throat but stopped when two larger men appeared at her side. Cami mentally assessed them and the situation as a whole. She knew that none of them was fighters at heart, with the limited exception of Imani. She knew that Cami and Richard together could defeat them. She also knew that they would not be able to fight their way through the entire household, and the attempt would sever the only ties they had to Mary. Despite her own rage and violent desires, she pulled Richard back to where she stood. "Whatever it is, you cannot do it yourself. So you need to hold our friend over us to get what you want, is that it?"

Imani looked pained. "Yes, that's it. Sometimes the end has to justify the means."

Cami sighed. The chance to find Mary was worth whatever it was that Imani wanted of them. "What is it that you want?"

Imani's smile returned; her eyes showed a hint of victory before she pushed the sensation aside. "There's a vampire in Juneau . . . and is not *one* of us."

Cami and Richard waited for her to continue, but she stopped as though the explanation was enough. "An eater then?" Cami asked.

"No, not an eater. She's rogue, and she's already killed seven people. The police are looking for a serial killer, but it will only be a matter of time before they begin to accept it as the work of a vampire. The newspapers are already calling her one, but that's just the press trying to get their headlines for now. Could you imagine, Cami, what would happen if they actually caught her, if they knew, if they had proof that vampires, that we, actually exist? It would only be a matter of time before the rest of us would be hunted down and killed one by one. I can't allow that to happen."

"You want us to kill her?"

"Yes, before she kills again. Maybe you do not understand why, but it doesn't matter if you do or not. The offer is very simple—destroy the rogue and we tell you where to find your friend. It's up to you. You know where to find me." Imani turned and walked toward the door, the other two in tow. She reached for the doorknob, and—

"Wait," Cami called. "We will do it."

. . .

Cami and Richard were in Juneau that night. The season was changing, and daylight was starting to become a factor again. They came in from the east; they joined Mt. Roberts trailhead and followed Fifth Street toward the capitol building. The night was clear, cold, and the streets were empty, which allowed the pair to enter into the city unnoticed. They caught glimpses of the ships resting in the port, which created a serenely beautiful backdrop to their terrible task.

"How will we know how to find her?" Richard asked.

"I do not know," Cami frowned. She had been wondering the same for some time. They only had a vague description to work with, which afforded little opportunity to create a functional plan.

"Do you think she's telling the truth, about knowing where to find Mary?"

"Yes," Cami lied. She had no way of knowing if Imani would uphold her end of the bargain, but she needed to take the chance to find out. Cami knew that they were essentially mercenaries, but Imani had been right about one thing—sometimes the goal warranted the method. "We will do what we have to do, and then we will go get Mama." Richard stopped walking. It took Cami a brief moment before she noticed and turned to him. "What?"

"What did you call her?"

"Mary, why?"

"No . . . you called her 'Mama.'" Richard was confused.

"You misheard, or I misspoke. It does not matter. We have bigger things to worry about. If we do not find what we came here to find, it is all a moot point anyways." She resumed her walk, while Richard stopped suddenly. Cami turned and asked, "What?"

Richard, looking confused, began, "Moot point? Where did you go to college?"

Cami looked a little shy. "University of California, Irvine School of Medicine. I slept in the basement of the medical school for a little while. I pretended to be a cadaver there for about three months. Nobody wanted to cut up a little girl, and when one would open my drawer, I would open my eyes and twitch a little bit. It really freaked them out." Cami giggled. "I could feed on the blood samples that they would leave in the refrigerator. They did not keep track of those as well as hospitals do because they do not really use them for anything, except to practice."

Richard attributed the "Mama" slip to their shared affection for the woman rather than to Cami's unspoken belief that Mary was the reincarnation of her mother. "I loved her too, Cami. We're going to find her, and we'll get her back. Don't worry, okay?"

"Love. You said 'loved,' not 'love.' She is still alive, we still love her."

Richard nodded and then changed the subject by repeating his earlier question. "If the police can't find her, how do you think we'll be able to?"

Cami's mind raced. She saw, considered, and rejected countless scenarios. She was now driven to develop a plan given the reward, but it was something in which she had no experience. *If Boian were here, he had known what to do. The psychopath always knew what to do when it came to killing*, Cami thought. As much as she hated the idea, she realized that she had to think like Boian, which was not difficult given the amount of time that he spent trying to force her to do exactly that. She allowed herself to see the world through his twisted perspective. Then it hit her. It seemed so clear to her once she accepted her rebirther's influence. "Competition," she said simply.

"What do you mean?" Richard asked. He trusted that she had a plan but had no idea what it could be.

Cami mentally tore through the police reports and news clippings that she had memorized, mapping the intricacies and contingencies of her plan. "She leaves the bodies where they will be easily found. She *wants* them to be found. She has not been caught yet, so she is smart, and she sent those letters to the newspaper, so she is arrogant. One thing she will not be able to tolerate is competition."

Richard could hardly believe what he was hearing. "Competition . . . us? You think we should become serial killers?"

Cami was lost in her plan. She focused entirely on getting through the competition and rescuing Mary. She was pragmatic. "No. A serial killer has three or more victims with some time in between. We should not need more than two to get her attention. There is easily that many in the city who deserves it, if we look in the right places. She will hear about it, and it will draw her out. She will be the one looking for us."

"It'll get the cops' attention too, don't you think? Having two killers in the same area?" Richard asked.

"They will not know the difference. It will look exactly like her work. That is part of what will get her attention, unless you have a better idea?"

Richard admitted that he did not. Like all Cami's plans, it was elegant, if slightly morally ambiguous. It fed them, it got unsavory people off the street, and it took out a rogue vampire and protected the good law-abiding people of Juneau. Cami started prowling, crossing the streets of the small city, and following the instincts that her existence had forged over centuries. She was proud of her plan, mostly because she knew where her plan differed from one that Boian would have developed. Her plan only targeted the evil of the world, while Boian always took a perverse pleasure in defiling innocence. She was not Boian, but she was using his perspectives and teachings against him. *I am coming, Mama*, she thought to herself.

Cami had little difficulty finding evil, knowing that a run-down motel would always provide a source in one form or another. She and Richard hid from the light of the moon in a small collection of trees just off Trout Street, watching the double doors of the entrance. They did not have to wait long. A woman emerged. She wore a mini skirt and a tight top, which could not have provided any significant protection from the harsh elements. She was young—Cami figured that she was seventeen at the oldest—and her beautiful face was covered with shame and fear. She ran across the parking lot, unsteady on her tall heels, desperate to reach the large black sedan that was left running and releasing warm exhaust in the far corner of the aging asphalt. She reached the car and pulled the handle for the passenger's side door. Nothing happened—the door was locked.

The girl stood and waited. Nothing happened. She knocked gently on the window, and Cami strained her hearing to catch the conversation.

"Please, Slim, please let me in. It's cold."

"How much you get?" The man's voice was muffled, but Cami could hear that it was cold and uncaring.

"F-forty." The girl shivered. She pulled four bills from her small purse and held it up to the window. She rubbed her exposed skin, hoping to force some small amount of heat into her arms and stomach.

Based on her expression, it was not working. "Please, Slim, let me in." She jumped when the window sank down an inch then stopped. She passed the money inside and let her fingers linger near the crack to collect the warmth that was escaping from inside. She shifted from side to side, trying to stay warm, until the lock disengaged and she was allowed inside. Cami could hear the muffled sounds of an argument inside, combined with what was coming from the radio. The man was yelling, the girl was crying, and Cami was scheming.

"Both of them?" Richard asked, pulling Cami from her thoughts.

"No," Cami answered. "She is the victim. He is the one we want."

"We need two," Richard reminded her.

"Not this way. She is being held against her will, and she is not the type we want to kill."

Briefly, she thought about the man at the rest stop. She knew that he had deserved what had happened, but she put the thought from her mind. She briefly explained her plan to Richard, who listened intently. Just as she finished explaining, the car door opened and the girl emerged. She lingered for a moment in the open car door, and the heat from the interior before a barked order from Slim made her jump, and she closed the door behind her. As she made her way back into the cheap motel, Cami wondered how many times every night she had to make the same painful journey.

Richard waited until the girl had entered the motel before he followed her inside. Cami waited until Richard was safely inside before approaching the car. Cami had carefully studied humans for centuries and had become exceptionally skilled at emulating those that she saw. As Cami approached the car, she became a very lonely and scared young runaway girl who was eager for independence but lacked the ability to survive on her own. She felt the man's eyes on her as she approached the passenger side window. He was judging her, weighing her, deciding. She gingerly knocked on the glass and smiled as it came down a few inches. "Hi, mister." She smiled. "It is cold out here. Mind if I come in?"

Slim looked around carefully; it was not often that such a gift fell into his lap. Cami could see the greed in his eyes. A premium would be paid for such a young girl due to a very specific clientele. "What's your name?"

"Stacey," she lied. There was really no reason for her to lie, but she wanted a greater degree of separation between the two of them.

The man grinned. "Yeah, I'd bet it is. Come on in, let's talk."

He hit the switch to unlock the door. Cami entered the sedan and closed the door behind her. The man launched into a well-practiced pitch, which Cami cheerfully ignored as she nodded and smiled. She looked for the opening as she remembered the facts of the previous murders. When Slim raised his chin to make some strange and unheard point, Cami moved in. She launched herself on him, careful to emulate the rogue's style. He screamed and tried to fight her off but was overwhelmed by her unexpected strength. Cami was careful to copy the police photos that she had seen. She tore at the man's throat with her sharp teeth and allowed the blood to spray on to his clothes. She held him in place while he grew weaker, and she drank her fill from his neck until death took him.

Cami met Richard in their agreed-upon spot. He had a fresh pair of clothes ready for her, and he turned his back when she changed into them. "Did you do it?" Cami asked.

"Yes," Richard answered. "You?"

"Yes."

They left the scene, trusting that the police would find the bodies before long, and made their way deeper into the city.

. . .

Michelle left the stranger's room and prepared for the cold outside. She was ashamed of the acts she had just performed for such a small amount of money, but at least his room was warm. She could feel her forearm swelling with what she knew would be a deep bruise—Slim was going to be mad. He would not be angry with the overweight and dirty man who gave her the bruise but at her for allowing it to happen.

She walked slowly down the stairs, rethinking every single one of her life decisions that had led her where she was now and wishing she had a way out of the hell that she lived every night. She thought of Slim's promises—that she would be taken care of, that she would be making enough money to live on, and that it would be better than home. Michelle sighed inwardly and made her way through the lobby. The night attendant, an older man named Thomas, had spent the last few days ignoring her as she came and went. He had kind but sad eyes, and she could feel his pity when he did not know she was looking. Other times, when he did not know that she was looking, she would see him take a long drink from the bottle that he kept under the counter. They were two sad souls, passing close to each other but never touching.

"Excuse me, miss?" the man called.

Michelle looked behind her before realizing that the old man was talking to her. "Me?" Her heart began to race, wondering why he would speak to her now after having ignored her for so long. She could only imagine that it was something unpleasant. Either he wanted something from her or he had planned to cast her out.

"Yes, dear, I'm talking to you." Thomas smiled. She had never seen him smile before, and it warmed her heart when he did. "What's your name?"

"Michelle," she answered. She generally lied about that, and the sudden truth surprised even her.

"Michelle, someone left something for you." He held a thick envelope in his hand, which he held as a form of validation.

Michelle approached the counter carefully; she could not shake the feeling that something was very wrong. She wanted to run for the exit but took a steeling breath and continued. "What is it?" she asked when she reached the counter. She stood just outside of reaching distance, just in case.

Thomas shrugged. "I dunno. A man came in just a little while ago and left it for you. He didn't know your name, but he described you well enough." He handed the envelope to Michelle, who opened it carefully and peered inside. There was money, more than she had ever seen in her life at one time. She held it, unable to believe what she was seeing. She looked through the thick stack, looking for a note or an explanation; there was none. She counted, and then she counted again. She knew that the money would change her life in ways she had only dreamed. It was not enough to live on forever, but it was enough to get a good start. That chance was more than anyone had ever given her before.

Michelle thanked Thomas and peeled off one of the bills, passing it to Thomas and thanking him for his perpetual kindness. She left through the double glass doors. She was wearing the same outfit she was wearing when she went in, and the air was just as cold, but she felt warm. She looked to the left, where she could see Slim's car idling in the parking lot. She looked to the right, which represented a brand new chapter in her life. She disappeared into the night and never looked back.

. . .

Richard followed Cami through the streets, racing against the steadily approaching dawn. He trusted her completely and saw no reason to disrupt her thought process with useless questions. She stopped when she found the phone booth and, inside, a phone book.

"Who are you going to call at this hour?" Richard joked.

Cami flipped through the yellow pages, looking for something specific. While concentrating, she missed the joke entirely. "No one," she answered. "It is an address." She found it and mouthed the information silently as she committed it to memory and then continued the way they were already headed. Finally, when they reached South Franklin Street, they stopped. Cami pointed down the block, directing Richard's attention to a specific building.

"We're going to stay at a homeless shelter?" Richard asked.

Cami smiled and, with a chuckle, said, "Not exactly. This particular shelter has a detox program. Where there are people trying to get clean, there are going to be people trying to keep them dirty and make some money off them. It is disgusting, so we will be doing the world a favor." The pair walked on the opposite side of the street, carefully probing the shadows with their superior night vision. "There," Cami started. She pointed into the alley that ran adjacent to the shelter. Richard strained his vision and saw a man sitting comfortably at the end of it.

"Him?" he asked.

Cami nodded. "He is number two. You can do this one."

"Why me?" Richard asked. He was still not accustomed to killing, although he understood the need and the reason for it. "Not that I'm arguing, but . . . you're just better at it, is all."

"He will be expecting an addict, not a little girl. If anything tips him off and he bolts, he will have a description of us. More importantly, it will completely ruin our plans. I do not want anything to keep us from finding Mary . . . do you?"

"No," Richard answered.

He thought about what Cami had told him, and the idea hatched. He thought of the movies that he had seen and the people whom he had met. He let his face relax and his eyes droop, and he slumped his shoulders, giving him the appearance of utter lethargy. He pulled his lips tight over his teeth and bit at his own lips. He removed anything that appeared valuable or could be sold for more than a couple of dollars. In a brief moment, he became a meth head in the middle of a crash and eager to score again. Whereas the dealer would see Cami as an oddity, he would see Richard as a customer.

When Richard walked into the alleyway, he was inwardly confident and assured. Externally, however, he was shaking and nervous. Cami watched him go, impressed with his improvisation. As he approached the end of the alley, the man stood up and smiled.

"Oh, bro, I know that look. You're jonesin' hard, aren't you?"

Richard nodded vigorously as he rubbed his arm. "Yeah, I gotta get a hit. Just one more, that's all, just one more to get me through."

The man nodded. His expression was compassionate and understanding, but his eyes betrayed his greed. "Sure . . . yeah, just one more. Tell ya' what, I'm gonna give you one free—little gift from me to you, you know . . . somethin' to help you on your way. If you ever change your mind, like, you want any more, you just lemme know and I'll help ya' out. Whadya say?"

A look of feigned relief spread over Richard's face. "Yeah . . . yeah, thanks."

The man held a small bag in his hands, much like someone who was offering a cherished gift. Richard rushed forward, in all appearances eager for his fix. So convincing was he that the man was genuinely surprised when Richard rushed past the offered bag and wrapped strong hands around his thin neck.

"What the fuck?" the man croaked.

Richard was careful not to squeeze too hard so as not to leave any prints or marks. He doubted that the forensics would be complete before the media made up its mind, but he did not want to take any chances—not with so much at stake. He leaned in and hesitated, trying to remember exactly how the rogue would do it. In that moment of distraction, the dealer pulled a thin knife from his pocket. While he tried to pry Richard's grip free with one hand, he pulled back and slammed the knife into Richard's torso. This was not the first time that he had to defend himself against a junkie on a bender. It was, however, the first time that they had no reaction to a knife in the gut. He tried again, stabbing Richard in the stomach, arms, and chest, but Richard ignored him. He could feel the pressure of the intrusions, but his unique physiology spared him from any pain that he would have felt a lifetime ago. A part of him—a very small but loud part of him—enjoyed the confusion and terror in the dealer's eyes.

He pulled his head back, away from the dealer, to look directly into his eyes. "Are you done?" Richard asked.

The man dropped his knife, startled at Richard's calm reply. He had thought that his attacker might have been high on angel dust, which would have explained his aggression and inability to feel pain, but he saw only cold clarity in Richard's eyes. "What are you?" he stammered.

Richard remembered Cami's speech when she spoke some sense into the abusive father. He tried to remember how it started—but could not. He was not eloquent, and he did not have Cami's broad perspective or emotional depth. Instead, he smiled and leaned in close to the dealer. He felt his fangs slip through his gum line with eager anticipation, and he could see the man's pulse and smell the nourishment flowing through his veins. He watched fascinated for just a moment as the dealer's arteries danced for him, carrying precious blood through wasted flesh. He used his free hand to cover the man's mouth and hissed as he bit down on the soft flesh of his neck.

The man struggled against Richard's viselike grip. He fought with all his strength, which became less fervent as the blood was pumped from his body into Richard's eager mouth, pulsing down his throat. As the blood flow to his brain was reduced, it became more difficult for him to concentrate. He started to forget where he was and why this man was holding him. He started to forget who he was, and what he was supposed to be doing. He started to forget everything and gave himself over completely.

Richard pulled back and watched as the last of the life vanished from the man's eyes. It was fascinating; they were the same eyes that he had stared into just moments before but without the spark of life. They were dull and empty.

"Do not let yourself enjoy it." Cami's voice startled him, and he dropped the dealer's body to the cold ground. "It is tempting when they deserve it so much, but do not give in." Richard nodded. He took one last look at the pale and lifeless form at his feet, turned, and walked away.

"Sun will be up soon," Richard noted. Cami nodded, and the pair walked silently, enjoying the clear night and the luxury of time.

. . .

Even after so many centuries, waking from death was a nightly traumatic experience for Cami. For her, death was still and quiet—a mere moment that passed by without her awareness. She allowed her body to reverse the rigor mortis process; her muscles relaxed and her joints softened, and the blood drew away from her lower extremities and into her core. She could see again, and then she could hear, and finally, she could move her fingers and toes. She heard Richard stirring beside her, and she waited for him to come around. It would take some time before he was accustomed to a daily death and revival, but it would come eventually.

Cami was eager to see if her plan had its intended effect, and she found the nearest newspaper stand. A light layer of snow had fallen during the day, some of which still covered the glass. Cami wiped the snow from it and smiled.

"VAMPIRE KILLER STRIKES AGAIN," the headline screamed. She skimmed through the article, which spoke in appropriately somber tones about the murders the night before, which represented a surprising escalation in the crimes. According to the article, police were warning residents to stay in their homes after dark and encouraging them to report anything suspicious to the proper authorities.

"That should get her attention," Cami said. She seemed almost giddy, and her age gave the appearance of a child at play.

"Now what do we do?" Richard asked. "If she has read the newspaper or watched the news on TV, she knows that we're out here. How do we find her?"

Cami smiled again. "That is the best part—we do not have to. She is going to be looking for us, and with everyone else staying indoors, we should not be too hard to find. Just give it time—we can end this tonight."

Richard had not thought it through, and he found that he was suddenly nervous. He knew what they were there to do, and he knew what they had done, but somehow, he had not considered that they would be fighting a creature that neither knew very much about. He thought of Boian, who had nearly overwhelmed him and Cami both, and wondered how they would fare this time. He looked at Cami, who walked confidently through the night, however, and allowed himself to relax slightly. He could trust her at least, even if he could not trust the conditions and circumstances in which he found himself.

He was not alone for very long to wonder what would happen next. Cami hesitated in midstride, and Richard nearly ran into her. She sniffed at the air and then continued walking as though nothing was unusual. Richard knew her very well and saw that she was tensed and alert. He also knew what that meant—the rogue was close. Since Cami was pretending not to have noticed, that also meant that the rogue was watching. They continued down the street until Cami took a sharp right down an isolated dark street. They were on the outskirts of town, and the few unlit houses were the only signs of life. Cami had chosen the battleground, but it was up to the rogue to choose the battle.

"What do you think about that house?" Cami asked aloud, pointing to the nearest dark home. Richard nodded, catching on to her ruse. They knew the rogue watched and was being taken in by their perceived intrusion into her world. She would not allow them to reach the home, which made every step agonizing for Richard. With each step, he grew closer to the porch; with each step, he expected her to attack. He wondered if she would attack the little girl first, to take out the smaller and weaker target before attacking the man, or if she would try to break the man with a surprise and then finish off the child at her leisure. A few more steps, the home grew closer. The anticipation was nearly suffocating to Richard now, and he almost wished that she would attack to relieve the tension. He remembered that Cami was able to discern vampire from mortal by smell, although he lacked the ability to do so, and wondered if the rogue was able. A few more steps, they reached the sidewalk.

Is she going to let us go? Is she just going to watch while we kill again? He wondered.

He did not have to wonder for long. Cami grunted as the rogue hit her from behind and sent her sprawling to the ground. Richard had not even seen it coming, and Cami barely registered the attack before it happened. The rogue was fast, and Richard was very justified in his fear. Cami stood. Richard swiveled his head, looking for the ethereal creature that seemed to have disappeared into thin air. The pair stared into the night, straining every one of their senses to find the creature that had attacked them, but they found nothing.

"Maybe she left . . .," Richard offered.

Cami shook her head. She knew that the rogue was out there somewhere, watching and waiting for another opportunity. She thought back to her battle with the feral child in the vault, where her opponent was contained in a finite space. In this case, her opponent could be anywhere at all. The method of the attack gave her some information at least. As the rogue relied on speed and stealth, Cami reasoned that she lacked raw strength. Of course, this was not a perfect assessment, but it was enough of a working theory to begin in developing her own strategy. Cami caught a brief scent, which was enough to guess the rogue's position. Despite every instinct telling her to rush at the creature and attack, Cami turned her back as though she were still searching for her target. She steadied herself and braced against the attack that was sure to come.

When the attack did come, it was violent and aggressive; the rogue intended to kill Cami as quickly as possible and then disappear again to wait until her next target made a mistake of his own. She leaped on Cami's back and used her staggering momentum to force her head into the asphalt. The rogue tore at Cami's back and neck, pulling the skin free in ragged, meaty chunks. Cami knew then that her assessment was right; the wounds, while fatal to a mortal, were largely superficial and failed to cause significant damage to her. Cami feigned incapacitation, knowing that the only way to defeat the rogue was by removing those aspects that gave her the advantage. Cami held until she heard Richard approaching, rushing to help save her from her apparent defeat, and felt the rogue tense her body in preparation for a speedy escape. She was going to run then come again for another attack. Although relatively unharmed, Cami was bleeding and torn and was not willing to face another attack due to a miscalculation.

Cami felt the rogue push off, using her body as an advantage, much as a sprinter would use a starting block. Cami was ready for this, and she spun her body until she was on her back, which destabilized the rogue for a single precious moment. The rogue hissed with surprise as she fell on to the suddenly alert Cami, who wrapped her arms and legs around her like a Venus flytrap ensnaring its prey. The timing was perfect. Richard held on to the struggling rogue, who bit and snapped like a cornered and injured wild animal. Cami tried to see the woman, to look into the eyes of the creature she was charged to kill, but was unable to position herself in such a way. Instead, she moved her hand to the back of the rogue's head and carefully forced it onto her shoulder so that her jaw was compressed between Cami's thin bone and her delicate but powerful grip. While the rogue struggled, Cami leaned in to open the veins of her neck with eager fangs, not to kill her but to drain away vital lifeblood that fed her speed. Then when she was slowed down, Cami would kill her. The rogue pulled away, trying desperately to keep her neck away from Cami's mouth. She screamed when Cami made contact and opened a small tear in the vein. The rogue screamed as the blood started to spill into Cami's mouth and renewed her efforts to escape. She was now fighting for her life—a fact that Cami knew made her far more dangerous than she was before. With the herculean strength that can only come from utter terror, the rogue worked her way free and disappeared into the night.

Cami rose and swore quietly. Her back had already started to heal, and she could feel the flesh closing over the wounds and knitting itself together. It was a slightly uncomfortable feeling, but she was grateful for the absence of pain. She stood next to Richard, and together, they surveyed the dark landscape, waiting for the next attack.

It did not come.

"We lost her!" Richard cried out. The rogue represented their clearest opportunity to find Mary, and losing her was devastating to him. He waited for Cami to reply or to console him, but she did neither. He turned to find her staring intently at the ground. "What are you doing?" he asked.

"Blood," Cami said simply as if that were an answer. She took a few steps forward, sniffed at the air, and repeated the process.

"What?"

"She is bleeding. She is not healing as quickly as she should either." Cami wondered what that meant, but she was thankful for it. She stared into the distance for a moment, studying the direction where the blood trail ran, then took off in a dead run. Richard followed, not quickly enough to keep up but enough to keep her in sight. Cami twisted and turned through the streets, following the diminishing trail. Finally, the scent trail ended on the steps of an old worn building with boarded-over windows and a crumbling exterior. On those steps was the rogue vampire. She had crawled halfway up before fatigue claimed the last of her strength. She was alive but starved of blood and was at Cami's mercy.

"Please . . .," she begged. Cami felt a moment of pity for the creature that lay face down on the stairs but, at the same time, was hardened by her purpose.

"Did they beg for their lives too?" Cami asked. "When you killed those innocent people, did they ask for mercy before you killed them?"

Richard finally caught up and stood next to Cami. He gasped when he saw the pathetic state of the once terrifying creature. "Are we really going to do it?" he whispered. "She's helpless, look at her." The rogue, however, seemed determined to prove Richard wrong. She pushed herself off the stairs and lunged at him, knocking him off his feet and on to his back. In her weakened state, she was no match even to the inexperienced Richard, who rolled, pushed her backward, and sent her sprawling against the stairs in a near sitting position.

That was when Cami got a clear look at the rogue's face. It was Mary. A thousand nightmares pressed against her mind like a relentless barrage. She thought of the pain she had inflicted on her. She wondered why Mary would try to kill them and how she had grown so quickly. She wondered why Imani had lied. Then she wondered when her mind had started playing tricks on her. She blinked heavily and looked again at the rogue. She could clearly see that she was not looking at Mary, but her eyes had deceived her into thinking that it was. She wondered how that could have even been vaguely possible. The weight of her fears and desires had betrayed her, shaking her to her deepest core. Cami leaned in close to the rogue, who was broken and beaten. "I am really very sorry," she told her. She knew that the woman would not understand nor particularly care about the reason that Cami had to destroy her. She hoped that she would find some measure of peace when it was over.

Cami grasped the stake that she had carried just for this very purpose. The stake was the one that nearly killed Richard. It seemed almost fitting that she should use it now. The woman threw up her arms in a futile attempt to block Cami's blow, but the stake found its mark and burrowed into her heart. She looked into Cami's eyes as death took her and nature claimed the years that she had denied it; it was not very many. She had been rather new, not more than a couple of years, so the process was very quick. Cami collected a small amount of ash and carefully sealed it inside a small plastic bag. The pair started the long walk toward Imani's estate, neither giving a voice to the very mixed emotions they were trying not to feel.

. . .

Imani paced in the great room of her estate. Those who had remained with her were somber, even morose. Many from their collective had left over the past few days, rejecting the notion that Imani had turned a little girl into a mercenary, with her only reward being mere knowledge of her loved one. Those that remained had convinced themselves that their noble goals forgave even the most barbaric methods, but regrets and remorse filled even their quietest moments.

"What if they don't come back?" Miguel asked, breaking the uncomfortable silence. They were all thinking the same thing. Miguel was just the first to say it.

Imani stopped pacing. "They'll come," she answered. As if on cue, the front door flew open. A chill wind blew through the entryway and caused the candles to flicker and the fire in the fireplace to surge. Cami and Richard entered and closed the door behind them. The small group only stared as the pair approached and stood in the middle of the room. "Is it done?" Imani asked.

Cami nodded. She took the bag of ash and held it above her head like a macabre trophy. No one spoke. Each pair of eyes was on the remains of a creature not much different from themselves.

Imani, upon seeing Cami's arrogance and halfway not wanting to give up the information, said in a matter-of-fact cadence, "How do we know that those ashes are those of the rogue?" Cami had prepared herself for a confrontation and possible double cross. "I could add my blood to the ashes and allow you to see for yourself!"

"She's in Barrow," Imani quickly offered. The pair accepted the meager supplies that Imani offered and left the estate. Together, they started the long and difficult trek north to Barrow.

CHAPTER ELEVEN

Boian Attacks

There are 1,098 miles between Juneau and Barrow, but the two pressed through each mile with a single-minded determination. They faced blinding snowstorms and hostile terrain, but whatever came against them would not deter them from their task. They carefully rationed the bags of blood that Imani had provided them, afraid of running out before they reached their destination. The fresh snow crunched under their feet as they traveled. Early in the journey, they were compelled to burrow into the snow in the daylight to avoid the sun, but as they approached then crossed the Arctic Circle, the night was extended to the point where daylight vanished entirely. Eventually, they saw the navigation lights from the airport—the lifeline of the small town—and closed in slowly.

The pair stopped just outside of the city, on a slope, which overlooked the surrounding area. They saw the steady, lonely lights of the small airport and the nighttime lights across the bay. A lone polar bear passed by and stopped to look at them before moving on. Richard had thought for a moment that they may have to fight this large animal and was not looking forward to it. He was thankful that the animal decided that it was not hungry enough to give chase. Cami had been spent the entirety of their journey creating and rejecting plans and machinations, but she still had no real idea how they would enter the hostile city and find Mary.

"What's the plan?" Richard asked as though he could sense Cami's uncertainty. He was used to her being the one who knew what to do—the one with a plan. The thought that she did not have one worried him.

Cami paused. "I do not really know," she admitted. Her admission confirmed Richard's fears. She ran through her previously discarded plans, hoping to identify the least objectionable among them. Nearly every aspect of every plan worked against the pair; Boian was stronger and faster than even Cami, and he had a willing ally whom he knew they would not risk harming. They were nestled in an unknown area, somewhere inside a hostile city filled with eaters, and Cami and Richard had already consumed their last bag of precious blood. In time, they would grow weaker while Boian, Cami knew, would find a way to grow stronger. They had to act, and they had to act now. Cami looked to Richard; his expression was trusting and hopeful. "I have a plan, and I know it will work." She smiled. The relief on his face was worth the lie that she told.

She continued. "There are only two down there that know our scent, and we know theirs as well. To everyone else, we are just a pair of new faces. We make our way in, try to avoid being seen, and hunt by smell."

Richard frowned. "That's it? Walk into Barrow and sniff?" He crossed his arms and shifted his weight from one foot to the other. He was clearly agitated, which was understandable given his hopes and fears. Richard had not developed his sense of smell as Cami had. He felt useless in this situation. He would have to follow Cami as if she were a bloodhound searching for a raccoon.

"Do you have a better idea?"

Richard thought, running through several scenarios but seeing the fatal flaw in each. Part of him—a very small shameful part—wanted to save himself and leave. Looking at Cami and thinking of Mary eliminated that possibility. "No," he admitted. He looked back at the city; it looked peaceful from the hilltop. A lone plane taxied on the runway, pausing at the end before opening the throttle and taking off into the night. Richard watched the lights slowly blink as the plane lazily flew toward the horizon. A car navigated the wide poorly maintained streets before stopping at the small hotel, which was one of the larger buildings in town.

Cami waited while Richard lost himself in his thoughts. They both knew that what she was suggesting was incredibly dangerous and that there was a very real chance that they would not make it. They both knew that they were going to do it anyway because they were doing it for Mary. She grabbed his hand and gave it a reassuring squeeze before they descended together into the outskirts of town. The open spaces between homes, which were much more pronounced than they appeared from the hilltop, coupled with the bright streetlights, made it difficult to stay out of sight. They darted from one home to the next, moving through the streets agonizingly slow as they made vague attempts to keep to the shadows, in hopes that they could make it in and out without Boian or Mary detecting their presence. Cami pressed against the side of a squat blue home with tinfoil-covered windows. She peaked around the corner and readied herself to run for the next before freezing in place.

"What do you see?" Richard whispered. He pressed his body against the wall, carefully emulating Cami's every movement.

"There is a small group sitting on a porch talking . . . They are from Imani's." Cami was a little bit sad to see that they had defected and aligned themselves with the eaters whom they had at one time feared. She could catch small snippets of their conversation that carried on the gentle breeze. They no longer talked about art and philosophy; instead, they talked about the city's politics and bickered over the selection of the town's blood supply. A small amount of rage boiled inside Cami when she realized they were talking about the town's human population, and she wondered how they were drawing from them undetected. She tensed when she caught the name "Boian," but she heard nothing else of interest. "Come on," she said finally, before darting to the next house. The new path took her further along the outskirts of town, but the direction was utterly unimportant without a destination.

They picked their way through the streets of Barrow, darting from one block to another. Periodically, Cami would stop and sniff at the air; Richard was incapable of detecting what she could, so he merely followed behind. While she relied on each one of her finely honed senses, Richard could only strain his hearing and glance nervously from one window to the next, hoping that they would not be seen. He had no idea what would happen if they were but suspected that strangers were not welcome in Barrow, Alaska.

"I smell something . . .," Cami said suddenly. Richard's heart fluttered with both hope and fear. She sniffed at the air then turned and did it again. She bent down and sniffed at the ground, muttering as she did so. "It is faint . . . not recent . . ." Suddenly, she stood upright and turned to Richard. Her eyes were wild, and she was filled with a burst of excited energy. "It is her, Richard! It is Mary. She *is* here, or at least she *was*, a short time ago!" She practically screamed the last part of her exclamation before she remembered where they were and that they needed to be cautious. The overall effect was strange— Cami looked like an excited little girl, so much so that Richard kept forgetting that he had seen her kill with a reflexive ease. She swallowed, breathed deeply, and whispered the rest. "Mary was here . . . at one time at least. I am picking up just a trace of her scent, so she is around here somewhere." She sniffed at the air again and took a few steps toward the heart of the city. "It gets stronger this way," she said, and she was off. She still darted from one building to the next, but she moved faster and was less cautious.

Had Cami moved more cautiously, she would have seen the young man walking along the opposite side of the run-down yellow building. When Cami rounded the corner, she nearly ran into him, which surprised them both. The man shook his head and narrowed his eyes. "Intrud—" he started to shout, but he was unable to finish the rest.

In one smooth motion, Cami clamped her hand over his mouth and drew her well-used stake. She pressed the stake into his chest, being careful to press against but not penetrate his heart. She then looked into his eyes and said, "Do I have to send you to your eternal rest, or can I trust you will be quiet?" He quickly nodded in panic. She tilted her head downward, looking up into his eyes. "Why do I not believe you?" She pushed his slight frame against the wall and quickly shoved the stake deep into his chest. His eyes grew panicked, but his screams were muffled under Cami's palm. She pushed again, forcing the pointed wood deeper into his flesh. He could hear the sound of his own ribs parting and cracking before the stake pierced into the soft muscle of his heart. He shook briefly in Cami's grip before exploding into aged remains. Cami slowly backed away from the scene and looked at her hands. Her hands were coated in grey ash, which she wiped on to the wall. With a last look at the dispersing cloud of dust, Richard and Cami continued their search.

After a moment, Cami caught the scent again. It was growing stronger, meaning that they were getting closer to Mary. Less so, she could detect the scent of Boian, as it intertwined with Mary's; he too was close. It took every bit of Cami's self-control not to run wildly through the city's streets as she grew impatient, following the intoxicating scent, but her patience was rewarded when she finally saw her. Mary stood just outside of the community hall. She was swaying slightly. Cami recognized the look—she had just recently fed. Cami stole a look inside, which was only possible because there were no covers on the windows. Men and women were restrained in hospital beds, all of which were occupied and which lined the walls. Boian was feeding greedily on one of the humans, who sobbed softly as the blood left her body. Cami watched as he left the woman and moved to the next bed, drawing only enough from each to satiate his hunger but not enough to kill the unwilling donor. She could see the difference between the two groups by how they fed—Imani's group relied on volunteers, while this group relied on force.

Cami and Richard each studied the approaches, hoping that they would remain alone long enough to convince Mary of the truth and escape with her. They knew that they could free her from Boian's deceptive manipulations if only they could have the opportunity, and that opportunity struck when Mary walked close to where they waited.

"Mary!" Cami whispered, appearing at her side. "You are in danger. You need to come with us!" Mary jumped. She looked at Cami then to Richard, who nodded in sincere agreement. "He has been lying to you, Mary," Cami continued. "He is the one who killed Samuel, and he is the one who turned me so long ago. He is using you to hurt me. He is evil."

"Boian told me you might come. That you would try to kill me, the same way you killed the others." She lowered herself into an awkward fighting stance. Cami recognized Boian's influence in her and knew that he had already begun training her.

"We are not going to fight you, Mary," Richard said. Although it was a statement, he was pleading with her to listen.

"Look around you," Cami added. "People strapped to beds? This is not right. Come with us, we will get you out of here. Please."

Mary's face contorted with a range of thoughts and emotions, which were internally warring for control. Cami and Richard looked on hopefully as Mary's face softened, but that hope was dashed when it hardened again. Boian's influence over her was still too strong for her to resist. She balled her fist and pulled back then released a punch with all her confusion and rage behind it. She connected with Cami's face, which snapped to the side. Cami was not physically hurt, but she was emotionally devastated. "You will not take me!" she shouted. "Boian!" she called. She continued her attack, hitting and scratching with a passionate fervor. Each of her attacks was easily blocked by the pair, but they refused to return the attack. They refused to do her harm. Instead, they took the weak blows, unable to accept that they had lost her.

"Mary, please," Richard begged, taking another punch to the face. "We're *not* going to *hurt* you . . . I love you."

Mary called out again. "Boian!"

Cami saw movement and spun around just in time to block Boian's sucker punch. He followed with a driving blow to her stomach, which would have stolen her breath if she had any. Instead, the force of it lifted her into the air before gravity brought her crashing back to the ground. Richard's attack surprised Boian, who had not expected his aggression or bravery. In a moment, Cami was on her feet and had joined in the attack. Mary beat uselessly against whichever of the pair came closest, but her weak strikes were barely more than a distraction. Boian, however, was given to shock by the coordinated blows, which nearly overwhelmed him. He could not believe how powerful the pair had become when they were fighting for the one they love.

Boian landed only lucky hits but did little harm. He pulled away and blocked what he could then leaned his head back and howled. The sound echoed through the city, and time stopped for a moment as Cami and Richard nervously surveyed their surroundings. Boian stood back and grinned. He did not attack, he did not cower, nor did he retreat—he merely waited. In a moment, they could see why. Vampires came pouring from the homes and the streets, convening on the foursome. Cami and Richard locked eyes and made a silent vow to each other. If they were going to die tonight, they were going to do it together, and they were going to do it fighting.

The closest of the creatures reached them and immediately attacked. Cami and Richard punched and were punched, tore and were torn, bit and were bit. She felt the stake pulled away from her and then felt the familiar ceaseless burning when it was forced into her chest. Although the tip missed her heart, the pain was incredible. They fought with every bit of strength and every ounce of courage, but the eaters kept coming. There were too many of them—more than the pair could handle. Richard went down first, buried under a writhing pile of eaters that tore at his skin as he screamed in agony. Another collective took a distracted Cami to the ground; she could only look at Mary until those who covered her blocked her view of the happenings. Fighting for Mary had made them powerful, but in the end, it was not enough to overcome the collective threat that was borne from the evil that lived in Barrow. Cami waited for death to come, but it did not. Boian barked orders at the mob, who obeyed without question. They changed their hold on the pair, pulling them roughly by their hands and feet until the mob could restrain them, next to each other, completely vulnerable to any attack.

Boian leaned in close to the pair and spoke low so Mary would not be able to hear him. "You betrayed me when you left me to die, dear Camilia . . . and I swore revenge. Today I get my revenge." He pulled the stake from Cami's chest, and she gasped when it was freed from between her ribs. He handed the stake to Mary, who tentatively accepted it. "Go ahead, Mary. Start with the girl."

Mary kneeled next to Cami and raised the stake high above her head. Cami struggled to free herself, but the firm hands held her tightly in place. Mary focused on Cami's chest, staring at the target just above Cami's heart. She brought the stake down, aiming for the spot, but stopped in midair. She raised the stake again and breathed deeply, fighting against herself. She looked in Cami's eyes. She did not know what she saw behind the lenses, but she could not take the life out of them.

"Please, Mama, remember," Cami begged.

Mary's eyes softened, not enough that she was completely free of Boian's influence but enough that she was once again able to think on her own. She lowered the stake and laid it on the ground. "I can't . . . Please, Boian. I don't know why, but I can't do it. It's like she's a part of my soul."

Cami whispered to Mary, "That is the same reason that I could not hurt you. I would rather that you kill me than leave me to harm one hair on your precious head."

The eaters were confused and looked to Boian. He sighed and picked up the stake. "You cannot be weak!" Boian growled. Cami watched as Boian raised the stake in a very slow motion. He smiled and whispered, "I told you it would be me." He brought the stake down, and Cami watched death approach. Mary watched it as well, and her body reacted in a way that she could not understand. With a scream, she threw herself over Cami's body. Boian's eyes opened wide, but it was too late to stop the stake's descent. It split the skin of Mary's back and pushed against her spine. The wound burned, and she screamed in fear, confusion, and agony. She was not done—she rose upright and attacked Boian with the ferocity of a mother bear defending her cub. She drove him back from the sheer unexpected attack, and she turned her attention to those who held Cami and Richard. They too, shocked by the sudden betrayal of Boian's protégé, showed shock and fear as they backed away from the pair. She continued driving at the crowd. Whatever instinct had awakened in her was more than they had ever seen before and far more than they expected. She allowed none to pass, leaving Richard and Cami clear.

"Do not hurt her," Boian growled, sounding like the devil himself. "It is those two I want!"

Mary ignored Boian. "Go!" she called over her shoulder.

"Come with us," Richard pleaded.

Mary looked at them briefly. "Please don't make me watch you die. Whoever you really are, I can't bear that. Please don't let *me* die."

Cami understood. Despite the sudden strength and courage that she had found, she could not hold them back forever. When they broke past her, they would joyously force her to watch as they tore Cami and Richard apart, ripping their hearts from their chests and burning them, along with their bodies, in front of her eyes. After that, they would destroy her as well. There were too many to fight, and there was no way that Cami and Richard could help the one they loved. "I will find you again," Cami swore.

"I know you will," Mary answered.

Cami and Richard turned and ran, dodging through the dark streets and empty homes. They heard shouting and fierce arguments as they ran, but that soon turned into a muffled murmur as they increased the distance between themselves and the mob. Soon, the pavement gave way to ice then to loose snow, which kicked up into the air as they ran. As the crystals crunched underneath their feet, they pressed on into the night. When they reached the hill that overlooked the city, they desperately searched for any indication that Mary was unharmed.

"We're going back," Richard said. He was firm and resolute, far more so than Cami had ever seen him. He had gone back for Cami once before, and he intended to do the same for Mary this time. He understood that leaving when they did had kept them alive and that it had given Mary a chance, but he refused to leave her in the clutches of the eaters when they had come so far to find her.

"Of course, we are," Cami agreed. She scanned the city, considering how they could assault it before Boian turned on Mary in his rage. "Look!" she squealed. Richard followed her eyes to see where she was pointing. The eaters poured through the streets as if they were desperately searching for something, but they were looking in the wrong place. A lone figure emerged from the outskirts of the city and bolted on to the runway where a single-engine plane idled on the tarmac. It was likely a private plane readying for takeoff. She pounded on the door, and the lone pilot flung the door open to let her in. Moments later, the plane was speeding toward the end of the runway and then lifting into the night sky like an angel ascending into the heavens. Cami's heart soared with the small craft, which banked sharply and flew south toward the welcoming horizon, toward safety, toward a new life filled with hope and promise. Mary had made it, which was all they had wanted.

Cami and Richard, however, had no idea where they would go or what they would do next. They knew only that they had each other and that Mary was safe—for now. They left the hill, stealing one last look at the chaos that filled the city of Barrow. The two turned away and left it behind them. They walked in the direction the plane had traveled, knowing they had the rest of their eternity to find her. For the second time in far too long, Cami cried, this time thanking God they were tears of joy.

Chapter Twelve

Furry and Fast

Mary's stomach knotted itself as the small plane lifted into the sky. She was not certain, if this was a physical reaction to flying—something that she hated anyway—or an emotional reaction to the chaos and bloodshed that she had just left behind. She stared out the window at the lights of Barrow. Cami was there, she knew, and Richard—she was afraid to let herself miss them, but then again, it was a reaction, which she had no control over.

"What are you running from?" the pilot asked suddenly, startling Mary from her thoughts.

"I'm not . . . I mean . . . I don't . . .," Mary stammered in response. She was suddenly very aware that she did not know anything about this man. He stared straight ahead, navigating in the night by sight and landmarks alone, while she tried to salvage her thoughts. "I was in a bad relationship. I needed to leave, to get away from him," she said finally. It was true, depending on one's perspective.

The pilot nodded understandingly. "Are you fresh, you know . . . baby vampire, or are you old blood?"

She noticed the point of his teeth when he spoke and wondered if she was any better off than she had been before they had taken off. Her eyes darted over both the man and his flight cabin, looking for clues or hints as to his intentions. He was wearing a thin T-shirt and jeans, despite the relative cold, and his obligatory aviator glasses reflected the dim lights of the panel. She was thinking that she should have been more attentive to his attire before. She thought, *Come on! He's a pilot, wearing sunglasses in the dead of night.* He manipulated the yoke with subtle practiced movements, and his mannerisms made Mary feel as though he were giving her his complete attention while also, somehow, watching the terrain slip by far underneath.

"Fresh," she admitted. "I see that you are . . . you know . . . one . . ."

"You can't smell it yet?" he asked. The question seemed to be more instructive than a challenge.

"Smell what?" Mary pushed herself a little bit tighter against the door, as though that small amount of space would equate to a measure of safety. She considered the fact that she had just battled for her own life and others', which was something that she had never had to do before, but she was tired and lacked the will to fight again if she could help it.

"You'll learn. Well, if you live long enough. I knew you were an eater when you came within ten yards. What I couldn't figure out is why you were in such a rush to leave." He left the unspoken question hanging in the air.

"Eater? I am *not* one of *those* . . . those *things*! I'm *not like them!*" she answered honestly, hoping that her answer was also the right one to give.

The man nodded slowly. He checked his instruments, he adjusted his watch, and he moistened his lips; however, he did not answer her for an uncomfortably long time, as though he were considering what she had said. "Well, what are you then?"

Mary looked out the window. There was a thick blanket of fresh snow, which covered the ground and reflected brilliantly under the pale moonlight. The trees slowly waved in the breeze that rocked the plane like a cradle. The stars shone bright and clear, but they only reminded her just how small she was in the scope of a very big world. "Alone," she answered. "I'm just . . . alone."

The man nodded again, solemnly, and flew on into the night.

Mary was not sure where they were when they landed, but she was grateful to be on the ground again. His birth name was Geoffrey (a common name for the period in which he was born, he explained), but he preferred the more contemporary "Jeff." The pair had gotten to know each other during the flight, and for the first time in far too long, she felt safe in someone's presence. She had no romantic interest in him, and she sensed that he had none in her as well, but she appreciated his company all the same.

They found a small motel—the kind of place where it was highly unlikely that anyone would notice two strangers, much less question them—and Jeff paid for the night. Naturally curious, Mary caught a glimpse of his billfold as he paid; either he was extremely wealthy or he carried everything that he owned with him all the time. She was grateful that he has specified that the room required two beds; that was, however, all that the room had to offer. It was surprisingly clean, a fact belied by the grimy exterior and lobby; there was a small broken television perched atop a pressed particleboard chest of drawers. The bathroom was small and functional, and a pair of lamps provided their dim light to the main room. Mary tried to open a drawer to find the Bible, but the front of the drawer fell off in her hand. She went into the bathroom, wanting to bath, but there were no towels. She would try every chance she got to wash the smell of her death off her but could never succeed. The most important feature of the room was that the curtains were thick and overlapped in the middle to keep out any traces of light.

"So what happened to you?" Jeff asked. He was trying to get the television to display anything but static, but it did not seem to be working for him.

Mary's memories flashed to Cami and Richard, to Boian, to her own death and resurrection. "I don't want to talk about it," she said meekly. "It still hurts a lot."

Jeff stabbed at the panel to turn the static off and sat down next to her. "It's not easy sometimes," he acknowledged. "Time makes it a little bit easier. Enough of it passes, and the memories aren't so bad."

Mary, with a grievous visage and irritated tone, said, "I was made into this *thing* that you see before you, by this Boian creature, and now I'm being told that all I have to do is wait! How long should I wait before I feel better—a year . . . a hundred . . . a thousand years?"

After she calmed down for a moment, she realized that something in his voice had piqued her curiosity. "What about you . . . what happened to you?" she asked, calming down, expecting him to offer some sort of bargain—a reciprocal agreement for stories. Instead, she was met only with silence. She began to repeat the question, thinking that he had not heard her, when he suddenly spoke. His words were memories from ages ago; it seems he may have been lying about it getting easier with time.

"I was in England," he began. "This was probably centuries before you were born. It was a simple time—a simple life. There were no telephones or cars, certainly no Internet—most of us could not even read anyway. I was a blacksmith's apprentice. I was very good too, nearly ready to strike out on my own."

Mary listened to Jeff talk about his life hundreds of years ago. At one time, this would have been odd for her. Now it was relatively normal. She did not stop to consider what that meant.

"My master—a short, fat, and elderly man named Wayland—he had amazing hands. I was lucky to work under him because there was no one more skilled than he was. Skill, however, was all that he had going for him. Not many really liked him, and of course, his gambling and drinking ruled his life more than anything else did . . . so it really did not surprise anyone when he failed to come into the shop one morning. I still remember it—it was on a Monday. I would always open up early in the morning, and he would come stumbling in sometime in the afternoon, still smelling like alcohol and perfume. He did not come in that day, however, or the next nor the next. I was not quite at his skill level, but almost no one even realized that he was gone. In addition to that, those who had realized it did not seem to care . . . but I cared. I looked for him every night and waited for him every day. He had become like a father to me, and I was worried."

Mary moved closer, drawn in by both the story and his earnest sincerity. He seemed comforted by her presence but also seemed to need a small amount of strength to continue. She thought of the unshakable man that she had gotten to know during the flight and realized that she had no idea of the depths that she hid. She wondered how many other surprises he had inside this man. "Did you ever find him?" she asked. It was less of a question than it was comfort. She rested her hand on his, giving him strength that she did not realize, until that moment, she had to give.

"He came back one night. I was closing the shop, and then suddenly, there he was. I still remember the feeling—I was surprised because I had not heard him even come in . . . but then I was relieved because he had finally returned. It only took a few moments to realize that he was not my master anymore. Something had . . . changed."

"What do you mean?"

"He was cold . . . He was literally cold. I touched him, and he was like ice. Then I noticed how pale he was. His complexion was so pale he was blue. He must not have fed for a long while. That was when I realized that Master was not in there anymore. He never could move quickly before, so he took me by surprise when he grabbed me. I did not even have time to scream or fight. He just had me. I tried to ask him or reason with him, I do not know, but it was too late. He bit me, sucked me nearly dry . . . and you know the rest."

"Yes, I do," Mary answered, noting their common bond. She subconsciously brought her hand up to her neck, where she herself had had her life quickly drained from her body. The wounds had long since healed, but she knew. She could even feel the scarred holes in her throat, which were no longer there. Then she continued questioning, much more gently, now. "So he took care of you? He taught you?"

"I don't think he had anything to teach me, not from his life before anyway. Maybe if he had, he would have lasted longer. He left me to turn and went back out to find more victims . . . or as I know it now . . . nourishment. I don't know if he was trying to feast or breed—I don't know what he was after . . . The fat man was greedy, and he was caught. The way I heard it later, he had attacked some old woman in her home, but he did not realize that her son was within earshot. The townsfolk—they were a superstitious lot. They knew what to do with evil, even if they did not fully understand what he was. He was drawn and quartered, and—"

Mary hated to interrupt, but she was completely invested in the story. "What does that mean, drawn and quartered?" she asked.

"It's not pretty, but it happened occasionally back then. Each of the limbs was tied to a different horse, and then they're run in different directions. If the person who is to be drawn and quartered is lucky, it rips the limbs clean off. If they use older horses, sometimes it is not quite so clean. Normally, it is punishment for treason, but those folks held their superstitions very dearly, and by that time, I was strong enough to watch—just barely. They used the old horses," he said matter-of-factly.

"On purpose?"

"Probably . . . But because they knew he was vampire, they attached a fifth horse to pull off his head. As long as the head stays on, and as long as the heart has not been either pierced by a wooden stake or removed from the chest and burned, he will remain alive, unless his head is also removed and either burned or the mouth stuffed with wolfsbane and the heart pierced with a wooden stake. Wolfsbane is really overkill, but most of the old-timers still do it that way. He lost his legs right off, but his arms took a little bit of pulling. I could not figure out why in the world he was not screaming. There he was, his legs gone, and the horses ripping his arms from their sockets, and he was angrier than he was anything else. He was cursing them and yelling . . . while the horse, which these poor, stupid villagers had employed to pull off his head, was running around, dragging his body, still screaming obscenities. The women were crying, and the men were resolute. If it had not been so horrific, it would have been comical. Imagine seeing a man with no arms or legs being dragged around by a rope looped around his neck, cursing and screaming, while the ones who did it to him were crying and pacing back and forth, completely beside themselves. It wasn't until they burned him that he finally died—everything else just seemed to make him angrier."

"So you didn't have anyone to teach you . . . anyone to watch over you?" Mary asked.

"No, I was alone. I didn't have anyone to guide me . . . well, not for a while at least. I just left. Eventually, I figured out how to eat without being caught and have, kind of, lived in the shadows ever since. Eventually, I found someone to take me in—to teach me how to hunt and survive. He taught me everything that I needed to know. I lost him a long time ago. I woke up one dusk and he was just gone. I've been looking for him ever since—just so I know."

"What are you going to do when you find him?" Mary asked.

"I'm going to kill him." The coldness in his answer made Mary's hair stand on end. It was a physical sensation that she had not experienced in some time, and it was decidedly uncomfortable. "That's what I was doing in Barrow. I'm not a monster, but thanks to the one who taught me, I can pass for one pretty well. He made me into a monster, and it took me a few lifetimes to overcome what he did to me. Everyone, whom I killed for fun . . . everyone who suffered at my hand . . . I will never live that down. All I can do is seek God's forgiveness, and hunting him, that is my penance . . . finding him, my absolution. Maybe, if I'm lucky, we'll kill each other."

A part of Mary wanted to run, a part wanted to hold him and comfort him, a part of her wanted to ask, a part of her did not want to know. "What's his name?" she asked.

"Boian."

Mary's eyes narrowed. She rested a comforting hand on Jeff's own. "I know him." She thought of what she had gone through through him. She thought of Richard and Cami. She had no idea where the pair had gone to or even if they had made it to safety. "He's in Barrow," she said. "We can find him." The thought of going back terrified her, but her short time with Jeff allowed her to reflect on her life, at least her undead existence, and what was important in it. Jeff looked at her with a mixture of shock and adoration.

. . .

Cami and Richard's celebration was short-lived. They had found Mary and allowed her to escape or at least convinced her of the need to do so. The irony of the fact that they would not have escaped themselves was not lost on them. They looked at the small town of Barrow; it looked like it could have been a peaceful place at one time—and perhaps it was before the eaters took it over. They watched the lights extinguish one by one until the town was completely dark. If not for their superior vision, they would not have known that the town was there at all. Otherwise hidden by shadows, concealed in darkness, the eaters began to spread out. Some searched the town thoroughly, while others spread out into the surrounding wilderness. They were looking; they were hunting. The light snow may have concealed their tracks, but there was no way to hide their scent. It was only a matter of time before they would be discovered, and when they were, the pair would be pursued to the ends of the earth.

"We need to go," Cami said. "Now," she added. Richard nodded, and the pair tore off into the snowy night. They had a head start, but that would not do very much against the dog sleds and vehicles favored by the town's de facto garrison. The sudden rise in voices and dog barks in the far distance told the pair that their scent had been detected and that running could only buy them time. "I am sorry," Cami called to Richard. She was sorry for putting him in this situation and sorry that he would be returning to it. More than anything, she was sorry for what she expected would happen next. He took her hand, and they ran together. Cami's mind raced, looking for a solution, a way to escape. When she stopped suddenly, with the pursuers only moments away, Richard briefly overshot her before returning to where she stood.

"What are you doing?" he shouted. "Don't give up now, we have to run!" He pulled her by the hand, but she held firm.

"Do you remember what I showed you, about changing your body?"

"I remember . . . I wasn't very good at it." The idea of their very lives depending on him terrified Richard.

"You have to be now, Richard. You need to try." Her eyes begged him.

Richard sighed. He listened to the sounds of the chase, growing closer with every passing moment. He knew she was right, that the transformation offered them a chance; he just did not believe that he could do it. "You do it," he said finally. "You change, you run—I'll do what I can to hold them off." He remembered the time when she had done the same thing for him so long ago and could only think to return the sentiment now. He pushed her away, in the direction that they had run, but she did not leave—she would not leave. "Go!" he yelled. Again, Cami did not listen.

"I am not changing until you do. If you are caught, I am caught too. So get your ass into something furry and fast!" She grinned. It was a strange sensation when one was facing death, and Cami had long since welcomed it. In her quieter moments, she wondered if she no longer feared death or if a part of her welcomed it.

Richard made one last desperate plea. It was not eloquent or convincing, but it was heartfelt and passionate. Cami smiled and sat down in the snow. She was not going anywhere without Richard. He resigned himself to try, if only to try to save Cami. He closed his eyes and focused, forcing the thoughts and fears from his mind. He willed himself to ignore the shouts and barks that were drawing ever closer. He tried, unsuccessfully, not to think about what would happen, what could happen, if he failed. He thought about his body changing and fell to his hands and knees as the transformation began. He felt each of his pores ache as coarse hair pushed through them to cover his body. His claws pushed painfully through his fingertips as they pulled back toward his developing paws, and his teeth grew into long and jagged points that pressed against his lips. In a moment, he made the transformation from man to beast. A grey-tipped wolf stood in his place. The wind pulled at his fur, and his paws sank softly into the snow. Cami looked at him, relieved and proud, and then forged her own change. She was naturally smaller—even in lupine form, she appeared more feminine than he did. Together, they ran, light paws dancing on the fresh snow. They dodged trees and rocks and pressed into the night, racing against the odds and pushing toward freedom.

CHAPTER THIRTEEN

She's a Little Bit Odd

Mary and Jeff sat in front of the bar's window. They each nursed a drink, which they held more for appearances than any other reason. They watched the light foot traffic pass by, comparing notes and making their selections. To Mary, it felt like they were window shopping—plotting the deaths of people that they had not met. She understood the necessity of feeding. Jeff's enthusiasm for the task, however, was somewhat off-putting, but she accepted it.

"That one—he's big enough for both of us." Jeff grinned. He pointed to an obese man in a jogging suit, who walked past carrying a thick hamburger and an even thicker strawberry milkshake. Despite the cool air, he was sweating.

Mary could see that he would be a very bountiful feast, but she declined. "Wedding ring," she replied as though it answered the unasked question.

"What? I didn't even notice, but what does that matter?"

"There's someone who would miss him . . . someone who would cry if he did not show up at home tonight. Maybe he has children . . . maybe two little girls, a nine-year-old and her twelve-year-old big sister, who loves and watches over her . . . We just don't know . . . He has a family. Doesn't that mean anything to you?"

Jeff thought for a moment. He looked at the man, who was huffing out of sight. "I guess I never thought of it. We have to eat. I guess I never thought about what happens after but just that I need nourishment. Does that not drive you crazy? I mean, what do you eat?"

"It's who, Jeff. We might have to kill them, but we can at least choose who we kill. People with families . . . good people . . . we do not need to kill them if we can help it. There are plenty of bad people in every city and town who don't deserve to take another breath, and those are the ones whom we need to go for whenever we can."

"Like that?" Jeff pointed out the window.

Mary followed his finger, her night vision piercing into the darkness outside. A man stood in the opposite alleyway, staring at the human traffic much in the same way that Jeff and Mary had been. The purpose was similar as well—they were both looking for prey. The difference is that Mary and Jeff had to eat, while the man was looking for the weak and vulnerable to exploit for his own purposes. Mary's eyes danced over his body; he was obviously well fed, and his clothes were expensive. Clearly, he was not, by any means, starving. Although it was not necessarily a defense, Mary knew that hunger could make otherwise good people do very bad things.

"Yeah, he's perfect," Mary answered.

They paid their tab and left, carefully circling around the block and back up the alley from the other side. They found the careful balance between moving quickly enough to reach the man before he found his next victim but not so quickly as to alert him to their approach. When they dropped into the alley and stealthily approached, they found the man waiting exactly where they had previously seen him. The pair was directly behind the man before he realized it, and he only turned around in a fierce panic when he felt the strong hands on his arms and shoulders. He tried to scream, but a hand clamped firmly over his mouth. He tried to run or to fight, but the strong hands of the man and woman, who had surprised him from behind, had firmly restrained him, held him tightly. A million thoughts ran through his mind—thoughts that he was caught, trapped, or perhaps that a past victim had found revenge. It never occurred to him that his life force itself was about to be drained from his useless body and consumed to prolong the existence of others. They pulled him further into the shadows. He struggled and fought against them, but it was no use. They were, however, stronger and more determined.

When they had dragged him deeply into the shadows, away from prying eyes and outside of the range of his muffled screams, Mary leaned in close. "It's not personal," she whispered. "We're very hungry, and you, well, your life seems to be useless unless you count taking advantage of the lame and elderly. Please, I pray you take this time to make your peace with God and save your useless soul . . . and be sincere. Otherwise, when we're done, your soul will be burning in hell. Of course, it's not for me to judge. After all, as the Bible says, 'Judge not, lest ye be judged' . . . And with that, I bid you adieu."

Jeff smiled and leaned in close as well. "I always enjoy it," he added with a smile.

It was a terrifying smile. He pushed the man against the dirty cool exterior wall and pressed his fangs against the man's delicate jugular. He could feel the slight quiver of his pulse against his lips and pressed forward until the tips pierced the skin and cut into the vein wall. The man fought even harder, struggling against their unbreakable grip. He begged aloud against the hand that covered his mouth, but it went unheard and unheeded. The feeling was terrifying—he knew that he was going to die. He knew that two people were watching him die. He knew, despite his pleas, that no one would help him and that he would receive no sympathy from them. If anything, they seemed to relish his anguished screams, even more than he had relished the fear that he himself had induced in others. He would die screaming in pain, with no one to care about him, and no one to usher him gently into death. His life flashed before his eyes. He saw his childhood—he remembered how his mother raised him after his father left. He remembered how he raised his siblings after his mother died of a drug overdose. He saw his first and last legitimate job and his first of many crimes. He saw a life wasted and was overwhelmed with the knowledge that he would never again have the opportunity to make amends for the wrongs he had created.

Mary joined Jeff in the feast, tearing through the skin on the other side of his neck and spilling his blood into her mouth. The sweet and salty liquid filled her mouth and washed over her tongue before spilling down her throat and into her stomach. There was a slightly tangy flavor, which the adrenaline gave, whenever they mustered up fear in a victim. It was a taste, however, that they would both happily endure. They thoroughly enjoyed removing this blight on humankind, all the while making him feel, for only a few moments, the fear that he had undoubtedly caused in many. They both ate hungrily as the life slowly drained from the man. Soon, both his screams and his struggles grew weaker until he fell still and slumped against the wall. Soon, they drained the last of the salty, sweet, and sour nectar from the man's body, drinking from the vein like an organic straw. They left him there on the ground in the cold alley but not before using a knife to remove the bite marks, and then they stole his wallet, watch, rings, gold necklace, and bracelet to make it appear that a drug addict had killed him during a robbery. They then returned the way they had come—Mary with a backward glance at the body and Jeff while looking toward the future.

. . .

Cami and Richard continued running through the woods, desperately looking for somewhere to hide or perhaps escape. They could almost hear the footsteps of their pursuers, and they ran quite literally for their lives. Richard followed close behind Cami, already tiring from the exertion. They rounded a small rock outcropping and skidded to a stop. Several of Boian's minions blocked their way. The minions outnumbered them by two to one at least—odds that the pair would not have a chance of overcoming. Cami and Richard turned and ran in another direction, feeling the noose tighten around their necks. They did not make it very far before they found their path similarly blocked by another collection of growling violent creatures. Again, they ran; and again, they were blocked. There was no way to break out of the encirclement—they had been surrounded, and they knew it.

They huddled close together, turning around and snapping at the closing mob. "We can fight . . .," Richard began. "Go out with a fight."

They were going to die anyway, Cami believed. Taking as many with them as they could only made sense. She nuzzled briefly against Richard and then bared her fangs and prepared to fight to the death. She took stock of the creatures that surrounded them. "Stay away from the bigger ones," she whispered through clenched jaws. "Go for the smaller ones. This is a battle of numbers. Pick the two smallest, get them first. I will be damned if they are going to come out ahead on this one. Are you ready?"

Richard nodded. In reality, he was not even close to being ready, but he also knew he never would be.

Cami whispered the countdown, mentally choosing her targets. "One . . . two . . ."

"You may want to reconsider your actions, dear little dove." Cami froze—she recognized the calm, frigid coldness of the voice. Boian stepped into the small circle that surrounded them. "Tell me, little Cami, which one of you would die first? Do you want to hear Richard's screams while my friends are ripping him apart? Or on the other hand, do you want him to see your blood in the fresh snow before he succumbs to the frigid grip of death?" Turning to Richard, Boian continued, "Richard, did Cami tell you what happens when a vampire dies while in form?"

Richard did not answer. A light snarl escaped his lips, but it did little to cover his fears.

"Oh, Cami," he sneered. "You should have told him." He walked close and ran his fingers through her fur. She bristled and snapped at him, but he was too quick—she did not make contact, and he merely laughed at the attempt. "You see, Richard, when a vampire dies in an alternate form, a wolf or a bat maybe, they revert to their human form. Think about that for a second, Richard. What will happen if Cami dies before you do? What do you think your final thought would be if the last thing you saw were her changing back into human form, bloody and broken, then growing to a 550-year-old woman before bursting into flames? Would you have the stomach for something like that? Cami, I know who you think he is . . . Do you want to watch him die . . . again?"

He waited for an answer, but none came. Cami and Richard snapped and snarled at the other vampires that drew even closer, but Boian's manipulations were effective—they did not fight. Before either of them could react, strong unexpected hands clamped on to them and held them firmly in place. Boian's minions wrestled them to the ground and restrained them securely. They were captured, and there was no hope for escape. Boian leaned in toward Cami's ear and whispered, "Caught you, my lovely. I wanted to see the fear in your eyes before we take you back to Barrow." He then leaned in and kissed her forehead.

. . .

"So what's the plan?" Mary asked. They had returned to the hotel room and were preparing to enter their deathlike state for the morning.

"We go back to Barrow, we find your friends. We find Boian, and we kill him."

She thought about the sheer numbers that she had encountered in the town. She wondered if Jeff had known exactly what was in the town or if he was overly optimistic about their odds of survival in it. "There are two of us . . . God only knows how many of them. There is no way we can do anything there, except die. If we are going to do it, we are going to need help, but you and me alone . . . no way!"

"Help . . .," Jeff echoed as rigor mortis took him. "We'll need it."

. . .

The next evening, after the effects of the rigor wore off, Jeff told Mary that he had a plan, a plan that would get them both the revenge they deserved. It would get them both the revenge they needed. He talked Mary into following him as he walked down a road that would lead them out of town. After an hour of walking, they arrived at a secluded wooded area.

"Where are we?" Mary asked. They stood outside of a double-wide mobile home in the middle of the woods somewhere deep in Oregon. They never would have found it if Jeff had not known exactly where to look and how to get there. They had landed at a small private airfield, at great cost, and rented a car to make their way to the home. "It doesn't look like anyone's home—there are no lights. We came all this way, and no one's here." She frowned—they had wasted their time.

"There doesn't even appear to be any electricity out here. Besides, she doesn't need electricity—she can see just fine without it." He waited for it to sink in.

"Oh!" Mary said after a moment. "She's one of *us*."

"Exactly." Jeff nodded. "We're going to talk to her and see if she'll help us. Understand that she's a little bit odd. Do not talk to her until she talks to you, and never stare at her."

"Why? What's wrong with her?"

Jeff smiled. "You'll see," he said as he walked to the front door. With Jeff in the lead and Mary following behind, they reached the

---

door. The door was open, and the woman watched them approach. She said nothing, nor did Jeff until he stood before her. "Emilia . . ."

The woman did not answer. She was very obese but moved with an unexpected grace. An intricate web of scars and damaged tissue covered most of her face, and then her right eyelid was missing completely. This left her exposed eye covered with a milky white film that seemed to weep constantly. She was missing the corresponding earlobe. Mary caught the gasp before it left her throat, but the cold stare from her good eye gave Mary the impression that the woman was able to determine or guess her reaction. She looked carefully at the pair that stood on her doorstep and then pointed at Mary.

"This is Mary," he explained. "She's a friend."

"A friend?" Emilia asked. Her voice was thin and raspy, as though from centuries of hard living. "What's her last name?"

Jeff glanced at Mary. "I don't know," he admitted.

"Where's she from?"

"I . . . I don't know. Emilia, we need help. I need help. You owe me . . . You owe me everything, Emilia. You know that."

Emilia sighed and moved aside, allowing them into the trailer. Mary stood near the door, but Jeff seemed immediately comfortable in her simple home. He sat on her couch, and she sat on the chair opposite of him. No one spoke for a long time; Emilia and Jeff stared at each other, waiting for the other to speak. Emilia was the one who broke the silence first.

"I appreciate what you did Geoffrey, but I have a life now, a home. It's not much, but it's mine." Each word sounded strained. Mary began to realize that Emilia was not much to look at from the outside, but there was a calculating intelligence inside her.

CHAPTER FOURTEEN

The Reign of King Anthony

Richard and Mary talked late into the night. Even though their words were guarded, they belied a measure of underlying affection. Cami sat on Mary's lap, curled up like a young child; Mary alternated between rubbing Cami's back and gently stroking her hair as Cami fed gingerly from a slit in Mary's wrist. There were no humans left as captives in Barrow. Their owners had freed them, and then they had been humanely put down like abused animals. There had been controversy over that particular decision, but it was evident that they could not be trusted with the secrets of Barrow. It was also quite clear that their captors had both mentally as well as physically abused them, and a peaceful death was the last mercy that could be afforded to them. The only humans left in Barrow were those who had not been used as blood bags.

"How did you know we'd still be here?" Richard asked. Richard was finally able to articulate the question that was on their minds.

Mary thought for a moment. "Boian is evil," she began and then stopped again to collect her thoughts. "There is more evil in him than I ever knew existed in this world . . . more evil in his heart than I can believe now, even after seeing it firsthand. He had built up an empire here—something that he could own and control. He was not about to leave that . . . not while it was still his. He had you two, and there was no way he was going to let you go, and he would have *never* let you just *die*. It was quite simply a matter of putting that all together."

Cami looked up at her, very impressed. "You knew we would be here, and you knew he would be here as well . . . Why did you come back? Why would you take such a risk?"

Mary frowned at a recently repressed memory. "It seemed as if I could feel that you were in pain. No, it was more than just feeling that you were in pain. I could actually *feel your pain* and know that it was *yours*. I can't explain it, but it was like I somehow knew what you were going through."

Richard leaned in, both interested and slightly afraid. "What did you feel? What was it like?"

"It felt like I was burning every time I thought of you . . ." She averted her eyes. "Both of you, I mean . . . And my stomach hurt, like it was"—she paused for a moment to collect her thoughts—"empty . . . even after I'd recently fed. I guess now I know why."

Cami marveled at the realization; there was a bond, just as she had thought, but she was not the only one who felt it. She locked eyes with Richard. He looked shaken. He felt it too. "So what do we do now?" she asked. "Where do we go from here?"

Mary looked around thoughtfully. "Barrow's ours now . . . This seems like a nice-enough place."

Barrow changed quickly after that. There was an election, and the people of Barrow voted a new mayor into office. The town had not had one in such a long time, and it took time and effort to convert the near palace into a functional government center. Guard stations were removed and replaced with administrative staff. Bars were taken from the windows, and the curtains were opened for the first time in a very long time. Humans and vampires roamed the streets freely and without malice. It was a new age for the town and a peaceful time. The town's council included humans for the first time since the eaters took over. The council agreed upon and passed new laws to govern their fresh city. In exchange for the safety and security that was provided, the humans willingly gave small amounts of their own blood to feed their new allies. To supplement their needs, the two species worked together to raise pigs; although the taste was not exactly the same, it was similar enough to a human's to be a viable food source in an emergency. Cami liked to joke that it took "three little pigs" to fill her tummy, but as they grew, more could be taken.

It was a good life—a happy life. They chose a home; there were many to choose from now, with the eaters gone or dead. The people accepted and treated them like normal citizens. They decorated the walls and arranged the furniture to make it their own. Despite the transformations, the town itself retained a nearly militaristic undertone; despite heavy losses, it was believed that the eaters, or even Boian alone, would come back to reclaim their territory. In order to protect against this happening eventuality, they established a schedule of patrols, both in and around the perimeter. The mayor, a relatively young vampire named Anthony, had a vision for the community and knew that security had to be assured in order to bring it to reality. He was fond of saying security involved certain sacrifices of liberty. What good was the former if your very life would be taken from you because of a lack of the latter?

As the community grew, Anthony demonstrated that the need for security had grown with it. To guard against infiltration or subversion, only Anthony could approve new members of the community. The town council, only reluctantly, agreed to the provision—and then only after an impassioned speech in one of the mayor's rare appearances at their meeting. Moreover, indeed, he had become increasingly secluded, giving his edicts and rules through intermediaries and assistance rather than directly. It was a surprise then when he emerged from his office unexpectedly and without fanfare. He was screaming and waving off those who tried to come to his aid when he stumbled and fell. He stood again, trailing blood as he made his way to the town's center, and collapsed. The crowd gathered around him and murmured nervously to one another. There were shouts and accusations as he was carried, limp but alive, back to his home.

Days passed. With no one to lead the town, decisions were left unmade; the council maintained the day-to-day affairs of Barrow but lacked the initiative or the will to enact major changes. It was not until Anthony regained consciousness that the story became known. He was being bathed by his trusted aide when he suddenly opened his eyes and spoke. Despite the severity of his injuries, he was surprisingly calm and lucid.

"What day is it?" he asked.

His aide, Samantha, was an older silver-tipped woman with a thick Irish brogue. She jumped when he spoke but quickly composed herself. She had taken care of his needs for so many days and had resigned to doing so forever if necessary. "Sat-Saturday," she stammered. "Are you okay?" She bit her tongue at the question, fearing that it was a foolish one. She loved and admired the man and had always tried to maintain the strictest composure around him. He clearly was not, but she stood nearby and awaited his answer.

Anthony groaned and pulled himself upright into a nearly sitting position. He ignored the question. "Has anyone been in here beside you?" he asked.

Samantha nodded. There had been many.

"Who?"

She named those who had come and gone while he was unconscious. He rolled his eyes upward and to the left as she spoke, mentally noting the names that she gave him. "Samantha," he said softly once she had finished. "Can I trust you?"

"To the death, sir," she replied. In her sincerity, she missed the irony in her own statement. Anthony noted it but only smiled inwardly and did not mention it.

"It was an assassination attempt," he said with only the slightest hint of a dramatic flair. Samantha gasped, her worst fears realized. "Someone . . . or some*thing* in our community . . . tried to kill me," he finished.

Samantha blinked at the revelation as though she could will it not true. She closed her eyes and opened them—the words were still there. She could not comprehend such a thing—not in Barrow, not anymore. "But, sir, who? Who would do such a thing?" she managed finally.

His eyes narrowed. She knew that look; she had seen it before, and it frightened her. "I don't know . . . but whoever it was, they did not act alone. Get everyone together . . . Now!"

Samantha's instinct was to obey immediately and act at his word. It was an instinct that manifested itself both in the workplace and behind tightly closed doors. Therefore, it was with some hesitation that she admitted that she did not understand. "Who?" she asked puzzled. "The council?"

"No. Everyone!"

. . .

Richard had found an old board game in one of the home's closets, and it had come to be a welcome distraction from the unexpected monotony of their daily life. It appeared to be a Russian version of Monopoly. It matched well with the uniquely regional decorations that were displayed prominently through the home. Although only Cami could read Russian, and even then only a very small amount of it, they filled in their missing knowledge with guesses and assumptions, which made the game playable. It was Mary's turn, and she was well behind. She rolled the surprisingly heavy dice in her hands and shot them across the worn board; they were doubles again.

"Jail!" Cami squealed. "You are going to jail!" She sounded very much like the little girl that she appeared to be.

"Oh nyet!" Mary groaned. They all laughed—it was a good night.

The knock on the door shattered the light mood. They rarely had visitors, and the heavy, slow rhythm conveyed a certain sense of foreboding. "I'll go get it," Richard said finally with a forced smile. He rose and walked to the door, with Mary following close behind. They gave each other courage, despite their unspoken reluctance. When they opened the door, it was only a crack.

The man's deep voice poured through the crack like a thick fog. He spoke slowly and purposely, as though he was having trouble translating from his native tongue. "Anthony wants everyone in the square. Go now," he said simply.

Cami did not recognize the voice but could hear him walk away before Richard closed the door. Cami looked at the home, and she looked at the game that was in progress. She knew that the game was over for now, and she chased the frown from her face. She cursed the realization that every time she found some measure of peace and comfort, it was taken from her. Richard and Mary closed the door and looked to her for guidance; once again, she was the centuries-old creature that guided them—the one whom they looked to for direction.

"What do you think this is about?" Mary asked.

Cami thought for a moment. There were very few things that it could be. "Anthony—either he died or he is awake, one of the two. Either way, I do not have a good feeling about it."

The trio joined the steady stream of their compatriots that were making their way to the center of town. There were confused murmurs, but each person complied with the voice that had similarly appeared at their own doorstep. After all, there was surely no reason for concern and nothing that should arouse suspicion. Cami, however, had lived a very long time due to mistrust and suspicion, and she approached carefully. She checked her waistband, where a small wooden stake was carefully stored. It dug into her hip, but the feeling was more comforting than unpleasant—at least she knew it was there if she needed it. She only hoped that she would not.

The square was filled with those who had arrived already, and more were coming in behind them. Cami was surprised by how much the town had grown in such a short period, as it had been a very long time since so many had gathered in the same place at the same time. She skirted around the crowd, losing sight of Richard and Mary, and worked her way to the front—or at least the direction that everyone seemed to be facing. A small stage and podium had been erected, but there was no one on it. She took in the scene, studying every minute detail and absorbing every subtle aspect. Those in the crowd nearest to the stage looked oddly uncomfortable and even frightened compared with those toward the back who were merely confused. Two large men, one of them she assumed to be the owner of the voice that summoned them, stood in front of the stage. They were alert and menacing, and the crowd pressed against one another but nervously kept a fearful distance from the pair. If only by their presence alone, Cami knew the news was not good. She glanced back toward where Richard and Mary stood, briefly met their eyes, and returned her attention to the stage.

The crowd grew, both in size and in impatience. This impatience was expressed through nervous whispers and collective fidgeting; no one had spoken out, and no one left. Idly, she noticed that no humans attended and wondered why they were not invited.

Minutes passed. Perhaps an hour, Cami could not be sure. She settled into her own thoughts, refusing to allow her own fears to overwhelm her. It was nearly a relief then when Samantha emerged from the government center and walked slowly to the stage. Only in seeing her did Cami notice that the thick steel bars had been returned to the windows and the door had been fortified with welded plates of steel. Samantha stood to the side of the podium and a half step back like a politician's wife.

A few moments later, Anthony also emerged from the building. He was led and followed by two men, each of whom carried himself as though unafraid of causing or experiencing death. Cami recognized the trailing man from the battle but could not exactly recall for which side he had fought. Anthony approached the podium and stared at the crowd without speaking. The crowd stared back at him, equally silent. He motioned, and on cue, serious men surrounded the crowd. They made no effort to advance and did not speak but merely stood and waited. Only then did Anthony address the assembled crowd.

"I was duly elected mayor of this fine community by the majority—nearly unanimously—of Barrow, Alaska. That is, as they say, the will of the people. I have always dedicated myself to preserving and protecting that will." His voice was loud and strong, and his presence seemed much larger than his stature. He moved his hands and arms in broad dramatic movements as he spoke, and his accented facial features further drew in his audience. "Yet the violent minority seeks to defy that will . . . seeks to defy *your* will.

"Just a few days ago," he continued, "one of those criminals tried to assassinate me." He paused for the collective gasp from the crowd.

"Tell us who!" came a disembodied voice, but Anthony continued without answering.

"I was stabbed, very close to the heart, so close that the tip tore into my right ventricle, the same heart that beats for each one of you. Yes, while I was lying in bed in quiet meditation, I was attacked. This small barbaric group . . . they know who they are. They're among you . . . They wanted to put one of their own into office! They wanted power, whereas I only want to serve. I offered you safety and security—a place where we could all live in peace and without fear, and yet there are those who would murder me to take that from you."

The members of the crowd began to look nervously at those who were closest to them. Seeds of doubt were planted, and a mistrust flashed through the town's center.

"The only way . . . the only way . . . that we can ever be truly safe is to root out the cancer that threatens us all . . . and the first cancerous cell." He waved his arm, broadly pointing with his hands toward his headquarters. On cue, two men emerged, one clearly in the custody of the other. The man, the prisoner, was nondescript in every way. He was of average height, if not slightly shorter, and was unremarkable in his build and features. What was remarkable, however, was the resignation on his face. There was no fear, no anger, and no defiance. There was only acceptance and knowledge of his fate. Something, however, seemed odd to Cami, although she could not quite place it. She recognized him from the community. She had never seen him dress in such a way. His body was completely covered with long sleeves and pants instead of his customary unseasonable shorts and T-shirt, which reminded Cami of an abuse survivor that covered their marks and injuries. He walked with a slight limp and climbed the stage only with great difficulty. He stood where he was left, and Anthony crossed the stage to where he stood.

"Steven," he said, addressing the man directly but speaking loud enough for the crowd to hear him. "You have betrayed me, and you have betrayed the community. You have confessed to your role in the attempt on my life, and you have given the names of the other conspirators." He paused there and turned to the crowd. "We know who you are," he said and gave it a few moments to sink in before returning to Steven. "You confessed to treason. Do you acknowledge this?"

Treason? Cami thought to herself. The word seemed unusually strong for the circumstances.

Although it was only for a brief moment, Cami caught the flash on Steven's face that betrayed his true thoughts. He wanted to deny the accusation but chose instead to confess. "Yes," he answered simply.

Anthony returned to the podium. His face was fixed with a carefully rehearsed mask of remorse. "It is then, with a very heavy heart, that I sentence you to the final death."

There was an immediate outrage from the audience—a cacophony of shouts and screams. Some screamed for Steven's blood while others for temperance. Cami could only pick out small snippets from the shouts, arguments and exclamations that included "Kill him now!" "We're not monsters!" "A trial! We need a trial!" and other words that formed together into an excited murmur. The crowd quickly turned on itself, with arguments and fights breaking out. Richard and Mary appeared at her side, and she held them close.

Anthony allowed the arguments for a short moment, watching carefully before interrupting with an unexpectedly loud shout. "Enough!" he yelled. His voice, like an explosion of thunder, overpowered the quarrels and brought each eye on to him. "There is a threat from within, and there is a threat from without. Each one of you . . . your friends and families . . . we are all in danger, without exception! You heard this man confess to attempting my destruction and take the town from you, and you dare argue on his behalf? You shout for mercy when he showed me none! We cannot be both weak and survive . . . And listen, all of you, who argued on his behalf, for many of them"—he paused and reached his long thin hand out toward Samantha; she handed him a piece of paper, which he held above his head—"are likely on this list that he himself provided when he confessed. There are ghastly dangers in this town, and I will keep the good people who deserve this homeland safe from those dangers."

Nervous eyes darted within the crowd. Each side of the argument suspected the other; the side that argued in favor of restraint and caution could easily see that they were in a precarious situation.

"Abagail Reece!" he called finally. A woman screamed as a man waded into the crowd to remove her from it. The crowd parted for him, and no one tried to stop him despite her cries and pleas for mercy and denials of the accusation. She was removed and led to the government center, where she disappeared inside to an unknown fate. "Amrita Gutpa!" he continued. She fought against the one who came to collect her, but he overpowered her very quickly and easily before removing her. "Brad Tarren!" he called next. He left willingly, trusting the town's judicial system to right the wrong that was his accusation.

The list went on, with members of the crowd being removed one by one. Those who were already fiercely loyal subjects were being whipped into a near frenzy, out of disgust, as the accused were identified and removed. Those who had opposed Anthony, either in thought or in the previous argument, watched those who once stood with them disappear around them. They were terrified that they would be next and grew desperate to demonstrate their loyalty to both the community and the town. It started with one; one man, afraid for his safety, called out his support for Anthony. "Long reign, Anthony!" he shouted—surely, such loyalty would not be met with an accusation, and indeed, it was not; instead, he was favored with a smile from Anthony himself. That very smile carried with it an assurance that the man was in his graces. Others followed suit, each determined to outdo the other in demonstrating their loyalty and dedication. Some shouted the names of those whom they suspected of disloyalty, while others clamored to show their support. Only then was the final name called, bringing a final cheer as the traitor was removed from their midst. All that remained were the very loyal or, like Cami, Richard, and Mary, the very wise who knew to avoid attention and, later, execution.

For those in the government center, there were no trials, and there were no charges. None was given the opportunity to explain or to offer their own defense. Instead, they were each summarily executed, one by one. Each was dealt with in a unique and particularly cruel manner. One, for instance, was taken between two trees, which were bent, crossing each other. The full-grown trees were secured with chains to make them form an X shape. Then the offender was attached to it, wrists and feet, and then the chains were released, pulling the victim's arms and legs apart, sometimes actually ripping their bodies apart. The executioner would then walk slowly to the body and form his hand into a spear then thrust his hand to pierce the chest of the guilty party, pulling out their heart and throwing it into a bonfire. This was the fate of the political enemies of Anthony—those who represented some form of threat to him or to his reign, and now they were dead, eliminating the opposition and completely solidifying his position within the town and the victorious army that had formed it. He, as he had planned, had grown very powerful, very powerful indeed.

CHAPTER FIFTEEN

Staked

There were rules that followed, supposedly done for the overriding good of the community. Anthony had signed off on each of the new rules and approved them without question or comment by the council. This process was publicly and loudly extolled as the pinnacle of a representative republic (which Anthony was so fond of calling the town), as the will of the people was surely being provided for in the closed-door sessions and unilateral decrees.

First was the curfew, in which the set time was established where each person was to be in their home. What they did inside was up to them, but the streets needed to be clear during certain hours, aside from the regular security patrols. This, the decree explained, was to reduce the threat of conspiracy—a goal that would be supported further by the rule that prohibited the assembly of five or more in any one place, with the exception being immediate family.

Humans were no longer equal to vampires. Vampires were now expected to give the humans fair accommodations, with all their needs met, provided the humans made no effort to leave. Of course, they did not have the means to leave even if they wanted, but that would not be specifically discussed. There were searches and raids, each broadly supported as necessary to maintain the town's peace and stability, and each authorized only in the most secretive of settings.

There were dissenters, though not many, not since the initial purge, but there were those who opposed the rule of law and the decisions of Anthony and his government. The following day, one of Anthony's cronies would explain that either they had chosen to leave the community in the night or they had been tried and convicted for some crime against the city. Those who were wise chose not to criticize; those who were frightened cheered the loudest.

Mary, Richard, and Cami gathered in the home's small bathroom; Cami turned on the sink and the bathtub's faucet and allowed them to run freely and drain immediately. This filled the bathroom with a dull roar that made it difficult to speak to one another, but the whispered rumors of surveillance and carefully hidden listening devices justified some measure of concern and paranoia.

"Things have gotten really bad," Cami started. Richard and Mary nodded. "One by one, we gave up our rights until . . . look at us, we are huddled in a bathroom just so we can talk freely without fear of being heard!"

"It is like boiling a frog," Mary replied idly. Richard raised his eyebrows, shooting the question to her over the sound of rushing water. "You put a frog in a boiling pot of water, and it'll jump right out. However, if you put that same frog in a pot of cool water, it'll swim around quite happy. If you very slowly heat it up, the frog will end up boiling to death before it knows what is happening. If Anthony—" She stopped and looked around nervously, as though she expected him to burst into the room any moment. She took a deep breath and continued. "If Anthony had started off with these same rules and laws, no one would have gone for it. They would have revolted right off the bat. However, he took an opportunity to purge any opposition and then slowly added one rule at a time. He turned up the heat just a little, and now the water is boiling. All of us, we're the frogs."

"It sounds even worse when you put it that way." Richard frowned.

"The worst part is I think he stabbed himself," Mary added.

"What do you mean? Why would he do that? He nearly died," Richard retorted.

"Did he? We can't really know that since not one of us was there and only a handful saw him until he woke up again. We don't really know what happened. Tell me this—where was he stabbed?"

"In the chest," Cami added. "Near his heart."

"Correct!" Mary replied. "He was struck *near* his heart and through the left side of his chest. In fact, the wound was pretty far over on the left side of his chest, was it not?"

"I guess," Cami said. "What are you getting at?"

"Is Steven right- or left-handed?"

Cami thought for a moment and looked to Richard who was doing the same. She replayed her memories of seeing the man in the community before he was taken away. She remembered seeing him in the store or fishing from the pier. She remembered what hand he favored, and it occurred to her in a flash of recognition. "Left. He was left-handed."

Mary smiled. "Correct! He was left-handed. Even if he *were* going for the heart, he would have stabbed closer to the right side of Anthony's chest. The wound was on the wrong side."

"What if they were fighting? Maybe Anthony turned?" Richard countered.

"Do you remember what he said? He said he was lying in bed, reflecting, or something like that. Then he said he was not expecting it. That means that the attacker would have aimed—used his dominant hand to get the most power."

Her reasoning completely amazed Richard. "How did you think of that? That was . . . well . . . that was incredible." He looked at her with even greater respect than he had felt before.

Mary blushed and smiled. "Thanks. I used to watch quite a lot of detective shows with my grandpa when I was a little girl. I just try to imagine what Perry Mason or Barnaby Jones would do."

"So if it was not Steven, who do you think it was?" Richard asked. Mary reached over to him and took his hand—his right hand. He allowed her to move his arm, watching carefully as he tried to understand what she was demonstrating. She pulled his hand away from his body; she then pushed it back toward his chest in a wide arc; his balled fist landed exactly where Anthony was stabbed. "He did it to himself," he whispered. "If that was a lie, what else has he been lying about?" The realization sat heavy with each of them.

"It could be anything . . . could be everything," Cami answered. "I think we need to get out of here while we still can. We never cheered, we never bought in—it is only a matter of time before we are on his hit list. We should start packing."

"No," Mary said. Her voice was surprisingly firm and resolute.

"No? No, what?" Cami asked, confused.

"No, we're not leaving. This is our community . . . This is our *home*. We're going to get it back."

Cami and Richard reluctantly nodded. Cami turned off the faucets in the sink and the bathtub, and they resumed their evening.

. . .

"This is our home and this is our community. We're going to get it back." Mary's voice came through the speaker. Alexei listened carefully,

taking copious notes based on what he was hearing. His intelligence background had been invaluable to Anthony and the community, and he had become a respected member of the town. For Alexei, however, he was just happy to find a place where he belonged. At that moment, his place was in a small room in the basement of the center. The florescent lights hummed overhead, and his cigarette smoke curled across the ceiling.

He finished listening and completed his notes then held them above his head, knowing that Mitchell was sitting near the door and would take them. He said, "Vot, voz'mi eti Entoni. On budet ochen' interesno." Here, take these to Anthony. He will be very interested. He understood English as well as several other languages. He could speak them passably but refused in favor of his native Russian tongue. It was a matter of pride, but it also served to reduce the number of people who would talk to him.

Mitchell paused. Alexei had chosen him to be his assistant because of his high-school-level understanding of the language, which was not much. What he did not know, however, he was able to look up in the worn and tattered translation dictionary that he kept with him for just such occurrences. He nodded, despite the fact that Alexei was not able to see him, and scanned the notes before him. He frowned; he liked those three and was surprised to find that they had turned traitor. Nevertheless, he had been surprised many times in the recent past. "Are you sure?" he asked. "Is this really what they said?"

Alexei turned in the chair; he then stood in front of Mitchell. Alexei was the smallest in his family at just over six feet, but he was solidly built and naturally intimidating. He replied, "Ya vsegda uveren." I am always sure. He returned to his seat and checked his watch before he tuned his equipment to receive from a different transmitter. The young married couple, whose name he did not know, was having sex again, right on time. He listened, appreciating this, as a distraction.

. . .

It did not take very long. There was a trial held in Mary's absence, and the jurors found her to be guilty. Within minutes after the verdict, a small group made their way toward their home. The curfew had not yet taken effect for the night, but the streets were still relatively empty. Those who were outside for whatever reason saw the group and knew exactly what their presence indicated. The already nearly empty streets cleared, with not one person willing to stand against the enforcers that walked lockstep toward the home.

Mary busied herself tidying the living room while Richard and Cami were out. Despite the restrictions in Barrow and their dedication to opposing them, the pair loved the town. They enjoyed exploring the surrounding terrain and the waterfront. Perhaps it was the restrictions on their freedoms that made them realize how much they valued them. She smiled at the pleasant memory as she stacked the board game with the others and sighed with mild frustration as she put the wineglass caked with dried blood into the sink. This was not the existence she imagined. This, however, was the existence that made her happy.

There was a knock at the door. She was certain that she had nothing to fear, but the sensation of caution and fear was there all the same. The thoughts ran through her mind; she wondered if the person on the other side had heard her or if they knew she was home. She wondered what it was that they wanted and who had sent them. She stealthily moved the heavy curtain to the side and looked to the porch where she saw the men standing. By their demeanor, it was very clear that they were not there for social reasons. One of the men turned his head, and they locked eyes—they knew she was there. There was another knock—louder, more insistent, heavier. She held her breath as she made her way to the door and quietly engaged the deadbolt. To her, the audible click was deafening, and she could only hope that the men on the other side had not heard it. She backed away from the door with the next knock, and she screamed when the enforcer ripped the door from the frame by his heavy boot. The men rushed in; Mary tried to run, but they caught her before she could get away. They pressed her into the soft couch in the living room and held there by firm hands and a knee in her back. She knew that it was perhaps possible for her to break away and escape, but that would be both admitting guilt and only delaying the inevitable. They pulled her, roughly to her feet; they then threw her back on to the couch. She sat upright, trying to look both confused and frightened; the former was more difficult than the latter.

"What are you doing?" she demanded, allowing the fear to creep into her voice.

None of the men answered, but one of them approached and stood directly in front of her. He was a thin frail-looking man with sharply defined features and a nose that made him look more like a bird than a human. The similarities extended to his behavior; as he moved, his head moved in such a way that caused Mary to stifle a laugh. She did not dare show her momentary amusement, however, knowing that this man had found himself in a position to destroy or save her, and marked him simply as Birdman until she learned a proper name or title. She could hear violent crashes and grunts as the house was searched without any care or consideration. Splintered wood covered the floor; and the beds were overturned; drawers were pulled out of the cabinets; dressers, chests of drawers, nightstands, and the bathrooms and their contents were emptied on to the floor. They opened doors and slammed them shut, causing the pictures that hung on the walls to bounce and shake.

"Mary Young, you have been found guilty of treason and sentenced to the final death. You will come with me for processing." His voice was high-pitched, and he spoke quickly, making him difficult to understand.

Mary was startled. On some level, she expected such a thing, but hearing the words felt very different from merely expecting them. "Final death?" she repeated. "This is America! Do I not get a fair trial? Don't I get a lawyer . . . someone to represent me?"

Birdman sighed at the frequently asked questions. "You had a fair trial," he explained. "You were not there for it, but it was held, and there was also an attorney appointed to represent your case."

"When?" Mary was outraged at the injustice but kept that feeling simmering below the surface.

Birdman shrugged. "I don't know. You were found guilty," he repeated as though that should answer her question and silence her argument. "Where are the others?"

"Why do you want them? I'm the one that's guilty, so you say."

"Maybe. The mayor wants to talk to them, so I'm going to bring them. Who knows, maybe they'll get a trial there," he offered as though it was supposed to bring some measure of comfort.

"I don't know where they are," Mary lied. "They moved out. We had a fight. I think they went to Oregon," she lied again.

She did not expect him to strike her. She certainly did not expect him to hit her so hard. The sound of his palm slapping against her cheek made her ears ring, and the force caused her face to shoot to the side. She looked back at him, expecting to see some measure of emotion on his face, but there was nothing. He was calm—eerily calm.

"You're lying," he said simply. One of the men approached Birdman from behind and whispered in his ear. Birdman nodded, without taking his eyes off Mary. "Close the door, keep watch for them. They'll come back sooner or later, so be ready for them."

The man nodded. "Um, sir, the doorframe's busted. It won't close."

"Find a way, get some goddamn paint if you have to, I don't care. Just be ready for them."

"Yes, sir, sir . . . I'll take care of it, sir!" the other man acknowledged. He left to do as he had been told, but Mary reasoned that his mental faculties would prevent him from doing a very good job at his task.

"Now where were we?" Birdman frowned as he tried to remember. "Oh right. You were going to tell me where"—he took a quick look at the small notebook that he fished from his pocket—"Richard and Cami had gone off to. They are not in the home, but they were recently . . . were they not?"

Mary looked away. The answer was obvious, but she refused to confirm it. Doing so, she felt, would be a betrayal to the bond that they shared and an affront to everything that they had been through together.

"Were they not?" Birdman repeated.

Mary still refused to answer.

"No matter," he said finally. "We'll find them, sooner or later . . . more likely sooner than later . . . And by the time we do, you'll probably already be dead. It is a shame, isn't it? I'm not one to judge, but that seems a little bit selfish of you, denying them the opportunity to say goodbye to you when the outcome is going to be the same. On the other hand, you could tell me where they are and we can delay your execution long enough for them to say farewell." He leaned in close as though sharing a precious secret. "Since you're going to die anyway, my sweet, you could probably take the whole rap—tell Anthony that everything was your idea and that they thought you were joking or that they did not hear you right . . . something. Anthony is a reasonable man—he'll let them go, but you have to tell us where they went if you want any cooperation, tit for tat as it were." He was lying, but it was a well-practiced lie that worked more often than not. The key, he knew, was to find out what drove a person. Learn what motivates them, and the lies to exploit them come very naturally.

Mary paused for a long time, considering what Birdman had said. She wondered if he would keep his word, she wondered if he was telling the truth. She looked him in the eyes and decided that he was a liar. She looked away and hoped that her silence could somehow give Richard and Cami a fighting chance, even if it was too late for her. The men pulled Mary roughly to her feet and out the door, with two of the men staying behind to wait for Cami and Richard. Mary saw frightened faces appear in windows and doorways, only to disappear as they passed. She locked eyes with a man who pressed his face into the crack of his doorway; she knew him—his name was Travis, and he had a wife and children. He did not talk about it, but somehow, they had all been rebirthed on the same day. He looked frightened and pushed back the child who appeared at the doorway. "You might be next!" Mary shouted. "Or your family! It can be any of us!" He looked down and shut the door quickly.

. . .

"A wolf? I guess I could see that," Richard said. The two were crouched close to the ground, looking carefully at the tracks in the snow.

Cami was pointing at the tracks with a thin stick as she spoke. "Mmm hmm. It is the front paw—you can tell, about five inches, the rear is much smaller. It was just starting to run right here, that is why the pattern started to curve."

"Amazing," Richard said. "I could hardly see the tracks at first, but you knew what animal they were from and what it was doing when it made them. How long ago do you think it came this way?"

Cami smiled. It was the smile that she showed when she was going to challenge Richard with something particularly clever. "When did it snow last?"

Richard thought for a moment. "We just left Barrow, so I guess about an hour ago. Why?" Cami looked at him, and the realization crept over his face. He smiled. "Oh! It came through this way after the snow, or else the tracks would have been covered!"

Cami smiled back, genuinely proud that his powers of deductive reasoning were getting stronger. "Very well done!" She beamed.

They stood and walked on, heading toward the shore. Richard loved the beach, and they spent a great deal of time enjoying the steady rhythm of the waves and the tranquility of the horizon. He had never seen the ocean before, despite having lived close to it in his childhood, and the first time he saw it up close was with Cami. She told him later that he looked just like an excited little boy, with his eyes opened wide and a broad grin on his face. They stood there together again, barefoot in the surf; the moonlight reflected on the water, which crawled up the shore to meet them and cover their toes before slipping away back into the ocean. They had danced together in that ocean and collected shells to bring home to Mary. They had talked about anything that came to mind, and they had simply sat quietly and watched nature. Despite the fundamental wrongs in the town's government, Cami was happy here. Perhaps, she thought, the significant wrongs were worth the substantial rights.

"We should probably get going back," Richard said. Cami nodded and took one last look at the ocean before turning away and walking back toward the town. They walked in silence for several miles, cresting endless snow-covered hills and passing through small collections of trees and vegetation. "You know, Cami," Richard began, seemingly out of nowhere, "I was thinking."

"Did it hurt?" Cami teased.

Richard laughed; Cami loved to hear him laugh. "No, I was thinking that maybe it is not so bad here. I mean, as long as we stay quiet, nothing bad is going to happen. I mean, I know it is really messed up what's going on, but there are going to be new elections sooner or later, don't you think?"

"I do not know," Cami replied. "I have not heard that anything is planned."

Richard considered that. "Well, there's gotta be eventually. I mean, there *are* terms, right? There are laws and rules that even Anthony is going to have to obey. Sooner or later, someone else is going to be mayor, and maybe it won't be so bad then."

"Yeah, maybe," Cami replied. She wanted it to be true, but she had seen too many tyrants rise to power to trust his adherence to the system, but at the same time, she knew that all tyrants would fall, eventually—sunrise and sunset. Anthony, by his very nature, was chasing after his own demise—chasing after his own sunrise. Cami remembered King Leopold II of Belgium; it took a very long time, but those whom he oppressed finally took their revenge. Officially, he died of natural causes. Then again, countless tyrants have died of the same *natural causes.*

Richard continued growing increasingly excited at the idea. He continued as though he was trying to convince Cami, but it seemed as though he were actually trying to rationalize the plan to himself. "We've been okay so far," he said. "I mean, we're still here, right? We're free to come and go as we please, and as long as we keep our noses clean, we should be fine."

"What about the others? What about everyone who have disappeared?"

Richard frowned. It was a thought that he had hoped to avoid. "It is not right, but . . . I mean, they are not us. Maybe they really did something—we were not there for the trials. They would not have been charged if there was not something there, don't you think?"

"No, I have seen it before," Cami replied. The look on Richard's face was pained. "Maybe you are right all the same. We do not really know for sure. We can see how things go, maybe talk to Mary about it when we get home." *Home,* she thought to herself. Maybe this really can be home. She looked at Richard, who now smiled softly; he wanted it to work, and Cami silently vowed to do everything she could to make it possible.

"Okay," Richard replied. They walked on together, with their feet crunching the fresh snow with each step. Richard's thoughts rolled through his mind, much like the waves rolled on to the shore and retreated into the endless sea. He pictured a home in a community, with a family, a *real* family—all things that he had never had before.

He pictured having those things for all eternity, as death would never quite take them. His mind started to wander as they crested the last hill toward town, and he thought about expanding his family—making something new. He wondered if Mary could possibly see him in the way that he was starting to see her. "Can we have children?" he asked, otherwise out of nowhere.

"What?" Cami asked, shocked. "I do not . . . we *cannot* . . ." She stumbled over her words.

Richard chuckled at her reaction. "Not us, Cami—no. I mean can our kind, those . . . *like* us. Can vampires have children?"

Cami thought for a moment. She had heard rumors that some had, but those were always dismissed as legends or lies. She had never seen it happen herself and had never even thought about trying. "I do not think so, Richard." A small measure of sadness fluttered unevenly over his eyes, like a butterfly with torn wings. "I am sorry. We are different now, we will live forever, but . . . we are just not human any longer."

Richard nodded slowly. He accepted it; on some level, he already knew it. He just wished that it were not true. "Mary can always get a bunch of cats," he said after a moment. The unexpected joke took Cami by surprise, and she laughed. Her laughter was contagious, and Richard noticed the sentiment and erupted into loud sincere laughter. By the time they crossed into the outskirts of the town, their laughter had settled into periodic chuckles and giggles, and their mood was infinitely lightened. They walked along the streets toward their home, their footsteps echoing off the cool pavement. "Where is everyone?" he asked. "It is awfully quiet."

Cami's eyes narrowed. "Yeah, it is," she replied. The town seemed almost deserted, even though curfew was still a long way off. Normally, there would be music playing or young ones running in the streets; there would be arguments about the latest books or loud games played from the porches. There was nothing, except for an oppressive silence. Cami whipped her head to the side, just in time to see a curious face disappear behind a curtain. She turned the other way, and a door closed quickly. "Something is wrong. They are all so full of fear."

"What are they afraid of?" Richard asked. He instinctively moved slightly closer to Cami, both for the protection that she offered and from the natural instinct to protect those whom he cared.

"I do not know," Cami replied. "Something happened. Maybe Mary knows." She ducked behind the outside corner of a house, and Richard followed close by. They each pressed themselves against the wall, and Cami stole a cautious look down the street. One of Anthony's enforcers, a particularly nasty man named Reece, passed by without seeing them. She avoided him out of some intuitive instinct that she could not name but had learned to trust. He was looking for something, and if it was either of them, she figured that it was best he did not find them. "Come on, stay with me."

Richard nodded gravely. "What about Mary?" he asked. He had a gnawing fear that defied any logic or reason, but he knew that it would not leave until he knew that she was okay.

"I do not know. Come on." They ran together from one house to the next, careful to avoid any detection—she had no idea whom she could trust, aside from who was with her, and whom they were going to see. She hoped that she was just being paranoid or blowing everything out of proportion, but it was very clear that there was something terribly wrong.

Finally, they made it to their home. They approached it from the one single angle that could be seen neither from the front nor from the side window. They moved slowly and cautiously. Each of them scanned for anything that was out of place or any hidden danger that lurked in the shadows or around the corners.

"Everything seems to be okay," Richard whispered, relieved. "Right? Everything's okay?"

Cami stopped. No, nothing was okay; she could not quite place it, but something was wrong. "No, there," she said after a moment of careful inspection. She pointed at the front door.

Richard strained his eyes but saw nothing. "What about it?"

"It is cracked, just a little bit. It is pressed back together as if someone tried to fix it. If the door is cracked, that means it was broken. If it was broken, that means they came after Mary. If it has been repaired, that probably means they have her and someone is still inside . . . waiting . . . for us."

Richard wanted to cry or scream—something. He was simultaneously terrified and enraged, and the only possible outlet for those feelings stood inside their home. "Let's kill that bastard and get Mary back," he said. His voice was even and oddly calm and very resolute. "What do we do?"

Cami crossed to the corner of the house and leaned against it; Richard joined her and kept careful watch of all approaches as she descended into deep thoughts. She considered the scenarios and their outcomes, reluctantly thankful for the times that Boian ran her through such exercises repeatedly. What if they kicked the door open and ran inside; whoever was waiting for them is ready for their entrance and can stab Richard in the back. Cami could turn and kill him, but that scenario will leave Richard dead. With that in mind, this scenario is not good.

What if they set fire to the house and whoever is inside can either die in the blaze or leave the house. They can attack him to get the information they need; however, the blaze will attract most of the town, and they will lose all elements of surprise. This scenario is not very good either. What if they announced their intentions to come inside to talk; whoever was inside will wait for them to come in and attack. Cami frowned, discarding each subsequent idea in turn until only one remained. "Richard, listen carefully. I need you to—"

"Whatever you want, I'll do it. Just tell me," Richard interrupted. He was eager and anxious.

"To be bait," Cami finished. Richard's face fell—the idea did not seem very appealing on the surface.

"Bait?" he repeated. "Okay, I mean, I'll do it, but . . . how?"

"Go to the front door and push it open. Do not go in. Pretend that you are confused, and pretend you do not notice that the doorframe is broken. Call for Mary."

"I thought you said Mary wouldn't be there."

"She will not be, but you are not supposed to know that. Talk loudly as if you are telling her that I ran off into the woods and you have not seen me. Whatever you do, do not go inside. Do you understand?"

Richard nodded. "How does that help Mary?"

"Whoever lived here last put a key in one of those fake rocks, near the back door. While you are shouting, I will open the back door and sneak in. You keep their attention, and I will do the rest." Cami was speaking as though there would be only one, but that was for Richard's sake. She hoped that would be the case but suspected that there may be more. Despite her forced confidence, she wondered how many she could take on and survive. "Okay, do your part so I can do mine," she said and then ran toward the back of the house, keeping low to stay under the windows. All the windows were covered with the blackout covering that was very popular in town, but it only took a moment of poor fortune for someone to move it aside and see her passing.

She reached the back door and silently lifted the rock from its place. She hoped that the key was still inside, despite the irrational fears that told her that it would somehow be gone. She nearly wanted to cheer when she saw that the key was still in place, but she kept her composure. It was a small victory. She heard Richard's voice resonate through the home, and she pressed her ear against the door to know when it was the right time to enter.

"Mary, it is me!" Richard called. Cami slid the key into the lock in one smooth motion, feeling the pins snap into alignment through the metal key. "Have you seen Cami? She ran off while we were exploring." Cami turned the key slowly, feeling the tumbler slide freely and the mechanism open. Richard continued "We had a fight about something stupid, and I guess I made her mad."

Cami pulled the door open, just enough for her thin frame to pass through, and darted inside before closing the door behind her. She was inside and, as far as she could tell, undetected. She could hear Richard carrying the story through, buying her the time that she needed. She did not pay attention to the words but could tell that he was designing a captivating lie that was keeping the would-be attacker at bay. Cami passed quickly through the home, briefly searching all areas without allowing herself to be seen.

There was a man waiting in the narrow alcove to the left side of the entryway. Like many of Anthony's most trusted assassins, he was large and muscular; his face was scarred, but the fierce ruthlessness shone in his eyes. He stood like a great jungle cat ready to pounce on its prey, and Cami had no doubt that he could easily dispatch the two of him in a fair fight. If only one were to be left behind, he was a wise choice. He carried two sharpened stakes—one for each of them. One, he held in his right like a sword, pointing away from his body; that one, he would use to thrust and stab. The other he held in his left hand, inverted like a dagger. That he would use to slash or crush. It was not often that Cami felt something as crippling as fear—she had lived far too long to be afraid of death. Something about this man, however, terrified her and only partially because she knew that Richard would be dead the moment he crossed the threshold.

The one thing that the assassin lacked, however—the single advantage that Cami enjoyed—was surprise.

"I saw a wolf's prints in the snow!" Richard yelled after a moment of silence. As Cami edged along the wall toward where the man stood, she saw him tilt his head as though confused. Richard was running out of material, and the assassin would not be distracted for very much longer. Cami moved quickly and quietly toward where he stood, afraid to make a noise but afraid to take too long and lose the only chance that she had. She reached the alcove, just out of his view, took a deep breath, and leaped.

The man screamed in surprise and anger when she came into view. Cami screamed with rage and hatred when she slammed into his solid mass. Her reflexes were fast—honed by years of survival and adversity. Cami violently latched on to his left forearm and pulled in down and toward his body; the tip of the stake lodged into his thigh and tore the muscle on either side as it nicked the bone, passing through the other side of his leg. The stake buried into his flesh, where it stayed, firmly planted. The man's reflexes were also good; even as the stake in his left hand was slicing through the skin of his own leg, he had inverted the one in his right and brought it smashing down into Cami's back. The sharpened end tore through the very thin skin, shattered her shoulder blade and pressed through until the tip had exposed itself on the other side. The momentum forced her to the ground, a short journey for which the man's heavy boot forcefully interrupted. He brought the steel toe upward in a reflexive kick, which caught her in the jaw and sent her flying backward to the ground in a very ungraceful and unladylike arch. She landed on her back, sprawled on the floor, and screamed as the stake pressed further through her body.

She stood shaking on her feet. The man seemed completely unfazed by his own injury and stood at his full intimidating height. The two mortal foes regarded each other cautiously, studying their opponent with a practiced eye. Cami saw that the man refused the trappings of overconfidence, a flaw that had saved her on more than one occasion. Some regarded Cami as a mere child, which made them very easy to surprise; this man, however, understood the nature of the vampire and had long since abandoned the very human notion of equating size and apparent age with capability. He cocked his head to the side when Richard ran into the room but did not allow Richard to distract him from his mission. He knew Richard's age as a vampire and, therefore, knew that Richard was far less of a threat to him than Cami and regarded his deadlier enemy with the reverence that she warranted. Of course, he was not foolish either, and he slowly moved until he could see both Richard and Cami at the same time and, conceivably, battle both.

"Oh Jesus," Richard gasped when he saw the stake protruding from Cami's back. "What did he do to you?" Cami did not answer but kept her eyes locked on the man. "What did you do to her?" he demanded of the man. The man similarly did not answer. Richard's entire countenance reflected the boiling rage that was just below the surface, and he charged the man with a strength and courage that he had never before felt. With an unexpected clarity, he saw that the man had left his midsection unguarded, and he dove directly for it. He would slip past his fallen defenses and tear into the man's soft stomach with everything that he had. Then once he broke the skin, he would simply reach upward through his intestines and grab his heart, pulling it free. It was a cruel and nearly sadistic strategy but one that Richard felt no remorse in implementing when someone he loves is in danger.

The point, however, was entirely moot. Richard did not leap past the man's weakened defenses, and he did not tear into his soft stomach. He certainly did not push through his body until he found the man's heart. Instead, the man caught him with a surprise right hook to the jaw, which sent him sailing into a nearby bookshelf. While Richard was relatively unharmed, the bookshelf splintered and fell against the wall. The fragile items on top fell on to Richard or on to the floor, and the books were scattered in an uneven pile. Richard pulled himself to his feet, no less angry but significantly more cautious.

Cami took advantage of the momentary distraction to reach over her shoulder and try to pull the stake free—if nothing else, doing so would give her a weapon to use against her attacker. She pulled, and the searing pain ripped through her body and dropped her to the ground. She stole a brief glimpse at the exposed tip of the stake and realized why; the man had fitted pure blessed silver barbs into the smooth slope of the rounded blade, which meant that the stake could not be removed once the barbs took hold. That, at least, explained the sensation when the stake first entered her back. It would be blindingly painful to pull the barbs free, which explained why the second stake remained lodged in the man's thigh. Cami thought for a moment, desperately looking around her for any sort of weapon. Finding none, she realized that the stake was her only option. The man watched her passively, neither retreating nor advancing, as she took a few steps toward him. Rather than attacking, as he expected, she ran backward as fast as she could go and slammed into the wall. This pushed the stake further into her body but also pushed it further out the other side—through the front of her shoulder. Cami groaned and did it one more time, pushing the stake far enough that she was able to pull it free. The pain was intense but subsided to a dull throb once the stake was completely removed.

The stranger's eyes widened. "You must be Cami," the man said. He reached down and pulled the stake from his leg; the silver barbs tore at his skin and pulled large chunks of meat with them. He winced briefly but otherwise took the pain with very little reaction. If his intent was to intimidate Cami, it worked very well. They were each now armed and stood unmoving, staring at each other. Cami saw Richard move slowly, slipping behind the larger man. Cami did not know what he planned, but his face was resolute. Before he could act, she saw the man's eyes slide to the right and knew that he was very aware of Richard's movements as well. Cami shot a warning glance to Richard, who froze in place.

"Yes," she answered finally. "I am Cami."

"That's Richard behind me then?"

Cami nodded. "Yes. Where is Mary?"

"We haven't staked her, don't worry. We were waiting for you two. If you come with me peacefully, you can see her. If you make me kill you, which I would prefer not to have to do, then she will never see you again, and you, of course, will be dead. Think very carefully before you make your next move, little kitten—the choice is entirely yours.

If you attack me, or if Richard attacks me, I will kill the two of you without hesitation."

Cami considered the situation. He was wounded, so he would move slower, but she was wounded as well. There were two of them and only one of him, but he was much faster and much stronger; she assumed that he would use his strengths against their weaknesses, killing Richard first quickly and brutally. She weighed the odds and arranged the numbers—they were not in her favor.

She closed her eyes; as she did more often than she would care to admit, she allowed herself to travel back to her tutelage under Boian. She despised him and everything that he stood for, but he did know how to survive. Right now, she needed to survive. In her memory, they walked along the moonlit dirt path that wound between two small rural towns. They had recently fed, and Boian was in surprisingly good spirits.

"Little Cami, do you know what you call someone who fights fair?" he asked.

Cami answered, *"Noble? Honorable?"*

Boian would laugh and shake his head. *"Dead. You call them dead. When you fight—and you will—you fight to survive. There is no honor, and there are not any rules when you are fighting for your life, and assume that every fight is for your life. Cheat, lie, deceive—whatever you need to do to survive."* Cami had heard it then and discarded his advice as jaded and cynical. More than once, however, his cruel lesson had saved her life. This would have to be one of those times.

"I know what you are . . . I know what you are after. If we go with you now, we are not going to live to see another dusk!" Cami shouted. As she spoke, she pulled the silver barbs from the stake. They burned as they cut into her fingers, but she dropped each to the ground. The expected chime of metal on the floor was overpowered by her screams.

———

221

The man shrugged. "Chance you take, I guess," he replied. "It's probably the best chance you have."

"Where is she?" Cami demanded.

"She's at the government center—you cannot get in there without me, if that's what you're thinking."

"What if we refuse to go with you?"

"Then you die."

"I am not going with you. If I die, it is on my terms. Neither you nor Anthony, not anybody, is going to take that from me!" She pointed the stake at the man. "I will see you in hell," she said. She brought the stake up in a high arc and plunged it deep into her own chest. The tip sunk deep into her flesh, and she fell to the ground in a sprawled heap. She fell on to her chest, which pushed the stake completely through her body, and it stuck out through her back. Then she was still—she was very, very still.

"Cami, no!" Richard shouted. He could feel his own heart being torn in two as he watched Cami fall to the ground. He pushed past the man, oblivious to any danger or threat to himself; all he could see through the tunnel of tears and pain was Cami's lifeless body on the ground. He threw himself on to her body and wept until the man pushed him aside like a pest. The man knew that Richard was no threat to him but needed to confirm that Cami was truly gone.

"That's odd," he mumbled to himself. "Why isn't she—" He did not have the opportunity to finish his own question. In a flash, Cami pushed herself off the ground with every bit of strength that she had left. As she jumped into the air, she closed her hand around the base of the stake, which was still buried in her chest, and drove her back against the larger man. For the first time in a very long time, the man was taken by surprise; and unfortunate for him, this would be the last time. With her one chance, Cami guessed at the location of his heart and quickly aligned her own blinding pain to it. Although the man tried to block her and dodge her attack, he was unable—the tip of the stake found its mark and tore through his muscles, spread his ribs, and slid cleanly into his heart, ripping it open and spilling its contents into his chest cavity. He fell backward; and now with the stake binding them together, Cami fell on top of him, further pressing the stake into and through his mortally wounded heart. He lay on the ground, Cami's small frame on top of him—she seemed much heavier than he would have guessed but quickly realized that his perception was being altered by the fact that his immortality was waning and his thick frame was decaying quickly. He felt the strength leaving him; he felt his blood leaking from his heart and pooling around the stake in his chest; he felt his dying heart convulse as though trying to expel the invading wood. He grasped weakly at the stake that he still held in his hands but could not raise it, much less kill with it. "That was . . . unexpected . . .," he whispered, and then the last of his life left him. Cami felt him age centuries in seconds—his body pressed against hers, and it grew weak and frail; his face became brittle and fell away in forced senescence; And then, like a very small explosion, he turned to dust.

Cami lay in his remains; the pain spread through her body, radiating from her newest wound. She struggled to speak or move but could only manage a weak groan.

Richard ran to her, confused and terrified but deeply happy that she was alive—even if only for a few more moments. "Why aren't you dust? What happened?"

She summoned the last of her strength and pointed at the stake in her chest. She pleaded with her eyes, but was unable to speak, to beg him to remove it before the pain overwhelmed her. She had seen it happen—enough pain, if not alleviated quickly, could drive even an immortal creature insane. Richard understood, and she was relieved, despite the pain that racked her entire being, as he grasped the handle and pulled the stake free from its organic sheath. Although the man's own body had loosened it, and again by the floor when Cami fell on to it, it was still difficult to work free from between her ribs, pulling some of her flesh, with the barbs, but that would repair itself soon. He threw the wooden instrument to the side, and it fell against the floor; Cami tried to muffle her own screams, but at least the pain meant that she had not suffered the eternal death. Already, she could feel her body begin to repair itself, and the pain level started to slide from unbearable to excruciating, but such injuries would take, even her body, some time to repair. She clenched her teeth and pushed herself into a sitting position. She wanted nothing more than to lie on the floor and wallow in the pain, but she forced herself to be strong for Richard's sake. "I am fine," she panted. Even speaking brought her a certain amount of pain.

"How did you . . ." His voice trailed off. He did not know exactly what she did, much less how she did it.

Cami thought, only very briefly, about the ways that Boian had tortured her for so long. How he had stabbed into her body, explaining sometimes that it was to give her a healthy fear of death, and other times telling her that he was teaching her not to be afraid of anything. He was sadistic and inconsistent, but she learned his lessons well— even the ones he did not intentionally teach. "I know . . . exactly where my heart is," she managed to say. "I made sure that"—she paused to work through her pain—"I did not . . . hit it." She gasped as though the few words had overwhelmed her.

"It looked like it was your heart," Richard replied. There were tears in his eyes. "My little raindrop, I thought I had lost you." He pulled her into a tight embrace; his tears fell on to her soft hair. "I didn't lose you," he said more to remind himself than for any other reason. "I couldn't bear it."

Cami had a look of shock come across her visage when she heard him call her his little raindrop, but Richard had closed his eyes, so it escaped him. No one had ever called her that, except her tata.

She turned her attentions back to Richard's well-being. "No, you did not," Cami consoled. He was unintentionally aggravating her wound, but Cami was happy to bear the pain because despite an otherwise deadly injury, she had never felt more comfortable than she did in his arms.

CHAPTER SIXTEEN

The Escape Plan

"How are we going to get her back?" Richard asked.

Cami had been wondering the same thing but had not yet developed a plan. She sat on the soft couch; her wound had continued to heal. This process had quickly accelerated because of the very fresh blood that Richard had provided to her. As the nutrients from the blood were absorbed into her body, she felt her mind beginning to clear. "We know where she is . . .," she thought aloud.

"Right, the government center," Richard answered.

Cami had not actually asked the question and did not allow his answer to distract her thought process. Slowly, the plan began to come together in her mind; the hazy concept slowly began to form into something solid and terrible.

. . .

Although Cami approached Anthony's quasi-fortress alone, she walked confidently. She carried no weapon, as she knew that it would do her no good, and instead clutched only a single plain white envelope. The guard was noticeably surprised to see her approach, both alone and willingly, but quickly regained his composure.

"Where's Oswold?" the man asked. He stood in front of the entrance, blocking the way.

"He suffered the eternal death," Cami answered in a snapping, uncaring tone. "Anthony wanted to see me." It was not a question; instead, it was a very direct statement. The guard stood aside and allowed her to pass; Cami crossed into the proverbial lion's den, and the door closed behind her. She was committed now—the brief moment that she had to escape was gone. She had now become sealed inside, and there was no way out. She was in the same building with the most loyal of Anthony's guards and staff, far too many for her to fight and win. She clutched the envelope, hoping that her nervousness was not showing; she imagined that everyone in the building, including those who could not see her, could somehow smell her fear, the same way that she could smell the fear in the living. She forced a confident smirk on to her face and walked casually down the narrow hallway. As she walked, she collected the loyalists—those who served Anthony eagerly. They came out of each room and followed as though she were a pied piper leading them down the hallway. She could hear them follow behind, and it took every ounce of her willpower to avoid looking behind her; she could not afford the luxury of showing her panic that she was trying so hard to deny. She heard them push closer to her until they were right on her heels, and she was sure she would be attacked then slow down to increase the space between them; they repeated this like some bizarre medieval dance, much like the advance and retreat of the waves that Richard loved so much. She could make out individual footsteps and the rhythmic click of claw on wood, and the sounds of wings breaking the air told her that some of them had changed into a more animalistic form. She forced her pace to be even despite every instinct telling her to run. By the time she reached Anthony's office, it was very nearly a relief.

Anthony's office was a large room, roughly in the center of the building. It had been, at one time, the massive committee chambers, but he had remodeled it into his personal office. It was very ornate, with expensive furniture filling the various sections, and dominated by the massive dark hand-carved mahogany desk at which he sat grinning. Cami took in the room, mentally noting her potential escape routes if her plan would fail. There were several doors along the walls, but Cami had no way of knowing which led to an exit and which led to an office or other room. There were windows, but the bars removed them from the equation. She also noticed, most urgently, Mary. Mary had been physically placed to stand behind Anthony's desk. She was attached to and supported by a strange contraption, the purpose of which Cami could not immediately determine. Her arms had been spread and attached to the crossbeams by silver bindings, and her legs had been fixed to the small raised platform using the same method. Wherever the blessed silver touched, steam would waft the air like little wisps of steam from a cup of hot tea. Her mouth was fitted with a gag, and her head was secured by a leather strap around her neck, similar to the one which kept her upper body pressed tightly against the thin wooden plank that covered her chest. Her discomfort and fear were obvious. In that plank was a single hole, which was set into a sliding panel. That is what gave it away. Cami realized this contraption must have been used to facilitate executions. She wondered if everyone who had died had done so in Anthony's office. Cami's outrage at seeing Mary bound in such obvious discomfort almost made her give way to a display of her rage, but she kept it in under control. She knew that if she allowed her emotions to get out of hand, she could not do anyone any good. She forced herself to remain calm, remembering that she had a plan that depended on her being able to keep her feeling intact.

Cami expected some degree of subtlety from Anthony—perhaps some banter or threats. She had prepared to match wits against the far younger creature and had considered the jeers and taunts that would demonstrate her capability and confidence. She perhaps overestimated him because she was completely unprepared for his childlike taunts.

"I got you!" he shouted, jumping up from his desk. "I knew I would, I knew I'd get you! I knew you couldn't resist an attempt at saving Mary! It was just like I planned, and—" He stopped, confused. "Where's Richard?"

Cami approached his desk and leaned forward while resting her palms on the surface. Although she was as close as she could possibly be without crossing to the other side of the desk, the two were still well out of each other's arm reach by its width. "Where you cannot touch him," she answered.

Anthony spoke over her toward no one in particular. "Find him!" he called. Cami heard several footsteps make their way toward the front of the building and leave through the way she had come in.

Good! Cami thought to herself. *The fewer, the better.* "You will never find him," she taunted. The flash of anger in Anthony's eyes told her that her taunt had struck a very sensitive nerve.

Anthony scowled but faked a look of calm reflection. His anger, however, simmered just below the thin surface. "It doesn't matter," he said. "He'll turn up eventually, but now I have you, and I have Mary— that should be enough."

Enough for what? Cami wondered. She mentally made note of what he had allowed to slip and considered how to work the rest from him. "Here is what is going to happen, dear Anthony," Cami began, calling on the intimidation techniques that Boian had used on her and others. Anthony sat back in his oversized office chair and crossed his arms with a smirk as though he were very amused. "You are going to let Mary go, and then she and I are going to leave. We are going to leave Barrow, and we are not going to come back. Nobody dies, nobody kills, and nobody follows us."

Anthony laughed. "You want me to let you go? Just release her and let her go, is that it?"

"Yes. It is very simple . . . even for a relatively young vampire like you."

"She had a trial, she was found guilty. Why in the world should I just let her go? What type of message does that send to the citizens if they see her walking about free as a bat?"

"Suit yourself," Cami replied. She slid the envelope across the desk, and it stopped precisely in front of Anthony. He frowned as he opened it and pulled out the single Polaroid picture. His eyes shot open wide with surprise then narrowed in anger. He put the picture down and stared at it again; it was a picture of Samantha also bound in silver. The message was very clear—whatever happens to Mary also happens to her. Of course, the silver was only symbolic on Samantha because she was not vampire, but the message was the same.

"Let her go," he said quietly while trying to be intimidating. His arrogance and overconfidence were gone.

"Let *her* go!" Cami replied, pointing toward Mary.

"If you don't let Samantha go, we'll kill you—kill you right where you stand."

Cami shrugged and smiled inwardly. "You are going to do that anyway," she replied. "So that is not really much of an offer . . . but . . . if I do not walk out of here with Mary . . . Samantha dies—she dies in an extremely gruesome and painful way, and *that*, my dear Anthony, with the Lord God Almighty as my witness, I *promise* you. If there is anything that I learned at the knee of my rebirther, it is how to be cruel!"

"A standoff, how exciting!" The hairs on the back of Cami's neck stood straight out like a threatened kitten. She recognized the voice and spun to where it had come from. Boian strode calmly and confidently from the nearest office door, followed by two demons of men. He crossed to Anthony and stood next to him, grinning at Cami's surprise. His presence altered her very delicate plan, and Boian knew it. More so, he relished in it. "Hello, my dear Cami."

"Boian . . ." She attempted to speak calmly and with authority, trying to hide her fear and confusion. "What are you doing here?" Cami demanded. She could not keep the emotions from betraying her voice.

Boian placed a hand on Anthony's shoulder. Anthony looked up briefly and then frowned again at the picture. Boian, however, did not give a moment's attention to him. "We have reached an arrangement, Cami," he said. "The good people of Barrow will give you up—all three of you," He snarled the last part, highlighting the fact that only two were present. "And I let them keep their town. Anthony here has worked very hard to keep me from coming back and bringing my eaters, but he knows that he cannot keep it up forever. So what is the ultimate form of security if not to eliminate the threat entirely?"

Cami's mind raced, trying to adapt to the new information. She opened her mouth to speak, hoping that something disarming would come out, but Anthony spoke first.

"Boian . . . they have Samantha," he said.

"Who?"

"Samantha, my . . . my assistant."

Understanding flashed in Boian's eyes then annoyance. "Why should that bother you? Just get a new toy," he replied dismissively.

Anthony bolted upright, sending the wheeled leather desk chair flying into the wall. He drew back and thrust his outstretched hand toward Boian, aiming his extended claws toward the much taller man's jugular. Boian did not move nor did he even react—he just watched with a smug smile. Before Anthony could connect or react, one of the men who had arrived with Boian appeared at his side. He caught Anthony by the wrist and squeezed with a viselike grip. Anthony stared, shocked, and winced when his bones started to crack. The man followed by whipping his free hand against Anthony's neck and pushing him face first into his own desk. Anthony did not resist—any movement on his part would only serve to pull his arm from its socket.

"Are you going to try that again?" Boian asked.

"Let me go," Anthony managed weakly.

Boian pressed down on Anthony's shoulder, straining the joint even further. "Are you going to try that again?" he repeated.

Anthony was silent for a long moment. No one in the room moved; no one spoke. "No," he said finally. Boian signaled, and the man released him. Boian reminded him that he was merely a *puppet* leader and had very little *real* power.

"Now," Boian continued, "as I mentioned, we had an agreement— you, Mary, and the other one in exchange for the town. I think that is reasonable but—"

"His name is Richard," Cami interrupted. "Whatever happens to us, you will not find him."

"Maybe not," Boian replied. "Or maybe he will come looking for *me* someday. If so, I will *just have* to be patient. It is a small matter. I have the two who belong to me." He turned to face Anthony. "Of course, that means you failed to uphold your end of the bargain. I will probably end up keeping Barrow just for the trouble. Of course, I will probably allow you to stay on to take care of the grunt work."

"Boian! We had a deal!" Anthony protested.

"And you broke it!" Boian replied sharply in a voice that made the room shake like thunder and the pictures bounce against the walls. Until this moment, Anthony had not known that the town was already no longer his.

Inside of Anthony was a war. His impulsiveness and pride fought against his fear and sense of self-preservation. It was his pride, which would win out. As quickly as he was able, he pulled his desk drawer open, grabbed what was inside, and stepped backward, increasing the space between the trio and himself. In his hands, he gingerly held a clear glass bottle filled with a pure liquid. He removed the cap and held it in front of him menacingly. "Do you know what this is?" Anthony shouted.

Boian nodded. His expression was one of annoyed amusement rather than the fear that Anthony had expected.

Boian took a melodramatic deep breath through his nose. "It smells like holy water, which would have been blessed at the Vatican by the pope himself. You come into my town and threaten *me* in front of *my people*? I invite you in to negotiate *truce*, and you choose instead to *betray me? I will not have it, sir!*" The word "sir" was dripping with disdain.

Boian snarled and tensed his muscles. Cami could see that he was only looking for an opportunity to attack. She knew that once he found it, Anthony would be dead.

"You want those two so badly . . ." He turned his head but kept his eyes on Boian and called over his shoulder. "Let her loose," he said simply.

"Sir?" One of the men, the one closest to Mary, was not sure how he should react.

"Just do it!" Anthony shouted. In that moment, Mary was free. She fell to the ground, physically exhausted but now free. Cami ran to her, clutching her in a brief but loving embrace, then helped her to her feet. They stood together, hoping for an escape. "Let them go," he called to his loyalists.

"Do it and you will die, young Anthony. Do it and you will *all* die!" Boian warned. He pointed at Anthony. "I will kill you first, with that holy water you hold so dear, and then each of your men. I will still kill those two, and then I will find that whore you are so fond of and kill her myself. Her death will be slow and painful. I will first drain her then rebirth her vampire. At the end of that first night, I will bind her in silver, snap off each of her fingers and toes, and place her behind a wall so that when the sun rises it will purify her, beginning where her toes used to be . . . And by the time it reaches her heart, she will have gone mad with the pain. Her painful eternal death will be on your hands."

"There are only three of you, you won't last. Perhaps you'll kill me, but you'll be torn to shreds."

Cami and Mary backed slowly toward the exit. Watching the two men challenge each other was much like watching two dogs preparing to fight. Anthony, however, was the much smaller dog. He was a feist who has no idea of his actual size relative to his opponent. Anthony would be dying tonight. If Cami was sure of anything, it was that, and she hoped they would be gone long before he did. Anthony, however, seemed destined to hasten his own demise. He flicked his wrist aggressively, which forced the liquid through the opening and straight toward Boian's face. Although not expecting such an aggressive move, Boian dove to the side and avoided most of it; a small amount landed on the side of Boian's face and burned deeply into his skin. It would be enough to harm him, possibly even scar him, but not enough to kill him. The man behind him, however, was not so fortunate. The majority of the holy water, though meant for Boian, washed over the face of one of the men Boian had brought with him. He screamed and clutched his face but quickly pulled his hands away when they started burning as well. The air filled with an arid thick smoke and the overpowering stench of burning flesh as the panicking man's flesh began to melt away. He tried to wipe the water off with his shirt but only succeeded in pulling large strips of flesh from his own face because his skin was actually boiling from the attack. It would take him several minutes to die, and they would be several long torturous minutes. He fell to the ground, screaming and begging for death as the water destroyed his face one cell at a time and only then moved into his brain.

Boian, however, was not concerned with the slow death of his companion. Despite the searing pain on the side of his face, he was free to strike. He leaped at Anthony and caught him in a violent embrace, spilling him to the ground and landing calculatedly atop him.

He clawed at Anthony's face, pretending it was for revenge for what he had done; but in reality, it was entirely for his own pleasures. Boian loved and truly enjoyed few things more than the feeling of pliable flesh giving way to his relentless fingers, and feeling that flesh under his fingernails was like no other feeling in the world. It was power, it was dominance, and it was his bliss. Anthony screamed through the horrible pain, which was music to Boian's ears. What he had intended to be words instead came across as unintelligible shouts, but it was enough to prompt his loyalists into action. No longer interested or even aware of Cami and Mary, they rushed at Boian and the surviving man, who met them with joy and humorless necessity respectively. As Cami ran toward the hallway, she stole a glance backward, hoping to find that Boian had finally met his match. Instead, they locked eyes as he eagerly tore at the soft flesh of a woman's neck with his razor-sharp teeth. She screamed as the blood flowed over his face and down her shirt. Boian's eyes burned into Cami's as he winked; it was far from a friendly gesture. Cami continued down the hallway with Mary close behind; they each silently resolved to put as much distance between themselves and the hellish town of Barrow as possible.

. . .

Mary broke down in tears immediately after exiting the building. Although Cami wanted to console her right then, she led them through a few twists and turns of the streets to provide some small measure of concealment and security. Only when she was sure they were not being followed did she stop and pull the much taller woman close to her. "It is okay, you are safe now. You are safe," she comforted.

"It's not that," Mary explained in between sobs. "I couldn't get away when they caught me at the house. I tried, Cami, I really did, but I couldn't . . . And when they had me, all I could do was pray that you wouldn't come looking for me. When I saw Boian again . . . I knew that he was waiting for you . . . I thought you were going to die, I thought Richard was going to be with you and you were both going to die."

"That did not happen though," Cami comforted. "We are all okay." She started walking again, prompting Mary to follow close.

"I just . . . I don't want to lose you again."

Cami stopped; she thought about that day so many centuries ago. *Does she remember it too? Does she know?* Cami thought to herself. She did not want to get her hopes up, but the thought that the stress of the situation may have triggered Mary's memory have a great deal of hope to Cami. "What do you mean 'again'?" Cami probed cautiously. "When did you lose me before? Do you remember?" She stopped herself, nearly forgetting her own pledge.

"Before, when Boian nearly ran the town," Mary answered.

Cami was disappointed but hid it. Cami smiled and pulled Mary close to her. "You never lost us, you never will." She hoped she was telling the truth.

. . .

Richard had very little experience as a hostage taker, but he did his best with Samantha. They sat together in a comfortable but empty home; it had once belonged to a group of young men—artists and musicians—that had disappeared in the night. He began the experience with firmness and a cold detachment, but his general good nature and concern for others quickly won out. He showed her a small measure of kindness when he was concerned about her comfort, which led to an open conversation. They talked about their lives and interests and were soon laughing like old friends. It never occurred to Richard that he was getting too attached to his hostage, certainly advised against in such circles, but he did wonder what would happen if Mary and Cami did not come back. He wondered if he could really kill her if they never returned, if he had it in him to do it.

He was lost in that very thought when he heard footsteps on the gravel walkway. He could tell that the footsteps were from more than one person, but he was not able to tell exactly how many. This meant one of two things—either Cami or Mary had made it out safely and returned to the temporary hideout or their mission was compromised and Anthony's men were coming for Samantha. He froze, unsure if he was about to live or die. He jumped with the knock at the door; Samantha's head shot up at the sound. They each watched and listened, with different hopes, different fears, and different thoughts. There was a pause then another single knock. There was another pause then three rapid knocks.

"Cami!" Richard cheered immediately and ran to the door to open it. He stole a glance behind the pair as he let them inside. He took them both into a warm hug while Samantha looked on; she was keenly interested in the interaction. "You're safe! You're okay, both of you!" He laughed. The stress and worry released in a sudden torrent of emotions.

"Yes, yes." Cami giggled. She wormed her way free from his embrace and closed the door. "We are okay."

Samantha stood and approached the happy trio cautiously. "Did you kill him?" she asked. Her voice was not angry—it was both sad and hopeful.

"Who?" Cami asked.

"Anthony . . . Is he dead?"

"You untied her?" Cami asked, ignoring Samantha's question.

Richard looked at her sheepishly. "She was not comfortable. She was not going anywhere."

"We did not kill anyone," Mary replied. "We're glad for it."

"We only wanted to get out alive," Cami added. "Anthony made a deal with someone—an old vampire named Boian . . ."

"Boian!" Richard said with an obvious shock.

"Yes, I know. He was going to leave the town alone. Anthony was setting up a meeting to discuss it."

"Did he tell you what he promised?"

"What do you mean?"

Cami led the older woman to the couch, and they sat together. Richard stood nearby, with Mary in his arms. "Boian was my rebirther—the one who caused me to be reborn a vampire. I left him because he was evil, and he can't to be trusted."

"He did not seem evil," Samantha interjected. She was not defending Boian but rather Anthony's decision. She still loved the vamp despite his alliance.

"I watched him drain a baby in front of its parents. He did not even need to feed—he only . . . wanted to see the expressions on their faces."

"Oh my lord!" Samantha exclaimed. "I had no idea."

Cami took the woman by the hand and patted it reassuringly. "I know you did not, and I am sure Anthony did not either, but the deal he made . . . he agreed to give us up. He agreed to hand us over to Boian, who would have killed us. He would have done that, only after he had finished torturing us. Why do you think he did not execute Mary right away? Why do you think he kept her alive?"

"What do you mean 'execute'? He was going to exile her to another state, like all the others. I mean, except for the first, but they were dangerous."

Mary looked at Samantha sadly. She had been very deceived. She slowly unbuttoned her top and exposed the top of her chest; her modesty was maintained by her brassiere. A large black X had been drawn on her skin using a red permanent marker. "Do you know what this means?" Mary asked.

Samantha shook her head. "No, what is it?"

"It marked my heart. That's where the stake would have gone. He said that I was being *packaged* as a gift for Boian and that he was going to kill me upon his arrival. If Cami had not shown up when she did . . . Samantha . . . they've done it before. They knew exactly what they were doing."

Tears welled in Samantha's eyes. What she had known had suddenly fallen apart. Cami saw her in a different light—she was not aligned to Anthony as she had thought. He had fitted her with blinders. She sat on the couch and cried silently, and Cami wondered if it even mattered anymore. Maybe Anthony was already dead. Cami gave Samantha a very quick hug, and the three made their way to the door.

"Wait, stop!" Samantha called after them. Cami turned slowly, wondering just how deeply Anthony's deceptions ran in her. "You'll need this," she said. She tossed a small metal object toward Cami, who snatched it out of the air before looking at it. It was a stubby key with a triangular head. "It's the key to the plane—Anthony's plane. It's the only way you're getting out of here without being followed."

"Thank you," Cami said. She meant it with all her heart. She glanced at Richard and Mary. "Come with us. We can leave together."

Samantha shook her head. "My home's here. I just . . . I don't know anymore."

They closed the door while Samantha had her head buried in her hands, sobbing softly. The streets were very quiet and still, which was far more disconcerting than Cami would have expected. They ran low to the ground for the airport. Cami had a thought as they ran. "Do any of us know how to fly?" Richard laughed. "Not in a plane!" Once again, with the chance of freedom opening up for them, their spirits were collectively high.

EPILOGUE

Time passed as it always does. Soon, Barrow, Alaska, was just a very distant memory. They would each relive the horrors that they had encountered once in a while, during the brief period where the mind comes to life before the body, but they learned to ignore it. They moved on with their lives together despite the unanswered questions that always loomed unspoken over them. They did not know if Boian was alive or dead for one; Mary and Richard allowed themselves to believe that he had died that night, but Cami had her doubts. She had seen him delivered to death, only to have him somehow escape it, far too many times to believe that this would be any different.

After a circuitous route and a great deal of something resembling life, they ended up nearly where they started. It happened when Mary shared a long-held desire to visit the former home of her grandfather's favorite musician. She remembered very fondly their time together when she was a child. She would watch his television shows, safe and warm in his comfortable lap, and then he would creak and pop his way to his antique record player. It was only antique because he had never replaced it—he always said that he would replace it whenever it broke, but it never did. Mary tried not to think about it, but that player had gone with her when he died. She had cried every time she listened to it up until the day that it was broken in the fight with Boian. She still remembered the record that she had played last, "How Great Thou Art," from one of Elvis's gospel records. She always kept it in its place, sandwiched right between her videos of Spinout and Double Trouble. She wanted to go to Graceland, and so to Graceland they went.

Cami and Richard found it to be a very different experience the second time around. They had Mary with them for one thing, which gave the city a very different appearance. Without the threat of Boian, they rested easily and enjoyed the city for what it was. They did not even have to stay in the crypt but instead settled into a small long-term hotel suite. It was not much, but it was home. By that time, they each saw "home" as something temporary and fleeting rather than a permanent arrangement, but the chance to rest and relax was welcome. Mary was disappointed to find that the hours the estate was actually open for tours were limited to daylight hours, thus precluding them from taking the tours, but Cami, of course, found a creative solution.

It ended up taking several days for Mary to grow accustomed to changing form, and learning to do so reliably, but she was eventually able to manage it. She preferred the form of a small pure white mouse; it stood in sharp contrast to Richard's own jet-black appearance and was complemented by the form that Cami chose, which was a meaningful amalgamation of Richard's and Mary's with a cute little heart shape in white on her back. They roamed freely through the massive estate, remaining in their much smaller form to avoid the ever-watching eye of the hidden security cameras. The added benefit of such a unique perspective was that it allowed them to see the home in a way that few, if any living beings, had ever been able. It was a near religious experience for Mary, who was finally able to live her lifelong dream. They avoided the king's bedroom, however, both out of respect and due to the reality that even a creature as small as a mouse was unlikely to find its way inside the sealed room, without chewing through the wall, and that would be disrespectful. They were, however, able to see Lisa Marie's room and her famed hamburger bed. The estate kept it, just as if she were coming home tonight with pristine sheets, crisp and smelling fresh.

They stayed through the night, relaxing and exploring, talking and cherishing their time together until the very early hours of the morning and the impending, dreaded sunlight. They left then and made it to the suite with enough time to bid one another a peaceful death and that they would see each other again when they come to life once again. It was an odd ritual perhaps, but wishing themselves a good and painless death had taken the same kind affection as when they would have once wished another a good night and sweet dreams. In neither case was finality expected. Each would take their turn saying to the other two, "Good day. May you both find your rest with little pain, and may God bless and keep us all safe throughout the day." Some may have thought it odd that a vampire, such a loathsome creature, would hope and even ask for God's blessing. Cami, however, as well as Richard and Mary, had all believed in and worshipped God before being rebirthed and saw no reason to stop now when they needed him the most.

Waking the next night was characteristically excruciating but mercifully short. Cami rose first, being more used to the process than the other two would be for many years, and made her way to the refrigerator. Only when she opened the door, and the last of the fog rolled away from her mind, did she remember that they were out—there was no blood left.

"I'm hungry," Mary said from the bed. Richard lifted himself with a groan, which sounded vaguely like an agreement.

"Looks like we are out," Cami said. "We are going to have to go hunting."

It did not take long for the trio to get ready—it is always amazing how fast one can move when they are motivated by hunger. They showered, dressed, and slipped into the clear night. Memphis was a wonderful place to hunt; it was large enough to provide a certain element of anonymity, and there was a never-ending supply of fresh prey. As with any large city, there was a darker side to it. There was another world that the city would not show in the brochures—one that it tried to pretend did not exist. It was a world where innocence was a liability and naiveté was a death sentence. It was also where they could hunt freely and drink deeply, for there was always, as in every large city, an abundance of those willing to hunt the innocent; and those would be the ones who would be Richard's, Mary's, and Cami's prey. Despite what they were, Cami, Richard, and Mary were not the evil in the world; but they knew how to feast on it.

They found that part of the city and fixed themselves into a representation of a happy family. Cami walked between Mary and Richard, who appeared to be her parents, each holding one hand of the seemingly young child. Like any skilled predator, they knew how to use camouflage when the situation called for it; they also knew how to attract the attention that they sought when required. Tonight they were very easy targets, and they merely had to wait for a nibble.

They did not have to wait long.

"Excuse me, are you lost?" Two men approached them from behind, moving up to them quickly. They held their arms loosely to their sides, with their palms open and empty, looking very friendly and not threatening in the least. That alone meant that they were dangerous. Their fishing expedition had been productive, although their catch was a little smaller than what Cami would have liked. No matter—it was important to feed, and these men seemed deserving of their role.

"H-howdy, fellas," Richard said with a practiced touch of fear in his voice. He had gotten good at the role, and Cami resolved that she would remember to congratulate him on his performance later on. "Yeah, I think we're a bit turned around—we could sure use some help getting back to the Peabody."

One of the men whistled. "Y'all are stayin' at the Peabody, huh? Fancy place. You're a long ways off." He smiled a predator's smile—at this point, he did not know that the roles had reversed. He looked at Cami, to him a little girl. "Have you seen the ducks march through the lobby yet?"

She let herself shrink against her *mother's* hip when he spoke; fear was like a drug to them, and they struggled much less when they were put at ease. "Yes, sir." She nodded. He waited for more, but she said nothing.

"All right, then you're in luck because I know a shortcut—get you right back to the hotel in plenty of time for bed." He turned and walked toward a nearby alley, and the other man followed.

"Should we follow them?" Mary whispered, loud enough for both men to hear. She was playing a role too and playing it very well.

"Sure, honey, they seem to be fine young men," Richard answered—again loud enough for the pair to hear but giving the appearance of trying to be quiet. "They're just being friendly is all."

They followed the pair, Richard in the lead, trailed by the two girls. The darkness of night gave way to the even darker blackness of the lonely alleyway. They barely made it halfway before the men stopped. One pushed past their intended victims, blocking their escape, while the other stood before them grinning. "You're a dumbass," he jeered. He closed in on the trio, drawing his knife as he approached. The man had a lust for blood and had long since moved from petty robberies to murder; the look of fear on his victims' faces, the feeling of puncturing the flesh, the joy of leaving a body and seeing it on the news the next day, there was nothing to compare it to. He had not murdered a child before though; he wondered what he would do when it was her turn. He rushed forward and stabbed the blade of his knife deep into Richard's stomach.

Richard could feel the pressure of the insertion, of course, but there was no pain. He smirked at the man, who stared back at him startled. He regained his composure and tried again, another stab into Richard's solar plexus. Richard laughed. "I would think that a smart man would realize what he was up against and attempt a retreat . . . but then again, look who I'm talking to." The happy sounds of laughter and lighthearted insults were not the sounds the man was expecting.

"What . . . what are you?" he stammered.

Footsteps, the clang of steel on cement, the other man dropped his knife and tried to run. In a flash, Cami caught him. She was prepared for him to run, at least one always did, and her plan did not allow for anyone to raise alarm, no matter how unbelievable their claim or how unsympathetic the victim. *As he struggled with every bit of his strength, she pulled him alongside his accomplice, and with a grin, she said in that childlike singsong voice, "Who is the dumbass now?"*

The men's expressions were somewhere between confused and frightened; they stammered out apologies and begged for forgiveness. Richard pressed each against the wall, holding each by the neck with superhuman strength. "How many have you killed?" he snarled in a much deeper, almost animalistic voice than before.

The first man lied. "I've never killed anyone, I swear!"

The second man closed his eyes and mumbled a prayer that he remembered from childhood. "Our Father, who art in heaven . . ."

"What was God doing while you were doing this before?" Cami asked.

He was even more panicked. "Hallowed be Thy name!"

Cami raised herself in the air and looked down at him. "He was crying!" She threw her arms out for dramatic effect. "You turn to God now, but how many lives did you ruin before this? Maybe if you had turned to him before now, you would not be about to meet him in person!"

The second man did not answer, but the first did on his behalf. "Dozens!" he practically shouted despite the constriction around his neck. "It was all his idea! I didn't want to go along with it"—he was now crying—"but he made me!"

Cami had heard enough. There truly was no honor among thieves, much less among violent murderers. She had no way of knowing how many people each of the men had killed; she only knew that they had both fully intended to allow or to cause a family of three to die tonight. Mary fed first, unable to refrain from changing her appearance into a combination between a bat and a tigress, wanting to strike fear into his heart. She quickly changed back just before tearing into the neck of the first man and greedily taking his blood past her lips and holding it in her mouth until it was full then taking it down in one large swallow. He did not go into shock or die right away but instead struggled uselessly against both her feeding and Richard's arm. Simultaneously, Richard lowered the other man closer to the ground to allow Cami to begin her feeding. It was not difficult to silence them—a hand over the mouth served that purpose, in addition to keeping their necks exposed. They tried to scream, but they could not; Richard held the pair in place while they struggled against them, bleeding heavily through their severed veins. They pushed against Cami and Mary, respectively, but even when they were at their best, they were unable to overpower the "helpless family" who had only recently been their intended victims. Their punches grew weaker and their faces grew pale as their lives were being drained from their bodies drop by drop.

Cami touched Mary's arm to get her attention. Cami, with a look of compassion, said, "Let us allow them to finish their prayers and hope that they ask God to forgive them for their sins. Since he has already started, it may be a sin to finish him before he finishes his prayer."

Mary looked back at Cami, as did Richard, with astonishment. Mary then stated to the pair of involuntary blood donors, "You may finish your prayers, and as my dear young lady has suggested, you should ask God for forgiveness in an attempt to avoid burning in the pits of hell for all eternity."

The one young man, who had been praying moments earlier, looked at Mary and said, "Are you nuts? You can both kiss my hairy ass! I'll see you in hell!"

The other hapless young man was eagerly taking full advantage of his prayer time and begged for forgiveness for every sin he had ever committed, down to pulling the wings off a fly when he was six years old. Upon his saying "Amen," Mary and Cami dove back into their meals and drank greedily, feeling the strength return to their own bodies. It was a strange tradition of sorts, one that was repeated time and time again. At the moment of death, both men looked in their killers' eyes as the life slipped from them. For each, the eyes of a vampire were the last things they would ever see. Without enough blood to sustain awareness, they each slipped into unconsciousness, limp and still in Richard's arms. He lowered them to the ground, and then Cami and Mary moved aside to allow him to enjoy what was left of the warm liquid. He too drank hungrily, "finishing the drain of the bodies," as he liked to call it, with the same contentment and enthusiasm that one would finish a glass of fine wine, stopping just before the hearts stopped—a skill that had come with time and Cami's tutelage.

They were small men, however, and the sustenance they provided would only last for a short while. They would need to feed again before long, but they no longer were left feeling physically empty and light-headed. Richard, using a knife that the first man had pulled on them, slashed their throats and cut out the bite marks. He left the bodies in the shadows after carefully arranging them. Cami carefully mutilated each neck a little more and added offensive and defensive stab wounds on each man as deception.

When she was done, both of the men appeared to have died in a vicious knife fight; each with their knife buried into the other, the illusion was complete. Even when drained through the active thruway that is the corroded artery, some blood always remained in the system, a relatively small amount, but it could be coaxed from the body when needed. The organs contained a small amount, and some of the blood remained in the body once the blood pressure dropped below the point at which it would be pumped through the body. This allowed Cami to construct a bloody scene that supported the scenario she presented. A great deal of blood would be missing, but she knew that an investigation was unlikely at best. The police would not be inclined to expend many resources toward solving the murder of two men who clearly killed each other in an alleyway knife fight. She stood up and admired her work, careful to avoid the puddles of blood and resulting footprints. They left through the opposite end of the alley, feeling much better than they had when they entered.

They did not get very far before they were stopped. Because of their curiosity, they observed something they were not able to ignore. Three men, each much older than would be expected, given the circumstances, surrounded a fourth. They shouted cruel names and taunts at their target—a younger man wearing a sun visor and an overloaded backpack. They did not see their new audience, but Cami doubted that they would have changed their behavior if they had.

"Hey, retard, can you lick your elbow?" one called. The other two laughed like jackals.

"What's wrong with your . . . with your face?" another slurred.

"Yeah, your face!" echoed the third.

It was a lame taunt but a taunt nonetheless. The other man, their target, laughed; he was trying to understand the social cues but had no idea how to respond to such a situation. He tried to walk away, but he was restrained. He tried to talk but was shouted down. Although he stood tall, he was left to cower inside his own flesh.

"Why is he laughing when they are being so cruel?" Cami asked.

"He's bigger than they are . . . He could probably take them all on . . ." Richard answered.

"I think he's autistic," Mary said. "I had a friend whose daughter was autistic. They've even made movies about it. He can't understand social interactions—the way the men are communicating, he doesn't grasp it. He likely thinks they're his friends, and he doesn't get why they're doing what they're doing. He could probably stop them. He just doesn't know that he should. Autistic people don't see the bad in people . . . only the good. We need to do something."

The men chased their target into the street, forcing an oncoming car to swerve around him. The driver leaned on his horn and shouted through the open window but kept driving. They laughed and blocked the fourth man when he tried to get back to the sidewalk. Undeterred, he sidestepped, but they blocked him from proceeding forward. He was clearly becoming frightened, which only encouraged the other men to continue what they were doing. His frustration was becoming more pronounced when he began, almost chanting, "I didn't do it . . . not me . . . Somebody did it . . . It's not my fault . . . I didn't do it . . . Uh oh!"

Cami narrowed her eyes. She had been a victim before; Boian had been cruel and merciless, and she knew how it felt to be helpless. She knew what it was to need a rescuer, and she knew how it felt when none came. "Yes . . . we do," she replied. She ran toward the men, her already extraordinary speed accelerated by her anger and sense of protectiveness over this stranger. She knew that Richard and Mary were right behind her—they always had her back. Unlike Boian, Cami had mercy—even for those who did not deserve it. Mercy allows for absolution, even for those who would not accept it. "Leave that man alone," she said calmly.

To Mary and Richard, that was sobering. They had seen Cami angry, enraged even—they had seen her shout for effect and scream for a reaction, but when she was calm and even in the face of an abuse, they knew that things would be very bad for whoever did not follow her requests.

The men spun around, not having heard their silent approach. There was a moment of surprise then a shared perverse glee and laughter as they found a new victim. Max, the fourth man according to the label tag on his backpack, took the opportunity to move around the man and stand on the sidewalk. The look of relief on his face was sweet and heartbreaking at the same time. He did not leave as Cami had wished he would but instead stood and watched the interaction, fidgeting and looking up then around. He looked nervous and unsure.

The man who stood in the middle was clearly their leader. She recognized him immediately—not personally but she recognized his type. He would have been the ringleader of his small group of friends in middle school; likely, they were all bullies, and he would have been the worst among them. Those who were with him were nearly certain to have been his friends back then, and they grew older together without actually growing up. Being small, he chose to prove himself by preying on those weaker or slower than him—anyone whom he could hurt in exchange for a boost in his own self-esteem.

"How 'bout you mind your own goddamn business, you stupid little bitch?" He laughed. After a beat, the other men laughed with him. "What, you think you can tell *me* what to do? You think you're better than me, or maybe you think you can mouth off with Mommy and Daddy here. I got news for you, kid—you're in the wrong part of town to be brave."

Cami could feel Mary bristle at the man's language, but she rested a hand on her arm to keep her in place. "Mary," she said, "will you please take Max to the ice cream place we saw around the block." She turned to the man. "Would you like some ice cream, Max?"

He shrugged. "Okay," he replied. "I didn't do it." He tried to appear calm and casual, but the excitement in his eyes was noticeable. Mary replied, "I know you didn't, sweetie." Then Mary said with a smile, "Let's go. What kind of ice cream do you like?"

"Vanilla," the man said. "I like vanilla."

She started to walk away, but the leader of the pack reached to stop her. "Hold the fuck on," he started, but he was not able to reach Mary as he intended, and she walked calmly out of his reach. To his surprise, Cami had caught his arm by the wrist in mid-extension. He tried to pull away, but she effortlessly held him in place. "Let go, before I kick your teeth down your throat!" he shouted. He tried to put an edge in his voice, but his eyes betrayed his fear. He was used to picking on those weaker and had never sought out a fair fight. He could not back down, especially from a little girl, especially in front of his cronies.

Cami moved around to face him, with her back to his cronies. She smiled broadly, bearing her fangs at him, and spoke through her teeth. "These teeth?" His face took on a look of total terror, which his friends could see but not understand. Cami began to squeeze slowly just above his wrist, compressing the muscle against bone. The gap between his radius and ulna bones started to close in an unnatural manner until they were very nearly touching. The pain passed from excruciating to unbearable until he dropped to his knees and whimpered for her to let go. She did not but instead taunted him by singing to him, "What is the magic word?" and waiting for him to whimper out, "Please . . . please . . . PLEASE!" to which she replied, "Well . . . since you said 'please.'" She then released her viselike grip on his arm.

The other men laughed at him, for now he had immediately lost his status in the group. His was a fickle position, and the alpha of this pack was in danger of being replaced at the slightest sign of weakness; being bested by a young girl was, without a doubt, a sign of weakness. They snickered, which only enraged him. He stood, trying to hide the pain in his arm, and moved closer to Cami to tower over her. "You're fuckin' dead!" he snarled.

She just looked back into his eyes and calmly said, "I know." Despite his apparent anger and tough talk, he seemed afraid to come any closer to her. Cami did not flinch and did not back down from the man. She stood against him, something to which he was very unaccustomed. "You can walk away," she said. "You and your friends can walk away now, and I will let you just leave . . . Or you can stay, and I promise you that you will die." She looked around at the others. "Each one of you will die. Make your choices." His friends started yelling, jeering him on, "Kick her ass! Are you going to let her talk to you like that?"

The man wanted to run; there was something very unusual about the girl—more than just her surprising strength and eerie calm. He had thought she and the ones who had come silently with her were merely a little bit stupid. Now he did not know what to think. Without knowing what to think, he defaulted to that which had worked for him so far in life—intimidation and violence. If he could not understand something, he could at least destroy it. He raised a fist and held it, expecting Cami to back away or flinch; she did not. He could not understand her reaction, so his only choice now was to destroy her. He brought his fist down, aiming for Cami's nose, intending to break it.

Somehow, he missed. His fist whizzed by, missing her nose by a fraction of an inch. He knew how to punch—he had done it many times before, but he had not seen her move, so he was now left even more confused, more nervous. He followed up his missed strike with a left hook aimed at her jaw. Once again, she did not appear to move, but he missed all the same. Each time, he stumbled—carried by his own momentum when his fist failed to find its target.

Cami took a slow very deliberate step backward; Richard followed, doing the same. She looked down the street, after where Mary and Max had gone—they were out of sight. She looked around; no one else seemed to be watching, but she feared the harsh light of day, both literally and metaphorically. "Please, don't hurt me!" she squealed in a very deliberate approximation of fear and then turned and ran away. Richard did the same thing simultaneously, although with a slightly more masculine "Just leave us alone!" They ran the way they had come but slowly enough that their attackers could easily pursue them.

These men knew how to play this game and were finally comfortable and in their element. When their victim ran, they knew how to chase—it was instinct. They ran after the pair, having completely forgotten about their previous victim. They were mere yards behind the two when they entered the alleyway; they knew that alleyway very well and believed the poor decision to be the result of unfamiliarity with the area. If the man and his daughter knew the area, they reasoned, they would not have gone down an alleyway with no means of escape, save for the exit on the other side. The girl's young legs, however, would not be able to carry her fast enough to get away completely, especially when they had closed so much ground already. The man smiled—he loved revenge. They tore into the alley and could see the streetlights and moonlit street of the other side. There were no silhouettes, which could only mean that they had stopped running in favor of hiding. It was no matter—the result would be the same, even if the method changed. Their deaths would be especially brutal, he promised himself, given the embarrassment that they had already caused.

"Come on out, little girl," he called as he made his way deeper into the alley. "We're not gonna to hurtcha." That was a lie—he definitely planned to do much more than hurting them. "How about you, buddy? Come out and take your beatin' like a man. You stand up and we'll leave your daughter there alone. Hell, we'll probably even get a beer together after it's all over—no hard feelings." That was a lie too, but he reasoned that time he could save a lot of time if the pair gave themselves up rather than forcing him to find them. He waited for a moment; there was no answer. He continued walking, with the other two men close behind them. He strained his hearing and his vision, looking and listening for any clue as to their hiding places, but all he could see were shifting angry shadows, and all he could hear were their own footsteps and his own breathing. He imagined that he could just make out the sound of his heartbeat over his own uneven breath but could not be sure. Other than that which he brought with him, there appeared to be nothing in the alley. As they made their way further into the darkness, he searched anywhere that two people could reasonably hide. "Where the fuck did they go?" he asked. "We were right behind 'em." He did not expect an answer, and none was offered. They all knew that the two would not have been able to make it to the street exit, and the fact that they did not seem to be hiding anywhere close to the entrance was unusual, to say the least.

"Shit, look at this," one of the men whispered. The other two joined him, and they stood over the pair of bodies that lay in a pool of blood. "Bastards stabbed each other to death, can you believe that shit?"

"Yeah, I can believe it," said the other man. He kneeled and started pulling items from their pockets, keeping whatever he found in them. "Around here, I could be—"

He did not have time to finish his sentence. His words turned into a guttural scream as Cami leaped on to his back from the tall rooftop, with a sound that could only be described as the scream of a cougar, and pressed her fingers deep into the man's eyes. She felt the delicate organs burst under the pressure and pressed her fingers deeper into the sockets. The fluids normally internal to the eye and fresh blood squirted from the sockets due to the pressure and ran down past her fingers and down his face, dropping on to the asphalt. The damage done, she removed her fingers and allowed him to fall to the ground, with his hands at his face. He shook and writhed on the ground, screaming and trying to stop the flow of goo from his freshly popped eyeballs and the blood coming from his now empty sockets by clasping his hands over them. It did nothing—his bright red blood flowed between his fingers, no matter how tightly he closed them.

Richard, meanwhile, landed on the other crony. He was perhaps kinder than Cami; his fall broke the man's back, which would have left him paralyzed and in pain. He lifted the man high above his head and threw him against the wall. His head hit the wall first, and the sounds of his skull cracking and his neck breaking were surprisingly loud. By the time he hit the ground, he had been completely paralyzed, and he lay very still at the base of the wall.

The leader of the pack was now the only surviving member. He backed against the far wall as though the distance would somehow save him. He looked at his friend, who was still and lifeless at the base of the wall. A trail of blood steadily advanced toward him as though it were the merciless finger of death itself. He heard his other friend's screams and sobs and saw him rolling on the ground in pain. He saw the other bodies and wondered if they were also lured into the alley in a similar way. With no better plan, he promptly urinated himself and cried softly. He tried to force himself to disappear—to pass somehow through the wall as Cami and Richard approached. He was, of course, unable to do so.

Cami smiled and held him by the arms, pressing him against the wall. This surprisingly strong child was holding him firmly in place. He knew that he was free to kick but had every reason to believe that it would do him no good. "I'm sorry, please, please let me go!" he begged. "We were just messing around. We weren't going to do nothin' . . . honest!" Robbed of his advantage, the murderous bully, like all bullies, had quickly been reduced to a sniveling coward.

Cami did not answer.

"This isn't fair!" he shouted. "I did not actually do anything. I have money. Let me go and I'll give you money. I'll apologize to the retard and everything. We'll just pretend this never happened."

His choice of words did nothing to reach Cami. Again, she said nothing.

He struggled against her grip as Richard leaned in, eager to fill his stomach with the man's fresh blood. He knew that it was purely an imaginary difference, but he felt that the blood of the unjust was the sweetest of all when spilled. They had taunted him so long, however, that the adrenaline will give the blood a tangy flavor that, although unpleasant, makes one remember why it is there, while feeding, making it not overly unpleasant.

"Wait . . .," Cami said.

Richard froze in place and then pulled back away from the man. "Why? What is it?"

Cami shifted her grip and lifted his arm to eye level. She studied the space between his fingers then cursed and showed it to Richard. "Track marks," she explained. She pulled his sleeve high on his arms to find that the tender network of veins in the crook of the elbow had been punctured repeatedly and had collapsed from overuse. "We do not need it that bad," she said. Richard nodded.

The man was confused but jumped on the chance to survive the encounter. He did not understand why the needle marks on his body would make a difference to them but was silently grateful that they did. "Yeah, that's me—I'm a junkie, you caught me. You really don't want it. I'm messed up." He did not know what "it" was referring to, but he hoped that they truly wouldn't want it.

Before Cami could answer, she was distracted by the sudden explosion of color from the end of the alleyway. Red lights pierced the darkness and threw the shadows into a chaotic dance of light and movement. A moment later, the same scenario replayed itself on the other end of the alley; they were blocked on both sides.

"Cops!" the man said. For the first time in his life, he was happy to see them. "You wouldn't kill me in front of cops, would you? You'd get caught!" His voice was filled with relief and hope and contained a small amount of gloating with pride that he could not completely hide. "Let me go—we'll tell 'em that one of them did it all. We'll walk away from here. Nobody has to know." He looked from Cami to Richard and back to Cami again, looking for some glimmer of agreement.

"You are a terrible liar," Cami said. She let the man go, and he rubbed his arms to restore circulation. She could hear the police cars' doors open and close and knew that they would be upon them in moments. She thought very quickly, and a plan formed in her mind. She reached into the man's pocket and pulled out the knife that she was sure he carried. She flicked it open with her thumb, and the man flinched with the sound. She hurried to the eyeless man, who had fallen silent when he passed out from the pain. She cut the vein in his neck expertly, slicing it lengthwise instead of across to allow the blood to run freely. He would be dead shortly—one less witness. She returned to the man and pressed the knife into his hand. He looked at her confused; unsure of what else to do, he held on to it and listened. She leaned in close and whispered, "You are finally going to be punished for everything that you have done. You are going to be blamed for all of these deaths." She could hear the police coming now. "You can tell them that a little girl and her father did this— overpowered you and killed all these men. Tell them that, if you would like . . . but they will never believe you . . . and when you die, I will be watching. One way or another, I will be there."

The man stared wide-eyed but did not answer. Nothing that sounded reasonable could be said. In a flash, Cami and Richard disappeared, running along the wall and escaping to the rooftops. The officers had not seen the pair—they saw only historically violent man whom they knew well holding a knife and surrounded by bodies; and he knew that the girl was right—no one would ever believe him. The officers shouted unintelligible commands across their raised pistols.

They told him to drop the knife, to lie on the ground—too many things for him to understand in his state. He would die one way or another—he knew that. Either killed in prison by an inmate or killed by the state—it did not matter anymore. He looked at the knife; he looked at the officers. He raised it high above his head and rushed at the officer closest to him; if he was going to die, he would not do it alone.

He did not make it, however. Before he could take a few rushed steps, the first burst of gunfire caught him in the chest. The bullet shattered his rib cage and tore off a small part of his spine. With unexpected clarity, he realized that he had not heard it hit the wall behind him, which meant that the bullet was still in his body. It did not matter. It did not hurt. He stumbled forward, partially due to momentum, partially to sheer force of will. He took another few steps before the next round struck him, this time high and to the left. He spun around, his shoulder shattered from the round. This one did pass through and whined off the wall behind him. He stood then a million thoughts ran through his mind as endorphins and adrenaline clouded it. He was confused, and he was cold when he finally fell to the ground. He heard footsteps and shouts, and he rolled himself on to his back. He looked up at the clear night sky, seeing the stars for the last time and, in reality, seeing them for the first. There, over the ledge, was a face; he knew it was familiar, but it took him a moment to place it. Finally, he remembered. She had told the truth, she had watched him die after all, and with that, he expelled his final breath.

Although not in the literal sense, a vampire is prone to reflection. As the centuries pass, such a creature tends to view their life with a certain fatalistic longing; they think about their loves and losses, as over time, both grow to be numerous and significant. Cami had found a great deal of both, and time had formed them into more of a feeling than a memory. Richard and Mary were still within a normal human life span, but Cami had imparted on them the macabre tradition of living one's life or, in their cases, their existence, with a sense of gratitude for each sunset and an acknowledgment that each could be their last. Far from being frightening or depressing, it made what they had—what they were—even more beautiful.

The trio sat on the moon-drenched shore of a lazy river. Cami enjoyed the feeling of the cool sand filling the spaces between her toes and listened to the musical language of nature. The water washed slowly over smooth worn rocks; a soft breeze whispered through the bright green leaves and thin branches of the proud trees that lined the river's banks. A fish jumped, narrowly missing the brightly lit firefly, which hurried back to the shore. The world was beautiful, and the world was right. She had seen so much in her very long existence. Her vampirism forced her to do things that she wished she could forget, but she had to survive by doing them, and she had made sure that those whom she cared about the most survived as well. These things truly were all that really mattered.

Only in that moment, as she sat quietly between Richard and Mary, did she realize that she had been wrong all along. Home was not a place that was temporary and fleeting. Home was not a place at all. Home was being with those whom you love and having every reason to believe that they would be with you the next night. She had a home all this time and had just not realized it until now.

Mary bolted to her feet with a horrified look on her face. "What's wrong?" Richard asked. Mary could not speak, and Cami now became concerned. "Are you all right?" Mary now changed her look to that of puzzlement. "I feel strange. I feel just a little queasy . . . sick to my stomach. This is the first time I've felt anything like this . . . since becoming an immortal. It's . . . it's like . . . If I didn't know any better, I would swear I was . . . pregnant . . . but that isn't possible . . . is it?"

Lost in that thought, paired with the shock of the possibility, Cami did not notice the pair of eyes that were watching her from the opposite bank. The owner of those eyes blinked once, turned, and walked away. This was not the time.

A SNEAK PEEK AT
THE NEXT BOOK

New Dawn—Chasing Sunrise

The train lumbered along the timeworn tracks like a wary beast in search of rest. Cami watched the world pass by through the window; lonely houses gave way to silent fields guarded by weatherworn scarecrows, which themselves gave way to vast and barren tracts of land too sparse in nutrients, even for weeds to grow. Although she saw these things, they did not really register for her. Her mind was many miles away; she wondered if Mary and Richard had made it out, and if they would be able to meet her at their rendezvous point. She wondered if they were safe. She wondered if she was. She frowned at the horizon; the sun was throwing a painted canvas of gold and pink colors into the sky as though it was wishing her a fond good morning, more accurately a painful death. She pulled the worn and tattered picture from her pocket and stared at it longingly; there had been good times once. She hoped that there would be again.

Money had not been a problem for Cami for many years. In her travels, she had collected valuable items and collectables that were stored for her use when she needed them. She had accounts in various names and personas that would be periodically refreshed to hide her true age. She had no problem with obtaining money, but spending it without drawing unwanted attention often was a concern. Human nature, however, gave her a great degree of flexibility when the availability of money was no object for concern. She had found that ticketing agents and other such individuals were often very eager to overlook small variances from law or regulation when the convenience would compensate them well. When Cami's ailing grandfather, in this case, was unable to purchase her tickets and make certain arrangements in person, there was always someone willing to bend the rules in exchange for a modest token of his appreciation. In the end, Cami had a private room with the appropriate accommodations for her professed condition. This condition, or rather the excuse, necessitated blackout curtains and absolute privacy. She closed the thick curtains and settled into the bed, allowing her daily death to take her. She wondered if it would ever stop being painful to be taken and awakened. Such was her lot, as it was for every other vampire.

The day came and left; the train and those on it continued their lives blissfully unaware that they were traveling with a corpse. In her waking time, Cami would often wonder how people would react if they found her that way—seemingly dead without a mark on her. However, hours had to pass before Cami was able to wonder anything at all. When she started to wake, it happened the same way it always did. A single synapse fired then another. They were random and chaotic but soon increased in frequency and intensity. Her brain came to life first, starting with the base functions, and then moving into consciousness and awareness then memories. Lately, Cami hated that part—only the brief period when she was aware that she existed but had no idea what had happened recently gave her any sort of peace. That, though, was short lived, and the memories washed over her like a wave of boiling water. She could do nothing but accept the unwelcome intrusion of thoughts and images until her body followed her mind, and she was able to move again. Her eyes snapped open, overwhelming her senses with images and colors. She allowed the feeling to pass and forced herself to move. She sat up in the bed and forced herself to concentrate on anything other than her own thoughts.

That is when she saw the note. Although that observation did a great deal to eliminate the unwelcome thoughts, it only introduced new fears and new thoughts. The door, which had been locked from the inside, indeed, the door still was locked. Strict instructions had been left to the contrary, but someone had taken it upon himself to go inside anyway. She did not want to know, did not want to read it. It was irrational, but she hoped that if she did not read the note, whatever it said could not have an effect on her. She knew that, no matter how much she wished to the contrary, she had to. She had to read it. She had to know. She reached out and grabbed the paper as though it were a deadly and aggressive snake. The paper was thick and textured, almost more like a cloth. She opened it and read.

You are in great danger. You must leave the train at the next stop. I will meet you.

There was no signature, no way to tell who had written the message. She turned the paper over, but the other side was blank. Cami had no reason to trust the writer, but she knew that if they wanted to kill her, they could have done so when she was helpless. She stared at the note and wondered what the warning meant and perhaps more importantly who it was from.

APPENDIX

The Battle for Barrow, Alaska

The planet Earth had seen battles—countless wars, skirmishes, and conflicts—which had been waged on its surface, two of which involved every continent on it, which collectively cost the lives of untold millions of its inhabitants. Some of those millions had died for a hill, others for an idea, and others still for reasons that they would never even know. Most of those battles were recorded and then measured. It was known who fought and who died, how many shells were fired or vehicles destroyed. The Battle for Barrow, Alaska, however, came and went without as much as a whisper. Although the stories of heroism and the tales of cruelty would never be heard or read about in a classroom, there were those who would remember every one. Some among them were still living them on a daily and/or nightly basis, if only in their nightmares and memories.

Barrow was naturally attractive to vampires. The nights were long during much of the year and perpetual for two months in the winter. Even the daylight was often closer to twilight, which made it survivable and only slightly uncomfortable. It was also a community that was accepting—even welcoming—of the vampire, and they came from all over the world to have a relatively normal existence within its boundaries.

Although the area was a haven to their kind, there were some among them who resented their lot, their existence. They saw their occupancy of Barrow as a form of confinement, albeit a willing one. They argued, quite passionately and persuasively, that the humans were weak in body and in will. They compared these traits, equally passionately and persuasively, to that of the vampire. The vampire was immortal, which gave perspective and wisdom. It was said that such a trait, and their superior strength, gave the vampire the right—or perhaps even the obligation—to rule over the humans, for their collective good. The state of the world was held as evidence of the decline of humankind and of their unsuitability to run the world. Those who adopted this philosophy wanted to overthrow humanity and to enslave or breed the survivors for their nutritional value.

Although the idea spread through the community like wildfire, there were those who opposed it. Generally, it was the older vampires who argued publicly and fervently that killing without a need to feed was murder; and murder was not the way of the civilized vampire. They argued for the traditions of the elders, who lived comfortably in the myths and fears of humans in relative harmony for countless generations. Human beings must not die, they argued; instead, they should be fed on but only enough to sustain the vampire. They would argue that being greedy was what happened to the dinosaur. They eventually ran out of food and starved to death. For all their many flaws, humans were skilled at survival—and even better at vengeance. Exposing themselves then in a direct frontal assault would be suicidal.

There were debates and arguments, which eventually led to fights and threats. The town was quickly divided, with each faction staunchly bolstering their own arguments and opposing the other. The topic was quite serious, and the undead citizens of Barrow soon lost sight of the difference between the individual and the idea to which they subscribed. Soon, those who wanted to take the world by force grew stronger in number and zealousness. They rose and took control of the town for themselves, ejecting those whom they considered weak and foolish. Neighbors forced neighbors from their homes; family turned on one another depending on their views or affiliation; children fought their parents who met them with ferocity.

Those were dark times in Barrow, and they were going to get much worse before they could get better.

Those who fled, or those who were being forced to leave, trekked south to avoid being persecuted. Those who had taken the town—those who believed that might made right—forced their opponents out into the unforgiving wilderness with full knowledge that daylight would be coming soon, but they sent them out to face it so that the executioners could be left with a clean conscience. They were meant to die, but they refused.

When daylight came, they buried themselves in the snow to avoid its rays. Not all of them made it; some simply refused to hide from the sun, understanding the arduous journey that lay before them. Others tried but succumbed to starvation or errant sunlight. They walked across the frozen tundra, mourning the dead and pressing onward. Some among them sacrificed themselves, giving their own blood to allow those for whom they cared to survive; those who saw the mother open her own veins for her children would never forget it. Those who were too late to stop the father who did the same to his own child would never forgive it.

The procession spread over many miles, with isolated groups traveling in roughly the same direction. Despite the separation, the sense of relief and hope spread through the survivors from the front to the back. Those who were further behind had no idea what had developed, but they hurried forward for the mere promise of relief. Those who were closest—the ones who had been able to travel more quickly—had reached a home, and the crowd in front of it grew larger as more arrived behind them. The home was massive and ornate as was the patriarch of the occupants. Clutching an aged rifle, the man stood his ground, shouting threats and warnings, in front of the double doors that led inside. His bravery stood in contrast to the worried faces that peered through the home's windows. The assembly of vampires pressed against the wrought iron fence and gate, shouting angry accusations and desperate pleas. There were arguments within the crowd—appeals to reason and arguments for sacrifice, but the majority prevailed.

The gate began to give way against the constant pressure from the unnaturally strong hands. The man backed into the doorway, trying to hold what was his without looking as though he were retreating. He raised the rifle and pointed it at the crowd in a last effort to cause it to disperse. He shouted a warning; it was unheeded. He shouted another warning, "This is an automatic rifle, loaded with blessed silver-cased bullets with seasoned apple wood cores!" and trained the iron sights on the closest man; the mob continued to press toward the home. The man knew that all he had were threats—there was no way that he could kill them all, and the first shot would unleash the hell that pressed around him. The delay, however, had cost him all his remaining choices—desperate hungry beings now surrounded the home. Nothing was more dangerous than the hopeless when offered hope.

The man took a final look at his loved ones inside. He knew at that moment it would be his final look. He aimed carefully as the gate started to groan and give way. He slowly squeezed the trigger, hoping for fate or fortune to intervene. The gate broke away, and the mob poured in, lost in a frantic fervor. A tear rolled down the man's cheek as he pulled the trigger; the shot echoed from the home and made his ears ring. The round slammed into the chest of the closest man and passed through to the other side; it whined off the stone pillar and disappeared toward the horizon. He stumbled back for a moment, recovered his balance, and pressed forward against the others. The patriarch chose a different target among the rapidly advancing horde, aimed and fired again. The round tore into the flesh of his target's neck and passed through to the other side with no effect. He took his final shot—the last one that he had time to make. Again, it did nothing to turn the tide. They reached the doorway, and the patriarch was quickly buried under a living wave. His body was torn apart and then feasted upon while the rest of the mob flooded through the opened gate and poured into the yard. One of them floated gently to the window, where the man's daughter was peering out at the horde. He turned his head sideways like a quizzical dog and pleasantly asked her to invite him in. "Please come in" was her only reply. He floated through the window and immediately drained her of every drop of life coursing through her veins.

Every person inside was killed, brutally and painfully. There was no malice in the act, but the overwhelming craving made their hunger indistinguishable from wanton cruelty. They were each torn apart, screaming and fighting, but not a single drop of blood was wasted. Each one of the humans inside was drained completely, leaving only torn strips of cloth and flesh wrapped around loose bone and meat.

Only then, when the frenzy died down, did the refugees of Barrow fully understand what had happened. Cooler heads among them had reminded them that they needed to feed—that it was natural and expected. They noted that no pleasure was taken in the act and that the massacre was in fact necessary for their own survival. It did little, however, to assuage the horrors that they had seen or that they themselves had committed. Between the servants and family inside, there was enough blood to sustain them, at least until they could find other sources.

They respectfully buried those who had saved them and marked their graves with stones and living plants. They reasoned that those humans deserved a place of honor because they sustained the clan. In memory of them, the home was left exactly as it was, although it was now occupied by the surviving vampires. Over time, the home defined them—it was cultured and warm, with a massive library and countless works of art. Their numbers grew as more left Barrow or they were denied entry into the increasingly rigid society. Their numbers grew, but space remained a constant; soon, they were crowded within the walls. The library, hallways, and even the pantry were pressed into service as sleeping quarters, and morale began to fade.

The clan, as it was, had no leadership and no structure. It was entirely democratic, with each member following their own conscience when decisions were made. There were those, however, that were looked to for their wisdom and advice, and their decisions were rarely opposed. There were times, however, when they disagreed among themselves.

"We have grown too large in number and can take in no more. Our population is simply unsustainable," Lucius proposed. He spoke with his characteristic calm, but his voice carried both authority and confidence. The great room was filled with spectators to the conversation, and they spilled into the hallways, trying to capture even portions of the conversation. The debate had not been planned or coordinated, but the weight of the decision that it heralded was understood by all.

"Then we must divide and spread, but Barrow is no home to us. We lost the city, and we are not equipped to fight a war. They have the numbers, and the invaders are always at a disadvantage," countered Ella. Ella was prone to fits of anger and generally aggressive as well as brash in words and deed; it was said that her very soul was as fiery as her hair, and she was most often quick to action. Her call for restraint caused a great deal of concern among those listening.

"For how long? For how long do we sit and wait for them to come and find us?" Lucius replied. "Each day, they grow stronger. More come to them, as they always have, attracted to the freedom and safety of the city. They merely choose the strongest, the most desirable, among them and discard the rest. You speak of history—of the challenge of the invaders. What of the warrior societies that are allowed to grow? What do they do?"

"They conquer, and they spread," Ella conceded.

"They conquered and spread in Barrow too. We already know what will happen—it's how we came to be here in the first place. They're raising an army. They'll grow strong enough to attack the humans, and the losses will be incalculable. Nevertheless, they'll not win. They can't win. The humans can fight in the night and in the day and the attackers only in the night. They'll be hunted, they'll be found, and they'll be destroyed. Those of us who have chosen not to fight will be hunted as well."

Ella argued, "We can hide. We've hidden for a long time."

"No, we can't. We're only able to hide now because the humans don't know that we exist. We may haunt their dreams and populate their myths, but they don't truly fear us. When and if they know—when they're shown that we are real, without a doubt,—we'll never be safe again. They'll hunt us down like animals, and we will be eliminated. Our lineage, our history . . . we'll be the last."

Ella remained silent. He was right.

"I don't want war," Lucius continued. "We've been left no option. We must fight so that we can live."

It was decided with that conversation. As a formality, a vote was held. It was decided collectively that they would take Barrow. There were some, a small number, who refused to fight. They would be left behind in the relative safety of the hidden home, with the understanding that they would not be welcomed in Barrow once it was taken. Those who were to fight, however, busied themselves in preparation for the attack. Some cleared the overgrown orchard of its trees to create stakes, while others developed plans and strategies. Others left for the larger cities, collecting enough blood for their march and seeking reinforcements. Finally, they were ready. It was far from an army, but they had been able to turn their nonviolent clan into a formidable force. Their force, coupled with the element of surprise, gave them a fighting chance.

They marched. They followed the same path that they had taken previously when they had been forced to flee Barrow. The path was largely symbolic and completely cathartic, allowing them to pay homage to their dead and to swear revenge silently. There were far more returning to Barrow than had left it, and the dense formation that moved steadily on went much further than the eye could see. The reinforcements who had been swayed to their cause swelled their numbers considerably. After several nights, the force reached the crest of the final hill, below which spread the town—the bright jewel in the otherwise barren tundra. The formation prepared, each moving to their assigned positions as they had practiced. Their movements were imprecise and clumsy but far better than they had been initially.

Ella and Lucius stood at the front of the ready line, which stretched from one end of the hill to the other; it circled the town in a shallow horseshoe shape, with the faster and more agile at the ends and the stronger and more aggressive in the solid middle. They each waited in place, waiting for Lucius and Ella to give the signal that would start the battle—the battle they hoped will be the last. That signal would have to wait. In battle, the enemy also gets a vote; the citizens of Barrow exercised that right.

"Wait . . . what's going on?" Ella asked. The question was rhetorical as Lucius had no more knowledge than she did.

A single figure emerged from the city and stood halfway between it and the hill. The figure waited, neither advancing nor retreating—just waiting. Lucius and Ella accepted the unspoken invitation and slowly walked toward where the man stood. Before they arrived, the army of Barrow left the town and took its position behind the apparent leader. They maintained their distance, ready and alert; their ranks were more disciplined, and their warriors were eager for the upcoming battle. Their formation nested perfectly into that of the attackers. They had focused the bulk of their forces to counter the main thrust of the attackers and positioned the wings at a forty-five-degree angle that was a negative slope relative to the main body. The reserves were kept at the rear, and the designated shock troops were kept in the center of the bulge. Each side waited.

"Lucius, Ella," the man acknowledged as they approached. As they got closer, they recognized him. He was the second in command, and his cruelty had known no bounds.

"Abraham," they acknowledged in near unison. They stared at each other, waiting.

"You can retreat. We won't chase you," Abraham offered, finally. "It's not you that we're after."

"You're after the humans?" Ella asked.

"Yes. That doesn't concern you," Abraham replied.

"It concerns all of us," Lucius replied. "You must see that. You can't defeat them—not all of them. When you lose, they'll come after the rest of us. We can't let you do this. If you can't listen to logic, we will stop you."

Abraham shook his head sadly. "You won't be able to. If you don't leave now, both of you, and all of those who followed you, will die."

Lucius leaned in close. "Then we'll take you with us." Lucius and Ella turned and returned to the formation. Abraham turned and did the same. Each stood before those whom they brought, and each waited for the other to move. Finally, as though on an unspoken signal, the opponents advanced to each other. With the benefit of gravity, the attackers covered the most ground, and the strong center crashed into the defenders. The battle was pitched and violent, with neither side retreating and neither side gaining ground. The defenders' wings swung outward to encircle the attackers' forces, but they were met and stopped in place by the faster and more agile flanks of the attackers.

The defenders were nearly overrun; they had relied on their strength and training to win the day but were unprepared for the zealousness and passion with which the attackers fought. Those in Barrow were fighting to preserve their army and their ability to attack; the attackers knew that they were fighting ultimately for their own survival. Might was losing to passion, strength to purpose.

The defenders' reserves rushed to fill the gaps created by the dead and dying, which exploited the strategic failure of the attackers, who had no reserves to draw from. The right flank of the attackers began to fall, and the defenders pushed them back, swinging the flank back toward the main body. The left flank fared better and pushed the defenders' wing against the remaining reserves, compressing the forces between them and the center. This resulted in a strange shape that no longer resembled the careful plans created by both commanders. A contingent broke away from the attackers' center to exploit the ground gained by the strong remaining flank and pressed forward as the flank fell away. It was too late for the defenders—they broke the flank, but the main body had already encircled them.

The battle raged, ebbing and flowing between victory and defeat. The air was filled with shouts and screams, the sounds of the dying and the sounds of murderous rage. The attacking force grew smaller but continued tightening its grip on the remaining defenders, with Abraham at the center. When he was surrounded, he laid down his weapon and surrendered. Those who remained did the same. The unthinkable had happened—they had been defeated. The surrender meant nothing—they were shown no mercy, and no quarter was taken. Those who remained were slaughtered in place, until none remained. The field of battle was left to the attackers, and with it, they took the town.

The town collectively decided that a policy of isolationism was the only way to survive. Humans were brought in and kept in the town to be used as a food source and guardians during daylight hours. They remained in Barrow, and the threat to humanity—and, thus, their own kind—was gone.

Appendix

The Child in the Crypt

Brian died in Elvis Presley's crypt at the hands of a girl who looked to be no older than he was. His final moments were excruciatingly painful and violent. In the briefest of moments between the feeling of the stake sinking into his heart and his explosion into dust, his life unfolded before him. The memories that flooded his mind seemed impossibly long, as though time no longer existed for him.

Brian could not remember how old he had been or when he was born. However, he did remember how he had been reborn. His parents had left him home with his young sister, entrusted with her care while his parents were gone for the evening. Where had they gone? A date—he thought he remembered that it had been a date, or maybe some sort of emergency. His little sister had recently turned two years old and was just beginning to make the transition from crib to bed. She enjoyed her newfound freedom, and keeping her in bed had been a challenge that her younger brother struggled to meet. Perhaps it was unfair to expect him to be able to do such a thing. The promise of a financial reward, however, gave him reason to try. Finally, he was able to convince her to stay in the bed and over the covers, and she drifted off into a deep sleep. Although she lived up to every stereotype of the "terrible twos," he loved his little sister. He kissed her forehead and descended the stairs to return to the television show that he had left paused. It was a child's dream: a full refrigerator, a nighttime television that had previously been denied him, and a late bedtime that could be cheerfully ignored. He ate popcorn, watched countless acts of violence on television, and enjoyed every moment of it.

Thump, thump.

He heard soft footsteps from the floor above. The floor of his sister's bedroom was the ceiling of the living room, so he could hear every time she got out of bed. "Go to bed, Tanya!" he called toward the stairs. His call was answered only with silence. Brian knew that silence was never golden when a toddler was involved and doubted that the sudden stillness on the second floor meant anything good. He sighed and paused his show once again then made his way up the stairs. "I'm serious—if you're out of bed, I'm telling Mom and Dad. You're going to be in so much trouble!" It was an idle threat. She was never in trouble with them. He reached the landing and started down the hallway. Her bedroom door slowly and quietly closed; he did not remember closing it, and she was far too afraid of the dark to have done it herself. "Tanya?" he called. He stopped and listened; there was no answer. "Tanya?" he called again. "This isn't funny— come out before I get mad." The reality, however, was that he was far too frightened to be angry. There was something unnaturally still in the air, although he could not quite identify what it was that he was feeling. He swallowed hard, as though the motion would help him find strength that he did not know that he had. He wanted to run away, to leave the home and scream as he ran down the street, but he held firm and continued. *You're being ridiculous*, he chastised himself, *and you're too old to be afraid of the dark.*

He pushed the door open and stepped back, allowing him a brief indulgence into his own panic and fears. He blinked to clear the illusion from his eyes; he blinked again when his eyes adjusted to the dark, and he realized that what he was seeing was real. A man was kneeling over Tanya's bed, crouched over her as though sharing some terrible secret. The moonlight filtered through the opened window— which had been closed earlier in the night—and bathed her pale still face in its soft light; her head had been moved to expose the soft skin of her neck, which was marred by two bloody holes. Her eyes were open, but she stared at nothing. With a sickening realization, Brian realized that his little sister was dead, and the man who killed her was still in the room. The man stood to his full height then turned around and glared at the young man. He was not very tall, not by adult standards, but he towered over Brian like an angry giant.

"Who are you? Get out of here!" Brian squeaked. He had tried to make his voice sound forceful and authoritative, but what came out thinly disguised his fear and uncertainty. He fumbled over the words, and his body language showed clearly that he wanted nothing more than to run and hide. "I called the police," Brian lied. "They're on their way, so you'd better get out of here!" he managed. It was a desperate gamble, but the best that he was able to manage under those circumstances.

The man merely smiled and wiped the fresh blood from his mouth. He advanced on Brian—two quick steps before grabbing for the boy, but Brian was quick and the adrenaline boosted his own reflexes. He spun around and ran for the door, feeling the man's fingers graze over his back and close on nothing as he ran. He cried and shook with fear as he ran into his parents' room, an instilled instinct that did him no good in the current moment; there was no phone in the room and no other way out of it. He turned to shut the door and saw the man bearing down on him—running down the hallway toward the bedroom like some sort of rabid creature or man possessed. Brian slammed the door and locked it, but even his child's mind knew that the door would not last very long. The man was very strong, and the door was very weak. Each time the man beat against it, it shook in the frame and cracked just a little bit more. Brian backed away from the door, instinctively grasping at the chance for life. Brian crawled under his parents' bed, wishing that the man would simply go away or that his parents would come home and save him. He tried to mourn his sister's death—it felt like the appropriate thing to do, but he could only see his own fears and worry about his own inevitable demise.

Crack!

Brian jumped when the door splintered.

CRACK!

He began to cry and pushed himself further toward the bottom of the headboard as the rest of the door gave way. He heard the door swing on its strained hinges, and the doorknob hit the wall behind it. The man walked in, moving slowly and methodically. Brian held his breath and tried to lie very still, hoping against hope that the man would somehow be fooled and leaves him alone, but he knew deep down that was not possible. The man walked into the room, sniffing at the air like a hunting dog and honing in on his scent. Brian could see his feet as he paced the room, moving in small circles and gradually closer to the bed. He noticed idly that the man wore thick and well-worn heavy work boots, much like the workers who had just completed building the addition to their home; he wondered if they were somehow related. The man walked to the edge of the bed and stopped. He sniffed the air once and then bent down. The two locked eyes; the man's were cold and emotionless as though there was no spark of life in them. Brian's were fearful and wild, filled with terror and tears. The man stood and in one motion flipped the mattress, and heavy metal box spring out of the frame and sent them crashing into the hand-carved cherry chest of drawers. It was an odd thought, but Brian heard his mother's jewelry box crash against the wall; he had given that to her, for her birthday last year, and it broke his heart when he heard it being broken.

The momentary distraction was his last indulgence. The man reached down, clamped on his upper arm with a viselike grip, and then pulled him into the air. Brian hit the man with small balled-up fists and kicked him with his bare feet, but the man either did not notice or did not care. He used his other arm to support Brian's head, which he pulled roughly to the side. He pulled him close and closed his mouth around the child's neck. Brian felt a brief sharp pain in his neck, which spread outward over his body as the man drank greedily. The pain gave way to a strange detachment, as though he were floating in a pool of dirty water; after that, he felt nothing then an almost euphoric feeling, one of total happiness and bliss then cold, very, very cold.

. . .

"You are still alive," came the voice. It called to Brian in the darkness; it was not a question but rather as if he were answering a question. "Open your eyes, boy," it said again; the voice was deep and scratched. Brian followed the voice, searching in the darkness for light—for anything that would help him gather his bearings. Only after a moment did he realize that the darkness was not external to him, but he was lost in his own mind. He found a small reserve of strength and forced his eyes to open. They did so only reluctantly, and the light that his opened eyes let in was blinding even though the room was relatively dark.

Where am I? What did you do? What happened? Brian tried to form the words, but he was not able to voice them.

The man answered, however, as though he had. "You are in your parents' bedroom." Then in a tone almost condescending, he added, "This is going to be hard for you to understand. I am a vampire. Do you know what a vampire is?" The shock and fear registered on young Brian's face as he nodded slowly that he did, all the while thinking that it was impossible and that he *must* be dreaming. "I have drained you of almost all of your blood. There is a very small amount left, and should I take a single drop more, it will kill you. I am willing to do that because I still have hunger and the want to feed. However, I will offer you a gift, just as the one who created me offered this new life to me and as it was offered to those who came before me. I will allow you to drink of my blood, which will replenish you and restore you to life. You will then be vampire like I. You will be cursed to walk the earth as an abomination, no longer welcome among the humans that you must feed on to survive. You will get used to that, but it will never be easy for you. You will have a life, however, but only at night, and you will have that life, such as it is, for all eternity. The choice is yours, boy. Do you want this life that I'm offering to you, or would you rather die and your soul to be flung into the void?"

Brian thought for a moment; even his thoughts were slowed by the loss of blood. He could feel his life draining away and his body shutting down as the moments passed by. He did not have much time, and his decision was being driven by fear and panic more than any other thought. "Li . . ." was all he could manage. "L . . .," he tried again but lacked the strength to say any more. He only hoped and prayed that the man would understand what he had meant and that the partial answer would be enough.

"You want to live—a wise choice."

Relief swept over Brian. Strong fingers pulled his mouth open, and Brian tasted a sweet and salty liquid being first dripping and then pouring into it. He became a little stronger and grabbed the man's arm, holding it tightly against his lips so that he could form a suction and was able to drink much more deeply from the wound on the man's wrist, accepting both the blood and the strength that came with it. The man put one finger into the corner of Brian's mouth to break the suction and then pushed him aside, sending him sprawling on the floor. Brian began feeling the most intense pains that he had ever experienced.

The man said, "Dear boy, what you are feeling are the pains you experience when your body goes through the throes of death. Each tiny bit of your body is dying. I apologize that you have to endure this, but it will be more than worth this small inconvenience."

Those sensations passed after what seemed like hours, but in reality, it only lasted a few minutes, and he was fully conscious again. He felt more alive than he ever had been, as though each of his senses had been dialed up much higher than ever before. The man smiled, proud of what he had done and of the gift he had offered. Although weakened by the loss of his own blood, he knew that he had brought another into the world and that he would no longer be alone.

He was not alone; he had Brian as a companion until the moment he died. That moment, however, happened very quickly. Brian grabbed a heavy and sharp piece of the broken bedpost and plunged the sharp splintered end deep into the man's chest. He did not know that a wooden stake was necessary for what he had tried to do—he merely grabbed the nearest weapon that had been available and was lucky that it was made of wood. He also did not know that he had to pierce the heart—he was simply fortunate in his aim. The man looked at Brian with both surprise and betrayal, and then his torso began to swell, convulsing and expanding to twice its normal size, and then he closed his eyes, smiling. The next moment, his body burst into thousand bones and flesh bits. The bloody mortal remains coated the room and Brian. Brian left that night, cursed to roam the streets. Without the benefit of a guide to educate him on the new existence that he now led, he grew to trust only his own instincts and pursue only his own desires. The first dawn taught him to fear the sun; he learned that the light, which set his skin ablaze and weakened his body, was something that he would need to avoid at all costs, so he took refuge during the day wherever he could. He learned that he could no longer swallow foods that he had enjoyed the day before. When he tried, his throat felt as if he had attempted to swallow broken glass, and if he did manage to get a bite down, it came right back up as if he were vomiting those same shards of glass. He would grow hungry and weak unless he fed and learned to do so quickly and brutally. He became more and more feral as time passed, focusing only on survival and not even on reasons for survival. In time, he became more animal than childlike and left a trail of pain and misery wherever he traveled. He was always running and always seeking but never satisfied and never happy.

That was how he met Cami. That was how he died. The story of Brian's existence ended with her.